DEVOUR THE WORLD

He was too fast, too graceful, and too clever to permit any of the other joggers in the park to touch him. As soon as one drew too near, he drove his feet harder and in moments was gone—leaving them shaking their heads and wondering if they had imagined it or they had really seen him.

They would know. Oh, they would know, but only one at a time, and after that knowledge, they would be drained and discarded, left behind like empty cartons. He was convinced they existed only for his pleasure and nourishment anyway. He suffered no guilt when he fed. Indeed, he felt it was coming to him. Why else were they there? Why else were they here?

Questions like that rarely bothered him. It was just as pointless to stop and wonder why there were mosquitoes. Don't wonder about them. Destroy them and go on and on and on.

Just like he was doing now. Like he would always do.

Filled with the wonder of himself, he glided ahead toward the rising sun and into its expanding pool of warmth.

Even that existed solely for him.

Also by Andrew Neiderman

ANDREW NEIDERMAN

DEFICIENCY

POCKET STAR BOOKS
New York   London   Toronto   Sydney

This book is a work of fiction. Names, characters, places and incidents are products of the author's imagination or are used fictitiously. Any resemblance to actual events or locales or persons living or dead is entirely coincidental.

An *Original* Publication of POCKET BOOKS

A Pocket Star Book published by
POCKET BOOKS, a division of Simon & Schuster, Inc.
1230 Avenue of the Americas, New York, NY 10020

Copyright © 2004 by Andrew Neiderman

ISBN: 0-7434-8321-9

First Pocket Books printing August 2004

10   9   8   7   6   5   4   3   2   1

POCKET STAR BOOKS and colophon are registered trademarks of Simon & Schuster, Inc.

Cover design by John Vairo, Jr.
Front cover photo © Anthony Saint Jeams/Getty Images

Manufactured in the United States of America

For information regarding special discounts for bulk purchases, please contact: Simon & Schuster Special Sales at 1-800-456-6798 or business@simonandschuster.com.

To Tyrah Stenftenagel, a future fan,
and all my future fans from Palm Valley

PROLOGUE

Paige Thorndyke paused just inside the entrance of the Underground. The Underground is a perfect name for this dance club, she thought disdainfully. The stairway descended a full flight below the sidewalk, and the moment she opened the door to the lobby she was greeted by a musty odor that reminded her of what the basement at home smelled like, especially when the humidity was too high and everything had that dank, awful, redolent odor. Whether intentional or not, the walls here were just as poorly lighted and looked like raw cement.

She crossed the small lobby in which two pumped-up wannabe television wrestlers strained their undersized tuxedos at every seam. As if they were really passing judgment on her qualifications to enter, they nodded their approval, each man's neck bulging like a pinched inner tube. Neither smiled. They looked as if they had superglue smeared around their lips, keeping them from relaxing.

Paige hesitated as she approached the second set of doors, but as if some modern-day Satan was watching her and pushing buttons, the doors opened automatically with a dramatic swish, giving her the feeling she had indeed descended into a region of Hades and was now being sucked into its belly. Inside, the dance hall resembled an inferno—the blazing pink and blue, red and yellow lights flickered over the crowd and up the pink stucco walls. The dance floor itself was a layer of glass beneath which a ruby-tinted liquid flowed, giving the revelers the sense that they were dancing on a stream of wine or blood. The fog generated by dry ice twisted and knotted above and around them, spinning a web of smoke that gnarled and curled like a snake slithering into itself.

Paige regretted agreeing to meet Eileen Okun here. She was never fond of barhopping and found hanging around in dance clubs even more uncomfortable and somehow threatening, especially this one. The loud music, the liberal pouring and drinking of booze as if it was water, the entire atmosphere changed people or perhaps liberated the wildness and evil that hitherto lay restrained within them. It reconnected them to their animal selves. To Paige, most everyone down here recalled a mole or some reptile. That tall, thin black-haired girl in the skintight leather mini wiggled as would a rodent working its way toward scraps of food. Her eyes even bulged. And that buxom redhead who wore a pushup bra hovered over her shorter companion like a cat about to pounce, her fingers bent into small claws as she swung her arms above and around him.

Of course she knew what Eileen would say—at least these girls were dancing; they had partners and more than likely, they would leave with someone. Unfortunately, Eileen was right. Men were so simple, always going for the obvious ones, she concluded. I don't know why I agreed to come here, she thought and actually heard herself whimper. She had merely stepped foot in the place and her mind was already in turmoil because of it. Why do I keep doing things I really don't want to do?

Because you're twenty-eight, she replied to her own question, and you're unmarried, unattached, and working in a travel agency where the only eligible bachelor is Clarence Tugman, a short, pudgy thirty-year-old who still lives with his parents. Most of the young men who came to the agency as clients either had someone already with whom they were traveling, or didn't seem to be interested in her. Maybe it was because she showed little interest. She wasn't good at flirting and was disdainful of it in others. I'm wound too tight, she thought, remembering a boy in high school who had accused her of being just that.

She had no one to blame but herself. Why had she come back to her hometown? Why had she let herself sink in the quicksand of complacent security by living at home like Clarence Tugman? Why hadn't she gone off to California like Adrian, or New York City like Toby and Betty? Her closest high school girlfriends were all married or into exciting careers. Her current best friend here, Eileen, really her only friend, at least had an excuse for being here. She was relatively new to the area. For Eileen, this place was some sort of an adventure. But Paige could easily see the future she was committing herself to when she had returned after four years at the state university in Albany where she acquired a degree in liberal arts to hang on her bedroom wall. She had heard the warnings and she hadn't heeded them.

Voilà. Here she was; here she had been for almost six years after college. This was the year of her first high school reunion, ten years later, and although she had sent in her check and said she was attending, she dreaded the thought. Most anyone else with whom she had been friendly from the class and who had remained here was at least married with a family by now, even "Slow Boat Shirley" who had simply been given an attendance diploma.

Her eyes went down; she sought out the darkest, most secluded spot by the bar and fumbled nervously through her purse for her money to buy herself a drink.

"Relax," she heard someone say. He was seated so deeply in the shadows himself that she hadn't noticed him. Actually, it was more like he had suddenly appeared out of thin air. "Your money is no good here."

"Pardon me?"

He seemed to rise out of the darkness like a fantasy out of the coils of a deep sleep.

"I said, your money's no good here," he said more authoritatively. "What will you have?"

She stared at him for a moment. Was this blond-haired, evenly tanned man with the most beautiful blue eyes she had ever seen actually talking to her, really to her?

"I . . ."

"You came to the bar. You wanted something to drink, right?" he said smiling. It was such a warm smile, and yet those white teeth, those sensuous lips sent tingles down her spine, making it more than merely a friendly smile. He had a small cleft in his chin, just enough to make it interesting. This was a very sexy, very handsome man, she concluded. Was she dreaming? Did she long for it so much that she had freed a reckless imagination and concocted this wonderful illusion? Am I talking to myself? she wondered, or am I talking aloud without realizing it, and being overheard?

He continued to stare at her, to hold his smile, to drink her in with such intensity, she felt undressed.

"It's not a hard question," he said laughing softly.

"What? Oh yes. Um . . . Vodka and tonic."

"Vodka and tonic," he said sharply to the bartender. Then he sat back, the shadows closing in around his face again. She moved to the black vinyl stool and placed her purse on the bar.

"Thank you," she said.

Paige wasn't comfortable permitting men to buy her drinks, especially men she didn't know, not that it happened that often. She believed that when a man bought you a drink and you accepted it, he immediately thought that meant he bought you.

Of course you would jump to think that, her other side quickly snapped. Always thinking negatively, especially when it comes to men.

Maybe she was being too harsh. Eileen wouldn't hesitate to accept a drink from a stranger, would she? If it weren't for Eileen, she wouldn't be doing anything tonight, she concluded sadly.

Anyway, she had no idea why she had so quickly and easily accepted a drink from this stranger. She surprised herself with her impulsive action.

"No problem. You looked kind of lost for a moment and I thought, there's someone who feels the way I do." He leaned forward again and smiled. "I'm a stranger in these parts," he added in a mock-western accent, pretending to tip back a cowboy hat.

"Oh." She laughed, a thin, wispy sort of laugh, a laugh she hated because it sounded so forced. "Well, I'm no stranger to these parts, but to be perfectly honest, I was indecisive about coming in tonight. Even after I had entered. Especially after I entered," she added with a frankness that even surprised herself.

"Oh?"

She gazed around as she spoke.

"A friend was supposed to meet me here and she's not here," she continued as if that would explain everything—

her whole life, why she was alone, why she looked and felt the way she did.

"Yeah, I thought you might be looking for someone who hadn't arrived." His smile turned into an expression of concern—thoughtful, deep. "It can't be easy for a young woman these days, especially one who's alone."

The bartender brought her drink.

"Well, I'm . . . I'm not usually alone," she lied. "Usually, I go out with friends, but it's just one of those nights where I was somewhere and my friend was somewhere and . . ."

"Sure," he said turning his palms out as if to say, "That's my point."

She felt herself relax, her body pour down to the stool as she sipped her vodka and tonic. Why worry about making excuses, creating a false front? Be yourself, be comfortable in yourself, she urged herself.

"It's very crowded tonight anyway," she said looking back at the dance floor. She felt a need to keep talking as if the silences between them would give him time to reconsider what he had done and he would move away quickly.

"Yes, it is. Apparently, the Underground lives up to its reputation. This afternoon I asked someone where was the hottest place in town, and he told me to come here. I got here only a few minutes before you did," he said. She thought he was explaining why he hadn't another girl beside him, but of course, she recognized that as her own insecurity.

"Oh," she said. And then she smiled and thought, if Eileen could see me now, she wouldn't believe it. Where was she? How could she not show up? Maybe she never would!

"My name's John," the dark stranger declared and extended his hand.

My mind is clouded with animal imagery tonight, she thought, for his arm seemed to slither over the portion of the bar between them and his long, graceful fingers rose up toward her like the head of a snake about to strike. She turned awkwardly on the stool to shake his hand, and felt the heat in his palm, a heat that seemed to travel with electric speed into hers and up her arm. Also, his fingers clung to hers, but not because he was squeezing hard; it was more like his skin was magnetic. She held onto his hand at least three times as long as she normally would hold onto someone's hand when she shook.

"John," he repeated, widening his smile. "Follow me and I will make you fishers of men."

"Pardon?"

"Christ's invitation to the disciples."

"Oh." She finally released his hand.

"Actually, I think I was named after Kennedy. My mother was in love with him."

She smiled. He was so warm and relaxed; he sat there

so casually and had such poise, while her heart thumped so loud she was sure he must hear it. She looked nervous and stupid, fidgeting with the plastic mixer stick. And, he made reference to the Bible. How many young men today even read any of the Bible?

"After all that, aren't you going to volunteer your name?" he asked.

"What? Oh. I'm Paige," she said. "Paige Thorndyke."

"Paige. Are you a page in someone's book?" he asked, smiling.

"Hardly. No. I'm no one's little story," she replied, and he laughed.

She laughed herself, but still nervously.

"I'm glad of that even though you make it sound like a fault," he said, suddenly looking serious. He gazed at the crowd. "Maybe it is. Too many of us become someone else's little story. People don't take each other as seriously as they once did. Everyone uses everyone," he added. "We're so accustomed to disposable things, we even treat each other that way," he concluded, turning the glass in his hand.

She was fascinated for the moment. She even held her breath. How deep, she thought, and how right.

He apparently realized his pensiveness and turned quickly to her.

"I'm sorry. I didn't mean to get so heavy. This is not exactly the place for philosophical discussions," he added smiling again.

"That's okay, I . . ."

"Would you like to dance?" he asked.

"Dance?"

"It does seem to be one of the main activities here," he kidded.

She had to laugh at herself. Sure, why not? she thought. She would be on the dance floor with this handsome man when Eileen finally arrived. Wouldn't her eyes pop?

"All right," she said.

He took off his jacket, folded and left it on the stool, and then reached for her hand. She gave it to him and stood. He was at least three inches taller than she was and broad shouldered with a narrow waist. His turtleneck, milk-white silk shirt emphasized his dark complexion and made his eyes seem positively luminous. She noted how snugly his jeans fit and how tight was his rear end, tight and very enticing.

Even though her aerobics gave her the stamina to dance all night, her nervousness shortened her breath and she was self-conscious about the way she looked in the lights. She was positive she appeared awkward and gangly beside these other young women who had moves that rivaled Broadway dancers. That was the main reason why she hated dancing. People weren't dancing with each other; they were competing for attention. Every move was a desperate cry, "Look at me! Me!"

But something odd happened once they began. He

focused intently on her and she felt herself drawn to him, held in his orbit like a planet held to the sun. He was a wonderful dancer, graceful and smooth, his body undulating in perfect rhythm to the music. Almost immediately, she began to move in synchronization with him, mirroring his movements. It was as if he had control over her body, as if there were some invisible cords binding them so she would move as he wanted her to move.

She lost track of time and even became oblivious to everyone else around them. Never had dancing been more exciting or had she felt so complete and fulfilled by it. They barely spoke while they danced, but he never took her eyes from her and she couldn't look away from him. After a while she felt as if she had slipped into a warm cocoon, a cocoon he had spun around her with his gaze, his movements, the wet sensuality of his lips.

They returned to the bar a number of times to refresh themselves with new drinks. They danced on and on, and even though they talked at the bar, she couldn't recall anything he said. His words were like music; she was mesmerized by the melodic rhythms, not the meaning. What he said almost didn't matter. Whenever he touched her, she felt an excitement building, and she didn't back away.

Vaguely she thought, something special is happening here and I feel so good about it. Perhaps for the first time, I like the sense of abandon, the freedom, the excitement.

So she let it go on and on and she even forgot that

Eileen never arrived. She didn't bother to even look for her anymore. The club had become so crowded anyway.

Hours later, (she really wasn't sure about time), they left together. He had leaned forward and whispered an invitation into her ear, only it didn't seem like an invitation from him, it seemed like an invitation from herself. The thought, the proposal came from her own dark thoughts, that promiscuous second self with whom she was always debating. She drew upon her own well of fantasies and indeed she felt as if she were moving in a dream.

Maybe she hadn't paid enough attention to how many drinks she had, too. Whatever, some time later, like someone who had been literally hypnotized, she was surprised to find herself in a cheap motel room naked in bed with this handsome and beguiling stranger. And just as unexpectedly she felt the blood drain from her face. Although his lips were on hers and she welcomed his naked body against hers with more passion than she thought possible, she was confused by the mixed physiological messages being processed in her brain. She wanted him, more than she ever wanted any man, but instead of feeling complete and pure ecstasy, she was now feeling more like someone about to lose consciousness.

She raised her hands from the small of his back and ran her fingers through her hair, pressing her palms against her temples as if she wanted to keep her thoughts contained or her head from exploding. He was kissing her neck and moving his lips down over the base of her throat to the valley between her supple breasts. She felt the tip of his tongue move over one nipple and then the other, but when she heard herself moan, she thought she sounded more like someone moaning in pain than in sexual delight.

She opened her eyes and he raised his head so she could look into his. They no longer looked light blue. Instead they looked blacker, deeper, larger. It was as if they were absorbing the rest of his face until he would be nothing but eyes.

Suddenly she felt a terrific aching in all her joints. It was difficult even to bend her arm without experiencing some pain. The back of her neck felt tight, as tight as it would if someone had placed a metal clamp over it and had begun closing the clamp. She opened her mouth to express her discomfort, but he pressed his lips over hers and his tongue jetted into her mouth and over her own tongue, attaching itself to it like fly paper.

She began to gag. She willed her arms to push him away, but they remained limp at her sides.

Vaguely she knew he had entered her and they were making love, but the initial pleasure was gone from his thrusts. There was a terrible ringing in her ears that grew louder and louder. She was struggling now to extricate herself from his embrace. The chill that had come into her face grew even colder. She felt her eyes going back in her head and she fought desperately to remain conscious, but it was impossible. Everywhere his body touched hers, it felt sticky.

The last thing she thought was, it feels as if he is oozing over me.

Then she went dark.

ONE

STAT!

Dr. Terri Barnard dropped Irene Heckman's medical chart and rushed from her hospital room. The seventy-two-year-old woman had just begun to describe her chronic back pain in a slow, monotone voice as if the aches had taken over completely and turned her into another one of the walking dead, aged zombies parading through the corridors of Medicare, haunting the consciences of doctors. Terri knew it was arthritis and there was little she could do in the way of a cure, especially an instant cure, but she was prepared to be patient and sympathetic despite Mrs. Heckman's laying all the blame for her aches at the foot of her doctors and an uncaring medical community. Terri had an especially good bedside manner when it came to elderly patients. It made sense for a doctor to have that quality, she thought. Most of his or her patients would be elderly, wouldn't they?

STAT!

It was originating from the emergency room, and the Community General Hospital serving the once-famous resort area in the Catskills had no doctor on duty during the fall months. The participating physicians were rotating the responsibility. Tonight, it was hers, and for the first time!

Tough luck, she thought. Only hours after beginning her rounds she was thrown right into a crisis. At age twenty-eight, she had just finished two months as an assistant to Dr. Hyman Templeman, a sixty-eight-year-old family physician who had become something of a fixture in the upstate New York community of Centerville, a village of just fewer than two thousand year-round inhabitants. During the summer resort months, it and its surrounding hamlets and villages used to jump to ten times their population. It still multiplied five or six times, and Hyman's patients did come from all the surrounding hamlets in the Fallsburg township and not only Centerville.

Terri Barnard considered the elderly hands-on physician a perfect mentor: a doctor who diagnosed almost as much from instinct as from knowledge, maintaining an almost gleeful distrust of the new technology, but willing to learn and seize upon any aid to diagnosis and treatment that proved itself. Hyman Templeman liked to refer to himself as a medical iconoclast.

Despite her youth and her high-tech medical education, Terri had an affinity for the human touch. She believed in her grandmother's adage: people get well faster when they feel the doctor really cares whether they do or not. Her grandmother always wanted her to be a doctor, but "a real doctor, like your great-uncle Abe, who thought a doctor was a man with a gift, not a man with an expensive education." It followed then that if someone was given a gift, it was ungrateful, no, sinful, for her not to use it whenever and wherever possible.

Terri seemed to be following the dream life design. She had been a brilliant student, and she had returned to practice medicine in her hometown, where it was presumed she would marry her high school sweetheart, Curt Levitt, who had himself come back to the community to become a successful attorney in his father's firm, now taking it over with two partners since his father's retirement.

"Mr. and Mrs. Yuppie America," her girlfriends called them, "the dream couple." They teased, but she recognized their underlying envy, too.

Was her life too perfect? Could such a thing be so? She thought about it often. Her grandmother had brought all of her Old World superstitions with her, not the least of which was a belief in the Evil Eye. Whenever things were going too well for you, some covetous witch could cast a wicked spell. According to her grandmother, it was best to be humble, even secretive about good fortune.

At this moment in the emergency room, however, she thought about nothing but the problem at hand. She was doing what she was quickly becoming noted for . . . concentrating so intently she looked like she had shut away all distracting noise and sight.

A young woman had been brought in by ambulance

and was on the gurney in one of the examination rooms. The woman had lost some of her teeth, but it didn't appear to be the result of a blow to the mouth. There was no trauma, no blow to any part of her face. It appeared her teeth had simply fallen out. In fact, the young woman's face seemed to age right before Terri's eyes. The emergency room nurse looked up from the young woman, her eyes pleading for Terri to do something miraculous quickly. She pointed to a large hemorrhage on the woman's arm, just above the blood pressure cup.

"I did that," the nurse said. "With the blood pressure cup. I'm afraid to squeeze the bulb. Pressure, no matter where I place it on her body, and no matter how gently I do it, immediately produces hemorrhages."

Terri moved quickly to her side and examined the woman's neck and chest. Her eyes were open, but they were glassy, the pupils barely dilating. She stared up at the ceiling light. Petechia appeared up and down her arms and legs and over her stomach and chest. It looked as if some madman had come along with a dark-blue Magic Marker and poked her body for hours and hours.

"There's barely blood pressure," the nurse warned.

"My God . . ." Terri brought her stethoscope to the young woman's chest, but before she could suggest a therapy, she heard the young woman's heartbeat thump into silence. She looked at the nurse and then started CPR.

Nothing helped. Death had too tight a grip.

Terri felt her own face whiten in disbelief.

"How long . . . was she like this?" she asked the nurse.

"I don't know, Doctor. The ambulance and the police just brought her in. She was found in a motel outside of Monticello. What is it? What killed her?" the nurse said, grimacing. She pulled herself away from the dead young girl as if she had already concluded whatever killed her was highly contagious.

Terri shook her head. The symptoms were clicking off against a computerlike memory bank, and what resulted made no sense.

"I don't know," she confessed. "Not without the blood work. There are too many possibilities. You better call the coroner," she said softly.

This was almost a nonstop trip directly to the hospital morgue for this woman, Terri thought. She felt like a toll booth operator, a modern-day Charon ferrying her patient across the River Styx, full of disease and illness.

Actually, this was the first patient to die in her care, as short as that care was, and although she was cognizant of the way she should react, she couldn't help what was going on inside her. Of course she was used to corpses from her medical training, and when she had interned, she had seen patients die, but this was different because it was so bizarre and had happened so quickly. And on her watch!

"Was there any identification?" she asked softly.

The nurse gazed at her clipboard.

"Paige Thorndyke, age twenty-eight. Lived in Mountaindale."

"Thorndyke?" Terri asked looking up. "Paige Thorn-dyke?" She looked at the dead woman. Her face was unrecognizable at this point, otherwise, she would have known her. "I knew her," she muttered. "I know the Thorndykes. Her father, Bradley Thorndyke, is a commercial airline pilot for American. They live in the Greenfield Park Estates."

The nurse nodded sadly and they both turned back to the deceased young woman. Terri recalled that Paige was in junior high when she herself was a senior. There was an older brother, too, Phil, who was a year behind her and Curt. He had been on the basketball team with Curt.

A little voice in the back of her mind threatened: "You're not going to be able to do this—you're not going to be able to practice medicine in a hometown community where you will get emotionally involved in every case."

She stared down at Paige Thorndyke for a few more moments and then covered her with the white sheet, her fingers trembling as she did so. Whatever it was that caused this, she thought, it was a horrible way to die. The emergency room was already buzzing around her. She sighed and dropped her shoulders. She had to recuperate and, after speaking to the policemen who waited in the ER lobby, go back upstairs and continue with Mrs. Heckman.

The rest of the night went just as badly. They had two motor vehicle accidents, one resulting in a fatality, dead on arrival. She couldn't believe she was looking into the vacant eyes of another corpse, two within four hours. She set one broken arm and patched up another motor vehicle victim. Then she had to pump the stomach of a four-year-old girl who had swallowed paint remover. By the time 6:00 A.M. rolled about, she was ready to check herself into the emergency ward.

But despite all the activity, she couldn't get Paige Thorndyke out of her mind. The diagnosis she had instinctively arrived at seemed ridiculous, but the symptoms supported it. When her tour ended, she walked out to the parking lot still reviewing the possibilities. She ambled slowly through the pools of cool white illumination dropped over the macadam lot by the globular pole lights and walked right past her black BMW convertible, a graduation gift from her parents. She shook her head and doubled back.

Talk about your absent-minded professors, she thought, and sifted through her pocketbook to find her car keys. As usual, she fished out her house keys first and panicked, thinking she had misplaced her car keys; but they were there, lost in the makeup case, the lipsticks, the piles of change, the hand mirror, Life Savers, and gums. How could she be so meticulous in her work and so messy and disorganized in her personal life? she wondered. Probably because I don't concentrate on myself as much as I should, she replied to her own question.

Curt had advised her to concentrate on putting her work behind her once she had left either the office or the hospital, but sometimes, that just wasn't possible, at least, not for her. Curt was wonderful about closing the door behind him. He could shut himself off so completely, it was as though he were indeed two different people.

In the beginning she thought that indicated he wasn't fully involved in what he was doing, but now she had come to believe his power of forgetting was an asset. Many a night and many a morning after a night, she tossed and turned for hours reliving what she had done the previous eight hours. She had little hope for anything different this morning, despite her physical fatigue. She imagined she looked terrible—pale, drawn, strands of hair flying this way and that. She certainly felt drained.

At five feet ten with olive green eyes, prominent cheek bones, raven black hair that was shoulder length when she wore it down, and a firm, full figure, she looked more like a *Cosmopolitan* magazine cover girl than a physician. Her sensuous mouth and alluring smile drew endless compliments, but at this point in her life and her career, she found that to be more of a burden than a blessing.

Despite the many inroads women had made, medicine was still a man's domain. Patients who could choose usually chose male doctors over female. Even women discriminated against female physicians. It was maddening, but if a woman was to be accepted as a physician, she had to look brilliant and be coldly analytical, whereas a man could look goofy, have a personality, and even flirt.

She did the best she could to deal with the problem. Whenever she was on duty or practicing, she wore her hair tied in a tight, "granny bun" behind her head and wore no makeup, not even a light shade of lipstick. She had a pair of thick-rimmed, very plain glasses, her doctor glasses, she called them, and she always wore these dull-colored heavy cotton or tweed cardigan suits with a flat white blouse. Usually, she couldn't wait to get home after work and take off her physician clothes.

She would brush down her hair, apply some lipstick and some eye makeup, put on one of her pants outfits or nice blouses and sweaters with her tight-knit skirts or leather skirts and feel like . . . Wonder Woman. Curt kidded her about it, and said, "You accuse me of being like two different people. What about you?"

But when she chased him down, forced him to be honest, he confessed he felt more comfortable with a male doctor than a female himself and if he went in to see a doctor who was female, he would be nervous if she was what he called "a looker."

They almost got into a heated argument about it, but in the end she concluded it wasn't his fault. There were years and years of social changes yet to evolve.

Wise old Hyman Templeman had lowered his bifocals, even though all he had to do was raise his eyes, and warned her about all this when she first came to see him about the position he had advertised.

"It's like coming to bat with two strikes against you, Terri," he advised. "You want to work in your hometown where people remember you as the girl next door, a cheerleader, homecoming queen, and ask them to accept you as their family physician. I got as far away from my hometown as I could," he muttered, shaking his head, a head still crowned with a full crop of angel white hair. "I was born and bred in South Africa, you know."

She didn't know that. Funny, she thought, Hyman had been a doctor in this community for nearly forty years, and not once had she heard anyone talk about his coming from South Africa.

"And the second strike?" she asked, suspecting the answer.

"That you're a woman, what else?"

"So you wouldn't think of giving me the position then, I suppose."

"Never suppose anything," he chided gently, his bushy, gray eyebrows rising and then shifting forward as his forehead creased. "Conclude after you review all the facts. Supposing gets you onto side roads that are often dead ends. Whenever my patients ask me what I think, I say, I think I'll think about it.

"So," he concluded. "I'll think about it."

She left, never expecting he would call, but he did.

"Things are a bit boring for me these days," he said a bit impishly. "I could use some excitement around here."

"You won't regret it, Dr. Templeman. I promise I'll work hard and . . ."

"Now one thing right off, Terri. If we're going to work together and you want people to accept you same as they accept me eventually, you start calling me Hyman. Understand?"

"Yes, Doc . . . Hyman."

She had it! Her parents were overjoyed. How proud they could be, but she lowered their balloon a bit when she announced that she wasn't going to live at home. She wanted to move into Grandma Gussie's house. It had been on the market for four months without a bite, much like most of the real estate around there lately.

"But why?" her mother questioned, her face grimacing as though she were suffering real physical pain.

"I've always felt comfortable there, Mom. I just would like it for a while."

"Let her do what she wants," her father said. "She's earned the right."

"But what about Curt?" her mother pursued. Terri knew her mother had been quietly investigating all sorts of wedding preparations, anticipating that she would get the position and would practice medicine here. Terri was not surprised. After all, as soon as Terri had decided to return to the area to practice medicine, whether she worked with Hyman Templeman or not, she and Curt had become formally engaged.

"It will be a while yet, Mom."

"But . . ."

"Doris!" her father cried holding up his arms like someone pleading with the Almighty.

"Okay, okay. I'm just asking. A mother can ask her

daughter questions, can't she?" she said and turned to her again, this time like a prosecutor who had overcome a defense attorney's objection. "Why wait now?" Her mother held her breath in anticipation of some dreadful news.

"I have to have my own space for a while," she told her. "It's important I feel independent."

"You've got your career; you're going to be married. Why do you have to feel any more independent?" her mother persisted.

Curt had wanted to know the same thing.

"Why can't we get married immediately? Why do we have to wait for you to feel secure in your profession? What does that have to do with our marriage?"

She explained as best she could that without a strong self-image, she wouldn't be able to give him all he deserved.

"Let me clean up my act first," she begged. "I'd like to be standing on my own two feet."

She knew it was difficult for him to understand. It wasn't something his mother would have ever said to his father, and despite his protest that he was just as much a modern thinking man as anyone else, he carried a great deal of old-fashioned baggage, even some he wasn't aware himself he was carrying, as his attitude about doctors had revealed.

But it wasn't all bad. She admitted to herself that she liked, even craved some of those old-fashioned values, especially Curt's reverence for the sanctity of marriage and the home. In this way Curt was more like his grandparents. Of all the grandchildren, he had been the closest to them. As a child he had worked on his grandfather's farm and absorbed his rural-flavored wisdom. He had been with both his paternal grandfather and grandmother when they died, and to this day, he missed them dearly. She liked that about him. It was one of the qualities that endeared her to him and overcame what she saw as some faults.

Terri knew that Curt sincerely believed that a man and a woman became one when they took the vows, each and every word of which he accepted and held sacred. He cherished the image of family, wanted children and a solid home life. And so, he was caught in a conflict she recognized and handled as delicately as she could. He told her he was proud of her, proud of what she had accomplished, and proud of the idea that he would be married to a doctor, but at the same time, she sensed he was afraid she would be one of these professional women willing to sacrifice the children and their needs when it came to being her own person.

"Not that I want to be like my father," he quickly emphasized. "And expect you to do everything and make all the career sacrifices like he expected of my mother. I want to be there for my kids all the time. I'm not paying any chauffeur to cart them around to their school activities and Little League. We're all going to grow up together," he promised. "Can you make the same promise?" he taunted.

"I don't know, Curt," she confessed. "I'm going to try.

I want the same things you want. I'm going to try, but at the moment, I don't know."

It was a more honest answer than Curt had wanted, and a little sour note resonated in the hall of their otherwise happy symphony.

Terri tried to be understanding. She believed that in many ways the modern world tested the bonds of love more than they had been tested in times when people had to struggle every day merely to survive. She had an undying faith that the love between her and Curt would overcome any and all obstacles. Was she being naive or perhaps as Hyman Templeman might say, "a little too doctor arrogant"?

Occasionally, she muttered a tiny prayer: "Oh please, please, don't let that be so."

Impulsively, she made a sharp right turn onto State Highway 17 and sped up, instead of taking County Road One down toward Centerville and to what had been her grandmother's home. She was going to Bridgeville because that was where Curt lived, in a home once owned by his grandfather. It was another wonderful thing they shared, she thought, both currently residing in their grandparents' old homes.

She glanced at the clock in the car. It was ridiculously early to pay a visit, but she relished the idea of getting him up to answer the door and then going back to his bedroom and crawling under the covers with him.

She wanted to make love very badly; she wanted to be

vibrant and sensuous and feel sexual ecstasy. She wanted to feel alive. That was it. There was no other way to get Paige's degenerating body out of her mind and to forget the glassy eyes of the dead.

Curt could barely open his eyes, and when he did, he had to squint because the old farm house faced the east and the rising sun peered over the horizon unobstructed. The house had been built on a knoll facing the long, flat fields that had once hosted acres of corn, a sea of it he used to think. Now it was all overgrown, the pale brown weeds swaying in the autumn breeze. But there were a number of beautiful large maple and hickory trees around the house, and the house had a wide and deep back yard that looked upon the mountains and woods. On the rear patio, one could feel isolated, peaceful, relaxed. Curt wanted to put in a pool, but he didn't want to go forward with any of the changes or restorations in the old house until he and Terri were married so she could be party to each and every decision. Actually, he hated the thought of changing anything in the old house, the house his grandfather had built himself.

Curt's grandfather had been a small farmer, raising dairy cows and chickens and the corn crop that once had glittered like gold out there. He and his hard-working wife, Nanny Lillian, had raised four boys and a girl. Two of the boys, Uncle Frank and Uncle Abe, now worked on Wall Street. Uncle Louie had become a merchant marine and was presently still a captain on an oil tanker. Aunt Charlotte married a banker and moved to Pennsylvania.

There was never enough money when Curt's father, uncles, and aunt were growing up. His father had to take on odd jobs and when he was old enough, work in the Catskill resorts as a busboy and finally as a waiter to earn his college tuition. But he never gave up and when he did get into law school, he graduated at the top of his class. Only after he had landed a good job with a New York City law firm did he marry Curt's mother, Marion Steele. Shortly afterward, when the opportunity presented itself, he went into his own practice, developed real estate deals in the Catskills and became one of the most respected and successful attorneys here.

There wasn't time in those days to worry about whether or not he was stepping on his wife Marion's own career goals, he once told Curt whenever they discussed Curt and Terri's long engagement. "Your mother knew that from the start. She once had some ambition to become a magazine editor and work in New York City, but she never really pursued it. Oh, she tried some freelance writing, but that didn't lead anywhere, and soon she was happy just being Mrs. William Levitt. I never heard her complain about the decisions she made. Of course, that was before all this women's liberation business, before women began to wonder why they couldn't have flies on their pants, too," he joked, half joked, actually. Curt knew his father was too much of a male chauvinist.

However, Curt's father loved and respected Terri, even though he teased her whenever he had an opportunity to do so. Curt was also aware that his father was a flirt and suspected that he might have had an extramarital affair here and there, but Curt would rather not think about it. He was like that when it came to his father—deliberately blind to any of his faults or willing to easily excuse and rationalize them away.

Yet Curt supposed, or rather hoped, he was like his father in many ways. After all, his father was a self-made man. Curt looked more like him than any of his siblings. His younger brother Neil, who worked with Uncle Frank on Wall Street, looked more like their mother, and his younger sister Michele, who was married to a dentist in Boston, was so much a cross between their mother and father that she had a totally different look.

He had his father's six feet two inch height and the same broad shoulders, but he had his mother's smaller facial features, her slightly turned up nose and soft mouth. His father didn't have the narrow waist he once had. However, he still had a rough and ruddy complexion, a farmer boy's forearms and hands. "Just shake hands with Bill Levitt and you know you've been shook," people would say. His father and he had glimmering rust brown eyes and reddish brown hair. Both had a splatter of freckles along their foreheads, too.

His habitual gestures, holding his chin between his thumb and forefinger whenever he paused to think, or nodding softly when he was in deep thought were gestures borrowed from his father. They had the same deeply resonant voice, good for trial work, and like his father, he was impatient with small talk and bureaucracy.

Right now, he tightened his robe around his waist and stared incredulously at Terri.

"Jesus, you know what time it is?"

"I'm sorry. I just got off my turn at the hospital."

"I'm glad I don't have to keep doctor's hours." He wiped his eyes and looked at her more closely.

"What . . . what's wrong?" he asked.

"Oh Curt, just hold me. Please," Terri said, a little surprised herself at how vulnerable and feminine she sounded. Curt pulled her to him and pressed her against him.

"What?" He closed the door behind her quickly.

"A terrible night in the emergency room," she said. "Two deaths, one right before my eyes."

"Really? What happened?" He wiped the sleep from his eyes when she stepped back.

"One was a car fatality, but the other, the first one . . . Paige Thorndyke. You remember the Thorndykes. Her father is an airline pilot."

"Sure. Paige's brother Phil Thorndyke was on the varsity basketball team with me. What about Paige?"

"She's dead."

"Oh no. Also a car?"

"No." Terri shivered. He put his arm around her again.

"Easy. Want some coffee?"

"No. Let's just crawl back into your bed," she said. He looked surprised.

"Sure, but . . . so what killed her?"

"I'm not certain," she said as they walked toward his bedroom together. "It seems ridiculous in fact. I'll have to wait on the lab tests and speak with Hyman."

"Well, what were her symptoms?"

"Curt," she said stopping and turning so abruptly to him in the doorway, his eyebrows lifted. "If I believed her symptoms, she died of scurvy."

"Scurvy? You mean . . . like sailors used to get because they didn't have enough vitamin C?"

Terri nodded.

"Only, taken to a bizarre extreme." She shook her head again, this time to shake the images out of her mind.

"What the hell . . . can't be, can't it?"

"I don't see how," she said and began to take off her clothes. "I don't want to think about it right now. I don't want to think at all. I just want to feel."

He nodded. He understood and he was glad she had come to him. He would make love to her as gently and as lovingly as he could. In bed together there were no careers to consider, no egos to stroke. There was just honest and sincere passion.

Terri was eager to lose herself in it. She drew Curt to her as she would draw a warm blanket over her body, and as she had hoped, she forgot the dead.

TWO

Dr. Hyman Templeman pressed his lips together and squinted at Terri as if the sunlight coming through the opened pale blue Venetian blinds in his private office reflected too brightly off her face. Templeman's medical practice was located in his large home on Main Street, Centerville. It was a Queen Anne–style Victorian house with a steeply pitched irregularly shaped roof, a dominant front-facing gable, and one side-facing gable. It had patterned white shingles and cutaway bay windows with Wedgwood blue shutters. The asymmetrical facade had a full-width, one-story-high porch that extended along both side walls. In its day it was one of the most expensive homes in the area. Now it was a remarkably well-kept historic whose spindle work detailing drew appreciative eyes.

"They just don't make houses like this anymore," people would say. And patients would add, "Nor do they make doctors like Hyman Templeman."

The two-story building contained fourteen rooms. Hyman and his wife Estelle utilized the rear and the upstairs for living quarters, which was far more space than the two of them now needed. Their three children were all married and gone, two living in California and one in Westchester. The front five rooms, including a relatively recently built waiting room, were dedicated to Hyman's medical practice. He had an X-ray room, three examination rooms, and a small lab.

The structure didn't have much land around it, but it did have a long front lawn that unfolded smoothly toward the street. There was never enough parking space around or near his offices, but the village police had an unwritten understanding that they wouldn't ticket the cars of patients parked at expired meters. Parking was enforced only during the summer months anyway, and just as in most small resort communities, the recognizable cars belonging to residents enjoyed a special dispensation.

"I haven't seen a case of Frank scurvy since I served in the army medical corps," Hyman remarked. "And that was in the South Pacific. Never seen one around here. Why even the occasional stump jumpers and rednecks who come down from the hills don't have symptoms that bad. Frank scurvy is rare in the modern world, but the occurrence of petechiae, spongy gums, and tendency to bleed, usually with other evidences of nutritional deficiencies, suggests the possibility of scorbutic purpura."

"I know how unusual all this is, Hyman, but if you saw her . . ."

"Of course, I've heard of women who have gone on one or another of these fad diets denying themselves necessary nutrition. And you are aware, of course, that patients with gastrointestinal disease, especially those on an ulcer diet consisting chiefly of milk, cream, cereals, and eggs, develop secondary deficiencies. Infections increase the physiologic requirements for vitamin C and people with poor dietary habits are likely to precipitate the appearance of symptoms."

"I don't know whether or not she was on some fad diet, of course," Terri said, "or if she was suffering from an ulcer . . ."

"Well, the Thorndykes have been my patients for years. I never treated Paige for anything like that." He shook his head. "We'll have to wait for the autopsy report to confirm it all," Hyman said sitting back in his high back, dark brown, wide-lapped leather chair. The mahogany arms were worn where he would run his palms up and down while he thought deeply or spoke intensely. It was a nervous habit Terri had noticed. What she didn't know was that it, along with some other chronic gestures, was growing more and more pronounced as Hyman approached his mid-seventies.

He was a tall, lean man with dark eyes and a dark complexion that made his crown of white hair that much more distinct. He had a long, thin nose, but a strong mouth with full lips and a hard, sharp jaw. Patients were usually set at immediate ease by his fatherly smile, a soft movement in his cheeks, and a radiant light around his eyes. They felt his compassion and concern and were reassured by his confidence and wisdom.

Terri knew it took years to develop the physician's

demeanor, especially the demeanor of a man like Hyman Templeman. She longed for the time when she would finally not have to wonder if the patient had any faith in her diagnosis and prognosis. No one need be arrogant and overconfident, but a doctor had to emit assurance and firm purposes.

"I saw a lot of scurvy in infants while I was stationed in the Philippines." He shook his head. "Such an unnecessary thing and the poor little things—you know," he said lifting his long right hand with its puffy fingers, "angular enlargements of the costochondral junctions of the ribs, swelling of the extremities over the ends of the long bones, swollen hemorrhagic gums surrounding erupting teeth . . ." His body shook as if an ice cube had been dropped down the back of his neck.

"You know there are things that deplete vitamins—alcohol, of course, antibiotics, anticonvulsants, antihistamines, even aspirin—but can you imagine the intake of one or more of these substances one would have to undergo to achieve this serious a condition?" he muttered.

She shook her head.

"In any case, what I really don't understand," Terri said, "is she not realizing she was this sick. Manifest scorbutic symptoms are almost always preceded by weakness, irritability, muscle aches and pains, and weight loss."

Hyman shrugged.

"She might have attributed all that to her fad diet," he suggested.

"Um. But you would think bleeding gums, gingivitis, loose teeth would have frightened her into stopping it."

Hyman shook his head.

"I've seen a lot of craziness lately. Just last week, they rushed Mrs. Menkos in with a palpitating heart. She had been living on celery stalks and diet pills. She was losing hair, too. What about anorexia?" Hyman asked.

"That's the thing, Hyman. Paige Thorndyke didn't look anorexic to me. She was undernourished, but not really underweight."

He shook his head and then looked at his watch.

"Let's call," he said. "If Julie's on duty, he'll skip the protocol and give us the findings."

He leaned forward and lifted the receiver of the brass phone. Terri remembered sitting in this office nearly ten years ago to talk to Hyman Templeman about her ambitions. He still had that wonderful painting hanging behind his desk. It was a picture of a doctor making a house call and putting the stethoscope on his own chest to show the frightened child it was nothing. Terri had accompanied her grandmother, who had to have a routine examination, and while they waited for the nurse to help her get dressed, Hyman had invited her in to discuss her plans. He knew she wanted to be a doctor. In Centerville, everyone knew everyone else's business; sometimes before he or she knew it. Of course, Terri's parents had been bragging about her and, on more than one occasion, had told Hyman about her ambitions.

Funny, she thought, how everything looked so much bigger to her in those days. Hyman's dark oak desk had seemed enormous, as well as the office itself. Even the examination rooms were bigger in her eyes. Or was it that she was so much smaller? Regardless of her accomplishments and her association with Hyman Templeman, he still loomed larger than life in so many ways. The family doctor remained an icon in America, she thought, whether he or she deserved the reverence or not. She wondered, especially at this moment, if that veneration wasn't as much a liability as it was an asset. They expect miracles, and all we can offer is scientific knowledge and some medical skill. There certainly wasn't very much she could do for Paige Thorndyke last night, she concluded sadly.

"Julie," Hyman said when he had reached the morgue, "Hyman."

Only someone with Hyman Templeman's standing in the medical community could slip past the hospital bureaucracy so smoothly, Terri thought enviously.

"My young assistant was on duty last night when they brought in Paige Thorndyke. Yes, yes, tragic. Have you had an opportunity for any preliminary findings?" He listened. "Really?" he said after one point, his eyebrows rising. "That's amazing. Negligible, you say? I know, I know." He listened some more. "It sounds like someone kept in solitary confinement for months." He listened and then looked at Terri while he asked the next question. "Any chemical substances, antibiotics, barbiturates . . .

"Okay. Appreciate it. Talk to you soon," he added and returned the receiver to its cradle slowly. Then he lifted his eyes toward Terri again.

"Normal plasma ascorbic acid level, as you know, is about 1.5 mg. per 100 cc. He couldn't get any reading . . . nothing."

"Low levels may sometimes be found in nonscorbutic patients," Terri said softly. "But nothing?"

"Right, and she had no reading in the white cell-platelet layer. She had epistaxis, conjunctival, retinal, cerebral, gastrointestinal, and genitourinary bleeding . . . all of it," he emphasized. "There's no doubt; this was a severe case of scurvy. It's actually one for the record books."

"What a freaky death for a young, affluent woman in the twenty-first century," Terri said, more to herself than to Hyman.

"She had sexual intercourse right before she was brought in," he added.

Terri raised her eyebrows just as Hyman's intercom buzzed.

"Yes, Elaine?"

"Mr. and Mrs. Thorndyke are here to see Dr. Barnard," the receptionist said, her voice cracking with emotion. Elaine Wolf had been with Dr. Templeman nearly as long as he had been practicing. Some older patients considered her evaluation of their condition as good as a preliminary examination. She was a fountain of information when it came to knowledge about families in the community. She asked questions with the forcefulness of a homicide detective and knew if someone came in with bad bronchitis, there were good chances this or that close relative wouldn't be far behind.

"Show them in," Hyman said. He sat back.

"What am I going to tell them?" Terri asked, not disguising the panic in her voice.

"All you know. What else?"

There was a knock at the office door, and Terri rose reluctantly to greet the Thorndykes.

Bradley Thorndyke was still in his pilot's uniform. He was a tall, handsome man in his early fifties with light brown hair and a light complexion that usually gave him a youthful appearance. Now, the weight of mourning and the personal tragedy had added years quickly. His eyes were dark; his skin pale, his shoulders slumped.

Geena Thorndyke was nearly her husband's height. She was an attractive, long-legged, slim woman with ebony hair and dark brown eyes. She clung to her husband for veritable support, her eyes bloodshot, her lips trembling.

"Bradley . . . Geena," Hyman Templeman said, rising. He went to them quickly and shook Bradley's hand and then put his arm around Geena Thorndyke's shoulders and guided her to the brown leather settee. "I'm so sorry," he said.

"Can you believe this?" Bradley asked. "It makes no sense to us and we couldn't sit at home and wait for something sensible, so we decided to come see the doctor who examined her," he said looking at Terri.

"We were just discussing it," Hyman said stepping back. "Needless to say, it's one of the most unusual things I've seen or heard since I began practicing medicine."

Bradley Thorndyke's gaze swung quickly to Terri again. She felt his sorrow, but she also felt his anger. There was accusation in those eyes. She quickly realized that in their need to understand what had happened to their daughter, the Thorndyke's were searching for a scapegoat, someone to blame so it would make some sense.

"You were on duty when they brought her into the emergency room, right?" he said in an accusing tone.

"Yes. I was with a patient and I heard the STAT and rushed right down. I had just gotten my stethoscope on her chest when she expired," Terri explained.

Geena Thorndyke groaned and began to sob.

"They're telling us it looks like she died of acute scurvy," Bradley said, his disdain and disbelief quite evident in his voice.

"Yes, Mr. Thorndyke. It's just about certain that will be the diagnosis."

"That's just ridiculous. She was found unconscious on the floor of a cheap, one-night motel room. She must have been drugged," Bradley insisted. "Someone picked her up and slipped her one of those Ecstasy things or something, an overdose, right?"

"The autopsy doesn't show that, Bradley," Hyman said softly. "There was some alcohol in her blood stream, but no chemical substances."

"Well let them do another autopsy, for Christ sakes! My daughter had to have been murdered. Murdered!"

Hyman Templeman shifted his gaze quickly to Terri and then nodded sympathetically at Bradley Thorndyke.

"I can understand why you would feel this way, Bradley. We're stumped."

"Someone had to have at least hit her or . . ." He turned to Terri, his hands out, "Or done something violent to her."

"Every hemorrhage on her body appears to have been caused by fragile capillaries, a classic symptom of scurvy. The autopsy reveals large muscle hemorrhages and petechial and purpuric skin manifestations," Hyman explained, when Terri hesitated.

Bradley shook his head.

"It's not the sort of thing that happens overnight," Terri added. "Not this severe, this quickly. Did either of you notice her becoming weak, irritable? Did she become black and blue at the slightest touch? And her gums . . . rapidly developing gingival hemorrhages give the appearance of bags of blood," Terri continued. Wide-eyed, both Bradley and Geena looked at her. It was as if she were from another planet.

Geena finally shook her head.

"No, nothing like that," she muttered.

"She wasn't being treated for peptic ulcers, was she?" Hyman asked.

"Ulcers? No," Bradley said. "Besides, you would know. You were her doctor, Hyman."

Doctor Templeman nodded.

"It's been a while since I've seen her," he remarked softly.

"That's because she was as healthy as a horse. You know she was into all that aerobics and exercise. Christ, she ate like someone in training. She was always complaining about our fatty diets, the chemicals in our food. We never ate the right cereals and she would go into tirades over the cholesterol we consumed, right, Geena?"

"What? Oh, yes, yes," she said smiling and wiping her cheeks. "She made me promise to buy this butter substitute because Bradley eats so badly when he's traveling." Her voice trailed off. She caught herself as if she realized she was adding the most inane details to the discussion.

"When did you see your daughter last, Mrs. Thorndyke?" Terri asked softly.

"Two days ago . . . we had lunch." She started to bury her face in her hands again.

"So what were Paige's dietary habits?" Terri pursued. "I mean, was she following any fads? I know that some people get caught up in these meditation cults and make radical changes in their food habits."

"Meditation cults?" Bradley cried. "This is ridiculous," he said turning back to Hyman. "Scurvy? That comes from a lack of vitamin C, right? A sailor's disease before they knew about vitamins, right?" he insisted. "It has to be a stupid mistake."

"The lab findings are pretty accurate, Bradley. What we were also wondering was had Paige gone on any sort of fad diet to lose weight," Hyman said.

"Absolutely not. I told you. She was into exercise. She didn't have to diet to lose weight. She was in great condition. I know I couldn't keep up with her on the jogging track," Bradley replied. Then he looked down at his wife. "Unless there's something I don't know about," he added. Geena shook her head.

"She wasn't dieting," she said.

"You say you had lunch with her two days ago, Geena?" Hyman asked softly.

Geena Thorndyke looked up.

"Yes, but nothing made me sick," she added quickly.

"No, that's not what we're looking for. Do you recall what you ate?"

"We had a salad . . . chicken salad."

"Paige was in the habit of taking a daily vitamin anyway," Bradley said sharply. "I know that for a fact because she was always criticizing me for not."

"Uh huh. What did you drink with your salad, Geena?"

"We had . . . cranberry juice," she said and shook her

head so vigorously, Terri thought she was going into a convulsion.

"Well, that's a source of vitamin C," Henry muttered. "And if she was in the habit of taking vitamins daily, she would get the minimum requirements of vitamin C and none of these symptoms would have been precipitated."

"So she couldn't die of scurvy. Right?" Bradley Thorndyke cried with frustration. He turned from Hyman to Terri. They simply stared at each other.

"I'm sorry but we can't explain this, Bradley," Hyman said. "The autopsy report doesn't show a reading of ascorbic acid at all." He sighed. "Dr. Barnard can describe her symptoms when she was first brought into the emergency room. She never had an opportunity to begin any therapy. You will see a copy of the autopsy report, of course, and you will see that all the findings point to scurvy."

"But what was she doing in that cheap motel?" Geena Thorndyke asked, staring down at the floor. She was really asking herself.

No one spoke; only Geena's sobbing broke the heavy silence. She realized it and stopped crying to look up at Terri. Bradley Thorndyke turned to her too, as if he expected she had the answer to Geena's question as well as all the others.

Terri felt like she was shrinking under their demanding gazes, and for the first time in her long journey to become a physician, she wanted to run away from the profession.

• • •

Nearly eight hours later, Terri emerged from the first examination room where she had seen her final patient for the day and handed Elaine the patient's file. She had had little time during the remainder of the workday to dwell on Paige Thorndyke. Before visiting hours had ended, she had seen twenty-five patients. The rapid change in weather characteristic of the Catskill mountain climate engendered the usual minor epidemic of coughs and colds. Many residents stubbornly clung to the remnants of summer, dressing lightly for the daytime and forgetting that the temperatures plummeted in the late afternoon and evening as the sun settled below the peaks and treetops. Shadows grew longer, deeper, darker.

But Terri loved the Catskill fall mornings. They had that wonderfully invigorating crispness to them. Immediately after stepping out, she enjoyed inhaling deeply and feeling the rush of air fill her lungs and wash away the cobwebs woven during another restless night. Her spiders were hatched out of every diagnosis and prognosis. She had an understandable anxiety, a fear of missing something significant, making the wrong diagnosis and therefore causing the unnecessary death of a patient.

"A good doctor is never completely free of that anxiety," Hyman told her when she confessed it to him during one of their frequent tête-à-têtes. "The trick is to recognize the gray areas and be modest enough to ask for a second opinion. Unfortunately, there are some pretty arrogant bastards in our profession. Even when they make a mistake, they refuse to recognize it's their mistake. They blame it on the symptoms being too ambiguous or something. Many even blame the patients, claiming they didn't tell them everything. They see and hear what they want. I suppose there's nothing as dangerous as an arrogant doctor.

"But mind you," he added quickly, fully cognizant of her relationship with Curt, "I'm not happy with all this malpractice crap. All you've done, in most cases," he interjected, lowering his bifocals, "is substituted one type of parasite for another. In the end the patients will suffer."

Of course, Curt had another view. "If it weren't for the malpractice suits," he claimed, "many unscrupulous and incompetent doctors would have free rein and woe-be-gone the unsuspecting clod who wandered into their waiting rooms."

Curt had already successfully represented clients in two malpractice suits. One was a clear case of negligence that Terri couldn't deny. A doctor had rushed a patient through a routine D and C in order to make a golfing date and had neglected to check her blood count. She hemorrhaged and died on the table in the hallway.

Nevertheless, she saw that Curt had been smitten, and like a shark with the taste of blood on his lips, he swam eagerly in the waters of the medical world searching for a new opportunity or, as Hyman would say, a new victim. It wasn't hard to foresee that this would be an area of argument between her and Curt. Her fiancé was a strong-minded, firm man, proud of his self-assurance and the old-fashioned grit he believed he had inherited from his father and grandfather. Curt was willing to make the necessary compromises when he had to, but he was always like a combatant dragged kicking and screaming to the negotiating table. He relented; he gave in and made sacrifices, but he didn't do so with a full heart. Even when his opponents won a point, they left the office feeling they had lost.

"There's a policeman here to see you," Elaine whispered sharply, taking her out of her reverie. The gray-haired little woman who always reminded Terri of Gracie Allen shifted her eyes to the left.

Terri was so tired she hadn't noticed the tall, blond-haired man in a dark-blue sports jacket, tie, and slacks standing by the window. He had beautiful blue eyes that fixed on her with remarkable intensity. Broad-shouldered, at least six feet two or three, he stood with a firm demeanor that suggested strength and purpose. Her clinical eyes concluded from the rich sheen of his hair and the robust color of his complexion that he was a healthy, vigorous man. He had a small cleft in his chin and a set of teeth that belonged in toothpaste advertisements.

"Oh," she said. "Thank you, Elaine."

She opened the door and stepped into the waiting room.

"Dr. Barnard, I assume," he said smiling. The twinkle

in his eyes made him seem years younger than she imagined he was. He extended his hand and when she placed hers in it, he didn't hesitate to give hers a firm shake. No timidity here, she thought quickly.

"Yes."

"I'm here to talk to you about Paige Thorndyke."

He displayed his badge and card identifying him as a New York State Bureau of Criminal Investigations agent.

"Clark Kent?" she asked, smiling and reading.

"I know, I know," he said putting his identification away quickly. "You can imagine the kind of kidding I have been enduring my entire life. Every time my friends and I approached a telephone booth, they pushed me into it. What can I say, I had parents with a sense of humor."

Terri laughed.

"Let's sit down," she said indicating the waiting room sofa on her right.

"Thank you."

"Why is there an investigation like this? Was something criminal discovered in relation to her death?" she quickly asked, actually hopefully asked.

"It's routine basically. I won't be long. Just tying up loose ends on the Thorndyke woman's death for the district attorney. You were the doctor on duty when they brought her in, right?" he asked sitting back, his long arm along the rear of the sofa.

"Yes, but there wasn't much for me to do. She died within moments of arrival."

"I understand. Did she say anything, anything at all that would lead you to believe someone had done something harmful to her? Perhaps she gave you a name, a description."

"No. I don't believe she had even the strength to speak. She was too far gone."

He nodded.

"The traumas you observed are characteristic of those caused by a vitamin deficiency?" he asked.

"As far as I know, yes, but Dr. Templeman and I both think this is going to take a far more expert opinion than ours. It's too bizarre."

"There was nothing that looked like a blow to the face or head?"

"I didn't see anything like that. I examined her face because she was missing some teeth, but except for the hemorrhaging in the gums, there wasn't anything, no contusions about the lips, no bruise on the jaw or cheeks. The autopsy has apparently revealed nothing of the kind either, but you would probably know that."

"Uh huh."

"So? Do you have reason for some suspicion of foul play?" she inquired again. "She did check into that motel with someone, right?"

"Well, yes, but he was gone by the time she was discovered."

"But can't you track him down? He signed in, paid for the room . . ."

"He signed a fictitious name and address and he paid in cash, no credit card."

Terri sighed deeply, the frustration coming over her like a chill.

"Didn't anyone see him with her earlier? Do we know how she met him at least?"

"Well, she was at this dance club, the Underground, in Monticello earlier that evening. As I understand it, she went there to meet a friend, but her friend never showed. I questioned some of the people who were at the club and they remember her leaving with the man with whom she had been dancing. The bartender said they met at the bar, and from what he had overheard, met for the first time. No one knows anything about the guy. I've got a description," he said, looking at his small notepad. "But not that concise. Some said he had light hair, some thought dark brown. The bartender claims he was in shadows most of the time.

"I was hoping she had said something to you. No matter how insignificant it might seem, it could be important," he emphasized.

"No, as I said, she was too far gone to speak. She didn't know where she was anymore."

Terri looked up at him.

"How was she discovered? In the state she was in when I saw her, I can't imagine her even calling out for help."

"The manager was walking by her room and noticed the door was wide open. When he looked in, she was sprawled on the floor. What about the nurse at the ER or the paramedics . . . did any of them hear her say anything?"

"Not that I know," she replied and wondered why he didn't just go directly to them.

He anticipated the question.

"I'm just getting into this. I haven't even had an opportunity to speak with her parents yet."

She nodded, imagining how hard that was going to be now.

"It's never easy to understand the death of a child, but something like this especially so. This sort of acute scurvy would have revealed itself through symptoms far earlier. Her parents were here this morning," Terri continued. "Understandably, they don't believe the cause of death was scurvy. I can't believe it myself, or can Dr. Templeman, but the medical evidence is quite convincing.

"I can't believe that whoever brought her to the motel would not have noticed something," Terri continued. "To begin with her teeth . . . she would have had bleeding in her mouth, black and blue marks . . . been tired. . . . Who would do such a thing, bring a woman that sick to a motel or keep her there once he saw that? Why not get her to a hospital? The therapy was simple and would have saved her life."

"I know. That's what I'd like to know."

"If someone kept a person from getting life-saving medical attention, he would as much as murdered her," Terri concluded.

"Exactly."

"Oh. I see why you would be investigating," she said nodding. "As I understand it, she looked well the day before. At least, that's what her parents say." Terri shook her head. "Everything I know about the disease would make that impossible. The whole thing seems impossible. I can't think of any medical explanation for a practically instantaneous case of acute scurvy. People don't develop something like that overnight, even if they neglect vitamin C for days."

"Maybe drugs caused it," he suggested.

"Haven't you seen a copy of the autopsy report?" she asked.

"Oh yes, but I just wondered. Maybe they missed something," he said quickly.

"There are many drugs that deplete vitamins, but nothing would work this fast and everything I know would show up in an analysis. I'm not going to pass myself off as any world-renowned expert on the subject, however. I'm just a family physician, you understand."

"Of course," he said smiling, "but I can appreciate your frustration."

"I mean her parents told me that she was an exercise fanatic. What can I say? It's a real medical mystery. You don't have any other situations like this, do you?" she asked.

"I don't know yet. I'll have to contact the FBI. I hope not," he said.

"Oh, I would have thought you would have done that already," she said.

"Not enough time. This is my first case on a new position and I get this," he said smirking.

"Oh?"

"I moved out of New York City because my wife wanted a quieter, safer environment for our children."

"How old are they?"

"We don't have any yet," he replied, "but my wife's pregnant."

"Do you live here?"

"No. We moved to the Albany area, a small community just outside the city. It's actually more rural than I had expected, but we like the stressless life, a world without all this urban turmoil."

"Normally this is a safe place to live," Terri said. "I grew up here."

"Really? And you returned to practice medicine here. I guess you do like it."

She smiled.

"My fiancé lives here. He has a successful law practice."

"Oh." He looked impressed.

She thought a moment.

"You're absolutely sure no one noticed anything unusual about her at the club?" Terri asked, still struggling with the effort to understand and free herself of this terrible frustration.

"The bartender claims she was dancing up a storm."

Terri shook her head.

"That would just seem to be impossible. I wish I could tell you something that would clear it all up, but I'm more confused than anyone right now."

"I understand. Well, Doctor, thank you," Kent said rising. "I'm certain we'll reach some satisfactory conclusion."

"Well," she said, "nothing is for certain in this world, but people don't die like this."

"No," he said, "they don't."

He said it as if he knew just as much about medicine as she did. He nodded, thanked her again, and left.

She turned slowly and saw Elaine Wolf seated behind the counter. Of course, she had been listening in. Only now she looked sorry about her curiosity. Her eyes were filled with terror.

It gave Terri a chill that she knew she wouldn't shake off until she had made herself a cocktail at home.

THREE

He hadn't slept late this morning because he was fully energized and his every sense was heightened, sharp and clear. Maybe he imagined it, but he thought he had been able to hear the movement of the birds on the branches, their tiny steps on the thin twigs of the birch trees just outside the motel window. All he had to do was concentrate and he homed in so quickly and completely, it was as if he were right beside the birds, his ear against the twig.

When he had opened his eyes and focused on the opening in the window curtains, he had caught sight of a small cloud in the distance, and like a telephoto lens, his eyes had brought the cloud closer, so much closer in fact, that he had felt himself drifting into it the way an airplane drifted through clouds.

Then he had thrown back his covers, inhaled deeply, and recognized that he still carried the scent of the woman he had fed upon the night before. Everything about her stuck to him, was in his very skin: the perfume she wore and the scent in her shampoo, especially, and when he had combined that with the memory of how she had tasted, how delicious had been the inside of her mouth, her juices, he sighed and stretched like a newborn baby.

How wonderful it had been to be able to feed on one so healthy, with blood so rich. The memory had stimulated him and had filled him with every kind of natural hunger. Today, he had eaten normally and he now recalled how the thought of bacon and eggs, soft rolls and butter, and steaming hot coffee had made his stomach churn in such anticipation that he had been unable to linger a moment longer in that bed.

He had also wanted to jog, to feel his muscles expand and his heart pound. And he had wished he had another woman beside him to make love to normally. He would take no more from her than he would give to her.

"I promise," he had said aloud, as if there had been a skeptical woman beside him.

Then he had risen from his bed feeling a foot taller as usual and had put on his exercise clothes. When he had first driven into this town, he had noticed the nice park with the jogging track circling it. Faces and names drifted in and out of his memory like leaves carried in the wind. For a moment they were there, and then they were gone and he couldn't recall them no matter how hard he tried or how much he wanted to remember. Yet incidental things, like the park, lingered long enough for him to recall them precisely. Why this would be so, he did not know, but he rarely questioned it. He rarely questioned anything about his life even though he understood he was different from every other human being around him.

He had stepped out of his new motel room and looked about with interest. Because he had come here so late, he had really seen it for the first time this morning—the scenery, the parking lot, the office, and the pool. He had arrived here in the dark, tired, but fulfilled and eager to pass into a restful sleep. But when he had stepped out and inhaled the clear, cool air, all of his systems went into full gear and he quickly became the wonderful and efficient machine he always knew he was capable of being.

In the park he had appeared to be just another one of them: rosy cheeks, heart pumping, legs moving in stride, his lungs expanding, his blood moving efficiently through his veins bringing oxygen, taking away waste. Of course, he wasn't really just another one of them. They didn't have his capacities and they couldn't reach his sensual heights.

Yet, they would never notice any difference simply by looking at him. If they could, they would be frightened away and he would die of starvation, age instantly.

He didn't know why all this was so and at the moment, he didn't care to think about it. What was important was he knew what things he was supposed to say when he went out on a hunt, and he knew where to go for whatever he wanted; but unlike everyone he met, he had no photographs of family, no relatives to talk to. If they pressed him, he made it up—invented parents and brothers and sisters. Actually, he drew from his victims.

Lately, much of it was getting jumbled and that worried him a bit. Was he really remembering his own past, or was he dipping into the well of identities he had absorbed in one way or another? One day it occurred to him that he might not exist at all, not in the sense anything else existed. He really had no personal identity. He was a conglomeration, a union of a myriad of DNAs. His body was so infused with the essence of his victims, their corpuscles, their genetics, that maybe he was merely the sum total of his prey. In an ironic sense, they had absorbed him; they had seized and possessed him and not vice versa. He was nothing without them.

Because of this he resented them in the same way an addict might resent the substance of his addiction. He couldn't deny the need, nor could he stop himself from seeking it, but he despised it at the same time.

What would he do if he didn't have the need? In what direction would he go? As it was, his periodic hunger controlled and governed his every move. It provided all his ambition for him and created the subjects and natures of his dreams. In his mind there was an overall design, a road map only he could see and follow. It had brought him here, to this place, these mountains in upstate New York.

If anything amazed him about himself, it was that instinctive knowledge of direction, that power, that force that literally took hold of his hands and arms and made him turn the steering wheel to the right or to the left. Sometimes, he thought he saw a red line before him leading the way, even in broad daylight. It disappeared as he drove over it. At night, it glowed with neon brightness, the light thumping, thumping, thumping behind his eyes. He was hypnotized by his destiny, mesmerized by the predetermined design set forth by some magical power. He reacted and acted on stimuli in a precise, given way each and every time.

Now, as hard as he tried, he couldn't even remember when he had first come here or how he had gotten here. Things just seemed to happen. Something had triggered him to leave where he was. He was being chased, and he had packed up and come here. It was the closest thing to fear he felt, this sense of being pursued. Something was out there that would do him harm and he had to make distance between it and himself whenever he could. It bothered him that he couldn't identify it specifically, but he blamed that on his difficulty to tap into his own history. He was truly an amnesiac.

Vaguely he understood that he had done many different things during his short but rich life. However, as soon as he had done them, he had put them into some dark closet in his mind. Whatever was necessary to do was done. It was as simple and as worry-free as that. In fact, he never once thought himself unlucky or freakish. He mourned no one, loved no one, suffered no anxiety except the anxiety that accompanied his hunger, for there was always the fear that he would not find suitable prey. However, he had come to recognize this as a natural thing, something to help drive him forward and be successful. If he were too nonchalant about his need, he would fail, and he could fail only once.

Again, that was something he knew instinctively. No one taught him. There was no mother, no father, no sister or brother beside him to advise him. When he bothered to think of all this, he wondered why not, but after a short while, he would forget why it mattered and stop wondering. There was too much to do, too much to enjoy. Just like it had been this morning.

How sweet the air had been, how bright the day. He had gone through his stretching exercises quickly in the parking lot at the park. Who could deny that he wasn't the paragon of all creatures, a higher form of life? Look at his face, as young and handsome as it was from the day he was created. And aside from the agony he experienced when his hunger came, he had never had a sick day or a bodily pain, at least none that he could recall. Why, he had never even experienced the common cold. There were no medicines in his bags, not even aspirin. That was significant in and of itself, wasn't it?

When he looked at himself in a mirror, he could see that he had never had a cavity in his teeth. Of course, he couldn't recall ever having seen a doctor or a dentist, so he assumed he was just as he was created, perfect, complete, the epitome of life itself. And it made him proud. He showed it whenever he ran, his head high, his chest out, his arms perpendicular to the ground, pumping the air as he took his stride, his feet gliding over the turf, a veritable Mercury sailing through the parks wherever he was, his eyes bright and fixed on the way before him. He always sensed that other joggers were looking at him enviously as he passed them so swiftly and with such ease.

He wanted them to look at him. He understood that vanity had always been a part of whom and what he was, for what was more a proof of his love of life than his love of himself? It was the nature of an organism to be self-centered, to spend its life searching for ways to satisfy its needs and keep itself healthy and alive. Animals that worked for other animals had shorter life spans.

This realization came to him one day when he stopped in a meadow and watched bees working around a hive. The individual sacrificed itself for the good of the whole. But what was its reward? It didn't live to see or to enjoy the fruits of its labor.

Enjoyment and fulfillment were the only reasons for life, and who could deny that both of these were enhanced when the individual cared only for himself? There was more of everything for him. He lived to please himself. The weaker and the infirm called that greed or lust, but they were hoping to feed off the success of the stronger, weren't they? In that sense they, too, were selfish.

He loved himself even more for being able to justify that love, and anyone who had seen him on mornings like this one, the morning after a feed, would step back in admiration, in awe, shaking his head, wondering who he was and how they could be like him. He had jogged through the park, past the inferiors like a beautiful fish swimming through a sea of covetousness. They had just wanted to touch him, to be beside him, to learn from him or take from him.

But he was too fast, too graceful, and too clever to permit any of them to do so. As soon as one drew too near, he had driven his feet harder into the soil and had lifted his body away. In moments he had been gone and he had known they had been left shaking their heads and wondering if they had imagined it or they really had seen him.

They would know. Oh, they would know, but only one at a time, and after that knowledge, they would be drained and discarded, left behind like some emptied cartons. He was convinced they existed only for his pleasure and nourishment anyway. He saw them the same way a bird sees worms. And just like a bird, he suffered no guilt when he fed. Indeed, he felt it was coming to him. Why else was it there? Why else was he here?

Questions like these rarely bothered him anyway, and whenever they did, he brushed them aside as he would brush aside some annoying insect. It was just as pointless to stop and wonder why there were mosquitos.

Don't wonder about them, destroy them and go on and on and on, he thought . . .

Just like he was doing now.

Just like he would always do.

Filled with the wonder of himself, he had glided ahead toward the rising sun and into its gradually expanding pool of warmth. Even that existed solely for him.

Late in the afternoon he had read the newspaper while he had sat in a booth in a small Italian restaurant and sipped some white wine. Every time he read a newspaper or turned on the news, it was as if he had been on a journey in space and had just returned to earth. He devoured the headlines and stories like one who had been kept hostage by terrorists for years. He knew that he needed the knowledge and the information in order to conduct himself well in the present. People wouldn't understand if he didn't know what month, day, or year it was, or if he didn't know who was president or what major events like earthquakes or revolutions had just occurred.

Most of the knowledge he had, he had inherited anyway, if *inherited* was the right word for it. *Inherited* implied so many things. It was all just there, at his beck and call. What difference did it make that he couldn't remember how it had gotten there?

When he came to the news story about the young woman who had been found dying in a motel room and read the details, he consumed them with a detachment that would cause anyone who saw him reading to think this was the first he had heard about it.

He sipped some more of his wine and then looked up to smile as the young, buxom waitress with light brown hair brought him his order of lasagna, the special of the day. She had guaranteed him it would be good.

"The pasta's homemade here," she pointed out.

He was charming; it came natural to him to be so.

"It's rare that you get a meal that tastes homemade when you are traveling," he replied.

"Where are you going?" she asked. Her name tag on her uniform said Kristin. What a nice name, he thought. Had he ever experienced a Kristin?

"Oh, Canada, I guess."

"You guess?" Kristin had a nice smile. She couldn't be more than twenty, he thought, still fresh and vibrant and full of promises. He envied the man in whose ear she would whisper them, and for a moment, just a moment, he thought about love. The concept flashed past him— wanting someone who wants you forever and ever. What a strange idea; it was like having a milk bottle that continually refilled itself after he had consumed its contents. Wouldn't he love that bottle forever and ever?

Kristin was still standing there, staring down at him, smiling.

"Huh? Oh, I'm on vacation. Sort of a free-wheeling one. I go wherever I have an inclination to go. No set schedules, no previously booked places. It's nice here. I might stay a while," he added and began to eat.

Kristin laughed at how casually he spoke about his future, but he saw that she envied such freedom, such abandon.

"I wish I could do something like that," she said. "But I've got to save up for college or believe me, I wouldn't be here. I ran out of money and had to leave for a year to earn some."

"Very ambitious of you," he complimented. She smiled modestly.

"How's the lasagna?"

"Very good. You told me the truth," he said winking. She blushed. What innocence. It made his heart sing.

Yes, he thought. He would stay here a while longer. There was something wonderful and pure about this area now. It was uncluttered, uncrowded, peaceful, and slow, the villages quiet and quaint, the inhabitants moving at a tranquil and serene pace, traffic nearly at a crawl. There was none of the hustle and bustle of the cities, and the people who lived here, because they were relaxed, were friendlier, more inviting. More important, they were more trusting.

"I just checked in some motel last night," he said, "but maybe I'll hang around a while. Know of a good rooming house or something, where I could rent a room for a week or more?"

"Oh yes," Kristin said, her hazel eyes brightening.

"My grandmother runs a rooming house and it's off season now so you could get one very cheaply."

"That sounds great."

She told him how to get there. And then she added, "I live there with my grandmother."

"Um," he said, enjoying every succulent bite of his homemade lasagna. "Maybe I can talk you into showing me around one day."

"On my day off," she replied. "This Thursday."

"Maybe we'll have a date. My name is Karl," he said, offering his hand. He was working his way around the alphabet again and he was on the K's.

She placed her small, soft palm and fingers into his, and he closed his hand over hers slowly, staring down at it as he did so, looking like one who couldn't believe his luck. The sensuous way in which he brought his skin to hers and held her hand sent a tingle through her breasts. She felt her heart quicken. Her physiological reactions took her quite by surprise. Never had she stood smiling so foolishly at a man before. She was very self-conscious and shifted her eyes from side to side quickly to be sure no one around had noticed. But everyone in the restaurant was busy with his or her own thing.

Finally, he released her hand, letting her draw it from his gracefully, the tips of his fingers grazing the tips of hers. It sent another tingle through her bosom, a tingle that seemed to escape through the tips of each nipple. He had such a soft, inviting mouth, she thought and imagined her mouth pressing against his, his tongue searching for hers.

"Hi," she finally uttered and giggled nervously, hating herself for sounding so young. "I'm Kristin, Kristin Martin."

"Kristin is a lovely name. I don't recall ever knowing a woman with that name," he said happily. The way he said it made her think that if he had known another Kristin, he would pay her no attention.

"My grandmother actually named me. My parents were arguing over Christie and Carissa and she suggested Kristin."

"What happened to your parents?" he asked. Parents always interested him, probably because of the vagueness surrounding his own.

"Car accident," she said. He could see that the memory was fresh enough to bring tears to her eyes.

"Oh, I'm sorry. Are you the only child?"

"Yes."

"So am I," he said.

She smiled.

The chef hit a bell.

"I've got another pickup," she said.

He smiled and watched her walk away, watched the way her hips clung to the light blue uniform, how her buttocks swayed and her shoulders turned. The female form was truly the most beautiful sight on earth, he thought. All of them, every one of them, no matter how tall or how thin, how short or how fat, were beautiful to him. He found something to admire and something to desire in each and every female he saw. That even went for young ones, especially girls just becoming women. Was that part of his special power, his ability to see the promise in a young girl's body?

Why worry about it? he thought and shrugged. Why worry about anything?

He finished his lasagna, had some coffee, and then went looking for Grandmother Martin's rooming house at the west end of this small hamlet called Loch Sheldrake. It consisted of one long main street and a number of side streets, most of the homes vintage late nineteenth and early twentieth century. Grandmother Martin's large home was no exception. It was easy to find because it was so architecturally distinct.

It was a three-story Victorian with rusticated stone foundation, lower story porch supports, and tower. The walls of the upper stories were clad with textured shingles. The steeply pitched roof had intersecting cross gables and multilevel eaves. The windows in the lower level of the tower had Romanesque arches and the windows of the third story were all Palladian windows. There were two gabled dormers, both with three ribbon windows.

He thought there were at least five or six acres of land surrounding the house, and noted a small pond in the rear with a gazebo beside it. How picturesque, he thought and for a moment had a flash of memory that suggested he had lived somewhere similar in his youth. Was that his memory or someone else's? What difference did it make? The important thing was it left him with a residue of nostalgia and made him all the more eager to rent a room.

Grandmother Martin greeted him at the door. She was obviously a feisty old lady with a hard firm face that had inquisitive eyes filled with suspicion. She kept her gray hair neatly cut just below her ears and wore no makeup, not even a trace of rouge to hide the paleness of her complexion. She looked like one who would not deny age nor tolerate anyone who tried. She was small-boned, not more than five feet four at the most, but she stood so erect and secure, it was as though she had a steel rod shoved down the center of her spine.

Old people were more than simply an anomaly to him; they were frightening as well. His world was a world of youth and vibrancy. Age was a disease, not a natural process. He saw it truly as decaying. Wrinkled and gray, toothless and forgetful, crippled and arthritic, old men and women were already dead in his eyes. They offered no sustenance for his well-being. He felt as though he were looking into the face of his own death should he ever fail to provide for himself.

Grandmother Martin sensed his aversion for her, and it triggered warnings, but he was able to manage one of his charming smiles and keep his voice soft, controlled, appealing. He quickly explained how he had come to knock at her door. She smirked.

"Kristin's as good as any booking agent," she said, but she didn't make it sound like something good. "It ain't the season no more, you know. Things is closed everywhere," she warned.

"Oh, I know that, but fall is so beautiful here, I thought I would linger a few days, maybe even a week or so and enjoy the scenery and the peacefulness. Life is so hectic these days. It's nice to find a real escape."

"Um . . ." she said still leery. Her guests were usually older people who had been coming to her rooming house for years and years. All she had to offer them was home cooking and a clean place. There were no facilities. The pond was too small for boating and too muddy for swimming. Martin's Rooming House was just a place to rest your tired old bones, she thought, and wondered why this young man would want to stay here, especially now.

"I don't heat the rooms, you know," she said, not quite sure herself why she was searching for ways to discourage unexpected found income.

"That's fine. I don't sleep with heat on much anyway. I like it better when it's cool. How big is this house?" he asked gazing up at one of the dormers. "It looks enormous."

"Eighteen rooms," she replied, her arms still folded tightly under her small bosom. In fact, she was pressing her forearms against herself so firmly, she felt she might crack one of her own ribs.

"Is there a room available in the tower? That looks like fun," he said.

"The tower? Yes," she said. "I suppose you could take that one. I got to get some fresh bedding together first. And it needs a good dusting. I've had the rooms closed down for nearly a month, you know," she said defensively.

"Oh, I'm sure it will be a lot nicer than the motel I was in last night. You know how they clean those places," he said. She grunted.

"Where are you from?" she asked. It was more like a demand. She still hadn't agreed to rent him the room.

"New York City. Upper Manhattan on the East Side," he said. It came to him as quickly as a line memorized from a play he had been doing week after week.

"What do you do, Mr. . . ."

"Karl," he said, but he could see she wasn't comfortable with first names. "Karl Stanley. I'm an accountant," he said. "A CPA," he added to impress her. She didn't look impressed. "I have a vacation now and . . ."

"What kind of vacation is it that you don't know how long you will stay?" she asked quickly.

He felt a chilling sweat break out on the back of his neck. Only old people could do this to him, make him sound and feel defensive. He took a deep breath. Her eyes grew smaller as she waited for his answer.

"Oh, I'm self-employed," he said. "I own my own business and can usually pick and chose my own schedule. So," he said, "will it be all right . . . the room in the tower?"

"I suppose," she replied. "You'll have to wait until I

get it ready, though. You can bring your things into the sitting room on the right here until then," she added, finally backing up to indicate where he should go.

"Great. I'll just get everything out of the car."

"Don't you care how much it will be?" she asked quickly. He had already turned and stepped away; he was that anxious and anxious people always frightened her.

"Oh . . . I didn't think you were going to rob me. How much will it be?"

"Forty a day," she said quickly. "Fifty-five if you take meals, too." He could sense it was more than she would have charged an older person off-season. It was her last attempt to discourage him.

"Fine," he said. "I'd paid a lot more for a dingy motel room and I'm looking forward to home cooking."

"Um," she said not hiding her disappointment. He flashed the best smile he could and retreated to his car to get his things.

Nearly a half hour afterward, she told him it was all right for him to go up to his room. She showed him the way and then she asked for two days rent in advance. He peeled off the bills from his wad, her eyes big when she saw how much he had. He had no idea himself how he had gotten it, but he imagined it came from his trail of feeds.

"Very pretty," he remarked, looking in at the queen-size brass bed and the light oak furniture. There were a nightstand, an armoire, and a dresser. He put his things down quickly and went to the window. It afforded him a sweeping view of the hamlet's main street in the distances. He could see a trickle of traffic. "So picturesque," he said.

When he turned around, she was gone and she had closed the door. Suddenly, he had another memory flash. He was locked in a room just like this and he was pounding on the door only his hands and his arms were all bandaged, and the window . . . he spun around to look through this one again, to be sure it was uncovered. The window in his memory was painted black so that no light would come through.

Who am I? he wondered with a new intensity. Was it because he was in a house that had such character and he sensed family? The ghosts of all the children, the parents, and the grandparents who had lived here still lingered in the walls, reminding him in ways he didn't want to be reminded that he had no one and was no one.

But the frustration passed through him quickly, like some muscle spasm. He could breathe freely again. It was all right. Everything was all right.

He returned to the window to gaze over the hamlet and way off, toward the end of the street, in the direction from which he had come, he saw beautiful, young Kristin walking home from work, walking toward him, coming closer and closer like the promise of light that came with the first rays of morning.

His old confidence returned.

He was in the right place. For now, as always, he was in the right place at the right time.

Invigorated, he began to unpack.

FOUR

Hyman adjusted their schedules so that Terri could attend Paige Thorndyke's funeral.

"Although," he told her, "during all the years I've lived here, Terri, I think I could count on my fingers how many of my patients' funerals I've attended. I know doctors who have never attended any. I suppose it's a touch of paranoia, something that comes with the territory. You sit there in church or synagogue and you feel the eyes of loved ones and you think they are wondering if you made a mistake or if there was something more you could have done. Ridiculous, I know, but nevertheless, you feel it. At least, I did. Still do.

"And I don't blame them," he added. "We're always second-guessing, wondering if we should have seen that heart attack coming or that stroke. I've often revisited patient histories with just that question. Even after years and years of practicing medicine, I do it on occasion.

"Of course in this case, you have nothing to second-guess. You never treated the woman for anything, and you had no opportunity to provide any medical diagnosis or prescribe any therapy," he concluded.

"For what it's worth," she said, "Curt is on your side. He and I had a bit of a quarrel about it last night. He thinks I'm losing my critical objectivity."

"A certain amount of aloofness is important. It helps you maintain the objectivity you need to do your best," Hyman told her. "I wouldn't even deliver my own children. Sent my wife to Crackenberg, who charged the full ticket, I might add. No professional courtesy. He was not what anyone would call a generous man. His was a funeral I attended, motivated by a bit of glee, I'm ashamed to say."

Terri laughed, thanked him, and prepared to get to the church. It was a heavily attended service. Most of the hamlet had turned out, as well as people from Bradley's airline, the entire travel agency, and various relatives of the Thorndykes. The bizarre nature of Paige's death gave the funeral an unrealistic air, a sense that everyone was moving within the same nightmare. Terri could see it in the way people greeted each other, shook their heads in confusion, and stared at the grieving parents and Paige's brother Phil, all three of whom now looked stunned, gazing occasionally at the faces of the attendees as if they were looking to see if anyone could tell them why they were here. Bradley Thorndyke held his wife tightly, supported and guided her along, but to Terri it looked like he was really doing it to hold himself together as well or even more so.

Phil Thorndyke held hands with an attractive brunette. They were comforting each other. Terri heard someone say her name was Eileen Okun and she had been Paige's closest friend.

Everyone stood while the coffin was removed through a side entrance to the waiting hearse and then everyone began to file out, no one speaking in anything above a whisper, greeting each other with nods or movements of their eyes.

With her eyes down, Terri marched behind the crowd of mourners and, like everyone else, felt she was escaping from under the shadow of death when they left the church.

It was one of those perfect fall days when the sun seems to be holding back in intensity, but not brightness, and every cloud in the sky looks as if it was whipped with fresh milk. The air was redolent with the aroma of apples streaming in from an orchard near the church. It was a day designed for backyard touch football games and barbecues, which all made a funeral seemed that much more jarring and unreal.

Terri paused on the street outside the church while the funeral procession was being organized and directed to proceed to the cemetery. There, she had a chance to speak with Will Dennis, the county district attorney. Tall and lanky with a Lincolnesque look of melancholy that Terri imagined was carved by twelve years in the elected position, seeing the results of one vicious act after another, Dennis had the demeanor and bearing of someone dependable, someone in whom you would comfortably trust the important things in your life. It was this charisma that made him invulnerable election after election, that and his uncanny memory for putting together faces and names, a politician's biggest asset. Be introduced and shake hands with him once and you were remembered forever.

"Dr. Barnard," he said, nodding at her.

"Mr. Dennis." She stood beside him and both of them watched the hearse creep away from the church, the line of automobiles following to snake slowly up to the cemetery in Glen Wild, a hamlet best known for its cemeteries.

She sighed deeply and then blew some air between her gently closed lips.

"Tough one," Will Dennis muttered. "Especially when it makes no sense."

He looked at her.

"Medically speaking, of course," he added.

"Yes," she agreed. "Have you determined whether or not there was a criminal act committed?"

"In what sense?" he asked, his heavy eyebrows turning in and toward each other. "There wasn't any violence. It was scurvy, right?"

"I was referring to the man who brought her to the motel, leaving her there."

"Oh. No, we don't have anything concrete about him and I don't know how we could indict someone for that. We'd have to establish that she was sick and he knew it, but everything we've learned suggests there was nothing wrong with her. On the contrary, she was a ball of energy if you want to believe the eyewitnesses."

"Right. So the BCI investigator is leaving the case?"

Will's lips curled up and in as he turned to look at her.

"What BCI investigator?"

"The one who interviewed me, Clark Kent?"

His grimace of confusion softened into a look of amusement.

"Is that some sort of joke? Clark Kent?"

"No. That was his real name. He claimed his parents had a sense of humor. How could he come see me without your knowing anything about it?" she wondered. "I mean, does that happen?"

"No," he said shaking his head, the grimace gone now. "Someone was obviously pulling a very, very sick joke on you, Terri. What did he look like?"

"Look like? He was tall, about six feet one or two, blond-haired, blue eyes. He had a slight cleft in his chin and he was well tanned, like someone who had just returned from the Carribean. I'd say he was in his mid-to late thirties."

Will Dennis nodded.

"There's no detective in this county I know of who matches that description. Let me know if you ever see or hear from this piece of shit again," he added angrily. "I'll have him indicted and prosecute him to the full extent of the law for impersonating a police officer."

She shook her head.

"He seemed so convincing and very nice. He talked about his pregnant wife and moving recently to upstate New York. I don't understand."

"Hang around my office for a day or two and you will," the district attorney said. "You'll quickly tell yourself you won't ever doubt how low humanity can sink. Well, I have to get back to the office. Take care," he said and walked to his waiting limousine.

She stared after him, her heart thumping. Suddenly, she felt violated, abused as if something had been taken from her. She looked about quickly when the cold chill at the back of her neck slid down until it settled between her shoulder blades. The remaining mourners clung to some conversation to help ease themselves back from the gloom. People shook hands. People hugged each other. Contact was very important.

A man hurrying away turned around the corner of the church, the shock of blond hair gleaming in the late morning sunlight. It sent an arrow of ice through her chest. She hurried in his direction, practically running, but when she turned the corner, too, he was gone.

Who was he?

Was that the man who had pretended to be an investigator? Why had he done such a sick thing?

Why would he come to the funeral, too?

How in hell could Paige Thorndyke have died of scurvy? It's a Third-World problem, especially to the extent it was present in Paige Thorndyke.

She felt like screaming the questions at the church as if it was truly a conduit that would bring her words to the ears of God and then bring back His enlightening response.

She heard nothing but the slamming of car doors and the starting of engines.

Walking briskly back to her car she angrily thought, Curt should have been here with me. He should have adjusted his schedule, not only because this was a person whose family he knew, but most importantly because he should have been at her side.

Why that suddenly occurred to her and with such vehemence was unclear. She looked back at the corner of the church. Maybe, if Curt had been with her . . . .

She jabbed her key into the car's ignition and drove off, her thoughts falling back like thunder against the front steps of the church.

He sat on one of the oversized, chipped, and faded wooden lawn chairs and stared at the murky pond. It was still warm enough for water flies and mosquitoes to practice their insane circling inches above the water. It convinced him that Nature was far from perfect. It was an unfinished work, still being developed through trial and error. What in hell could be the purpose for this sort of maddening life? Food for frogs, bats? And who were they food for and if there were no mosquitos, would we need frogs and bats? One mistake engendered another. That's all. Simply and sweet, a fuckup of global proportions.

Man had been created to fix all these mistakes, he thought. He was here to work through science and correct, improve, and perfect the world. Weather must not be permitted to remain random and whimsical. Every disease had to be cured and eliminated. Sources of energy that were restorable had to be discovered and perfected, and all these vermin had to be exterminated.

From where all these ideas came to him, he did not know. All of it was just there. It was like opening a closet or a cabinet and finding all sorts of food and not having the slightest clue as to how it got there. However, even though not knowing the origins of things that pertained to him did bother him from time to time, it was only in a small and momentary way. He didn't dote or dwell on it, and he certainly didn't toss and turn at night worrying about it.

Why worry about anything? All problems were solvable eventually, and the solutions were never more than an arm's length away.

He was so lost in his thoughts that he didn't hear Kristin come up beside him until she actually began to speak. He didn't jump with surprise, however. He lacked that weakness he saw in other human beings. Nothing could surprise him and if it did, it never frightened him. Only one thing frightened him, malnutrition, and that was easy to starve off. It would always be easy.

"Hi," she said.

He turned slowly and looked up at her, giving her his best smile of hello, warm, full of delight at her presence, a smile designed to deliver a compliment and instill pleasure and confidence in its recipient. He was a master of smiles, a magician who could turn an expression into a look of wonder and innocence or just as easily, a look of sophistication and innocence. His eyes could almost change color to please. Like any successful performer, he could read his audience and reach into his repertoire to produce the look, the words, the very body motion to please. It gave his prey the sense that he was there solely for her. His whole body was truly a web and he was never so proud of it and what it could trap as he was now.

"Hi," he replied. "Thanks for recommending your grandmother's place."

She shook her head, smiled, and looked at the pond, the expression on her face turning quizzical as she looked at the water and the surrounding birch, maple, and hickory trees. Earlier heavy rainfalls had practically stripped the trees of their beautiful fall foliage, leaving the forest stark and dreary. She was surely wondering why was he sitting here so contentedly and looking at the surroundings? What could he possibly get out of this?

"It's so peaceful here," he said anticipating her question. "You're lucky."

"Lucky? Hardly," she said grimacing. "This is like dead-endsville. Peaceful as a cemetery. Things don't grow here anymore. They just rot, people included."

"Really? I thought it was a very busy, exciting resort area," he said.

"It's still busier than it is most of the year, but only for about ten weeks in the summer. Nothing here is like it used to be. It's dying. Look at my grandmother's place. She doesn't bother to spruce it up anymore. She's getting what she can out of it and then it, too, like so many similar small rooming houses, small hotels, and bungalow colonies, will either be bought up by some tax-free religious group or left to rot. I'm not interested in inheriting it. I can tell you that. If I don't get myself out of here soon either to return to college or just travel . . . ."

She left her words hanging in the air like someone hoping some mysterious and wonderful hero would come along and scoop them up, taking her and them off on a magic carpet of promise.

He turned and looked back at the pond. She's so perfect, he thought. He felt blessed. He really was blessed. Something more powerful than anything was ensuring that he would always have what he needed.

"Where would you want to go if you didn't return to college?" he asked, not taking his eyes off the pond.

"Anywhere but here," she said and followed it with a small, insecure laugh.

He nodded.

"Too bad we can't stand still and have everything come to us," he said.

"Excuse me?"

"You know, all new things, exciting things come to us. We partake of them and then they move on and something new arrives. We'd never be bored."

She shook her head.

"I'm not sure I know what you mean."

"Well," he said turning back to her. "You're here and now I've come."

She held her smile. Her face was still bubbling with confusion.

"It takes time," he explained. "Time to understand. I'm still in the process myself." He gazed at the pond.

"What if it takes me too long?" she asked, following it with a giggle that sounded like a pocket full of change.

He looked at her again. "I wouldn't worry, Kristin. You're too special to be left behind."

"Right, sure," she said. She glanced at her watch.

"Going to work?"

"Yes. I don't go in until noon today. I'm off at eight," she added, obviously not just to provide trivial information.

"Why don't I come around about then? Maybe we can go for a drink somewhere and you can relax and tell me more about your future plans. Would you like that?"

"Sure," she said.

"I'll be waiting for you outside the restaurant," he promised. "I'd go back for dinner, but your grandmother looks like she would consider it a capital crime for me or anyone to reject one of her meals."

Kristin laughed.

"That's for sure."

"I'm looking forward to it anyway. I never had turkey meatloaf. I hope she is a good cook. I have a ravenous appetite," he said and added, "in every sense of the word."

She raised her eyebrows and released that small, thin laugh again.

"Just tell her how good it is and she'll pile your plate sky high. Flattery, will get you everywhere. It's a family weakness," she added and started back toward the house.

"Flattery will get you everywhere? It's a family weakness? How original," he muttered.

He stared ahead. Water flies caused ripples. They seemed to continue forever in his head.

"Will Dennis said that?" Curt asked, stretching his lips as if he had just bitten into a rotten piece of fruit. "When you told him about the investigator, he said that?"

She stared at him. It was on the tip of her tongue to ask him what part he didn't understand. It wasn't in her to be sarcastic and short with people, especially him, but at the moment, she didn't feel anything like herself. Her stare made him squirm in the booth.

"I'll make a call," he said. "Something doesn't sound right."

She couldn't resist.

"No shit, Dick Tracy."

He started to smile, thought a second time about it, and glanced instead at the menu. Before the death of Paige Thorndyke, they had made the date to have dinner at Melvin's Trout Reserve this particular evening. Originally, he was supposed to pick her up, but his court schedule and her delays at the medical offices made it better for them to meet at the restaurant. They were coming to it from opposite directions.

Terri had always hated going to and from a date alone, especially if she arrived before he did, which was most often the case. Heads turned and she could read their eyes, especially the eyes of the men with their legs dangling over bar stools as if they were riding horses. She imagined third eyes situated right at the center of their crotches.

Curt wasn't as bothered by separate arrivals, and she wondered if it wasn't simply a male-female thing. She hated that sort of explanation for anything. It truly made it seem as if they were a separate species, one more tolerant of something than the other. Men cringed at the sight of a rat just as much as women did, she thought.

But were women more romantic? Was that why it bothered her to come here alone and leave alone? In the end after the years of medical school, the degree and the professional accomplishments making her just as big a wage earner if not a bigger wage earner than Curt was, didn't she still want doors opened for her, chairs pulled out for her? The feminine in her would not, could not be denied?

He lowered the menu, deciding he would explain himself after all, her Dick Tracy remark gnawing at his ego like a termite in a heart made of wood.

"What I meant was, Will Dennis wasn't being truthful, and that suggests something to me."

"Why wouldn't the district attorney be truthful, Curt? What does it suggest?"

"I don't know. Maybe there's something going on undercover and he doesn't want to blow it."

"The man who came to my office wasn't under any cover, Curt. He was out front with a badge and all."

"Well . . . what the hell was he, a private detective posing as a state officer, someone hired by the Thorndykes, maybe?"

She looked up, her eyes bright.

"Yes, maybe that's it." She put folds of skepticism in her brow. "But so soon after, even before the funeral, they go looking for and hiring a private detective?"

He shrugged.

"People don't have faith in their hometown police. It makes sense to me. It takes too much effort and imagination to really investigate something as complicated as this appears to be.

"Look, Terri," he continued, reaching across the table for her hand, "you've got to put this behind you. If you let every death, every patient get to you like this, you'll soon become a patient yourself," he concluded.

She nodded.

"I know. You're right, of course. Hyman is with you on that, too."

"I always liked Hyman. I think I might even have trouble suing him."

"If you even thought of representing someone who would want to do that," she said, her eyes growing big with a fury he thought could consume them both.

He laughed.

"Hey, I gotta do what I gotta do, don't I? You can't turn away a sick person just because you don't like him or her, or because he or she is a criminal, can you?"

"I sure as hell could discourage him or her from using me," she fired back and then sadly thought, *and that's the difference between us.*

Before the waitress returned to their table with their cocktails, Terri saw Eileen Okun enter the restaurant holding hands with a red-haired man who looked familiar. As they stepped down to follow the maitre d' to their table, the man glanced at her and smiled. She immediately recalled the strikingly hazel brown eyes and realized he was a nurse at the hospital and he, in fact, had been one of the nurses on duty the night Paige Thorndyke had been brought into the ER. How strange to see him with the woman Terri had been told was Paige's best friend, the woman on Paige's brother Phil's arm at the funeral.

"What is it?" Curt asked, noticing how she was staring at the couple.

She told him who they were.

"So? This is a popular restaurant and there aren't all that many good ones open this time of the year. I'm not surprised," he said with a shrug.

He was annoying her so much tonight, she thought. Usually, she had more tolerance. She recognized just how much she was on edge.

"Have you decided?" the waitress asked.

"I have," Curt said. "Terri?"

"The poached salmon," she snapped.

"I'll have the same," Curt said. The waitress took their menus and Curt ordered himself another cocktail. He smiled at her.

"So, have you given thought to remodeling our bedroom? I have Frank Curtis coming over tomorrow to decide how we would go about cutting in the patio door. I thought, if we could cut it on the west end, we would build the balcony and be able to see the sun set over the Shawangunk Mountains. Huh?"

"That does sound very nice, Curt."

"Can you make it over, say about ten? Or better yet, sleep over tonight?" He reached for her hand again.

"You want to hear something funny?" she said instead of replying. "Hyman had four calls from patients today asking about the daily requirements for vitamin C. Like they thought a scourge of scurvy was about to descend on us. Despite all the information over the Internet, education, television, whatever, most people are relatively ignorant when it comes to their own bodies. I guess part of the reason is there is so much conflicting information. First, coffee is no good for you, then it is. First, you should take more supplements, then a study shows it could be harmful."

Curt stared coldly.

Then he leaned back.

"So I have this case involving a mother who has illegally tapped into her own children's trust funds. The children have hired me to sue their own mother. Now, of course it gets complicated when you begin to consider the defined benefit pension plan her husband had created and then there is the matter of the family trust fund and IRS code . . ."

"Okay," she said putting up her hands in a gesture of surrender. "I get the point."

The waitress served Curt his second cocktail. As soon as she left, he leaned forward, smiling.

"I'd rather talk about us than anything, Terri, anything."

"I know. I'm sorry." She put her hand into his just as Eileen Okun stepped up to their booth.

"Excuse me," she said. "Mark, who's a nurse at the hospital, just told me who you are. I'm Eileen Okun. I was a very good friend of Paige Thorndyke's and . . ."

"Yes," Terri said quickly. "I know. I saw you at the funeral."

"Oh, you were there?"

"Yes, she was there," Curt said sharply, his eyes on her.

"How can I help you, Eileen?" Terri asked, trying to overpower his stern tone.

"I just wanted to tell you that I was with Paige twice this past week. We had dinner together the night before, and that was when we had made plans to meet at the Underground. I was unable to get there because of a family problem. Anyway," she said her eyes moving nervously from Curt to Terri, "I don't mean to bother you, but I wanted to tell you that there was absolutely nothing wrong with Paige."

"Are you in the medical field?" Curt asked.

"No. I'm a marketing consultant for Scanlon Insurance and . . ."

"So how can you make a diagnosis?" he followed, as if she were on the witness stand.

"Oh. I just meant . . . she was . . . she looked fine and she ate well and . . ."

"We're all confused about it," Terri confessed. "I wish I could tell you something that would help you understand it. I haven't learned anything new."

She nodded.

"I'm just trying to keep myself occupied and not think about it, but I was wondering if there was any possibility of there being something contagious or anything," she said, smiling weakly at Curt and then looking at Terri.

"Why don't you ask your boyfriend?" Curt said.

"He's not really my boyfriend and he's not a doctor. I just thought . . ."

"It's all right, Eileen," Terri said, her eyes soft and friendly. "Scurvy is not contagious, no. It's a disease caused by a deficiency of vitamin C. You don't have to be concerned because you were in contact with Paige shortly before," Terri added as reassuringly as she could.

Curt, either by reflex or because he was annoyed, followed with, "What sort of contact did you have with Paige?"

Terri's eyes went large.

Eileen looked as if she were about to burst into tears.

"Just . . . friends, having dinner. We hugged at the end of the evening. That's all," she said. She shook her head. "It just didn't make any sense. Even Mark says that, so I wanted to talk to you. I'm sorry. I didn't mean to intrude."

"It's all right," Terri said. "When something crazy like this happens, it makes us all a little terrified."

Eileen smiled her appreciation, threw a colder glance at Curt, and then returned to her table.

"Well, you were right," Curt said quickly. "The amount of ignorance and stupidity despite the improved technology and communication . . . ."

"And the lack of compassion," she added. "She's just a frightened young woman, Curt. What happened to her friend is devastating."

"Right," he said.

The waitress brought their food.

"I'm sure there is a sensible explanation waiting out

there. Or else it's just a freak accident of some kind. We've all just got to take a deep breath and think next and go on. Doesn't this look good?" he concluded nodding at the food.

"Yes," she said, but she had lost her appetite. Eating became mechanical.

"I hope there's some vitamin C in here," Curt kidded. The untimely crudeness of the remark made her eyes glitter with steel.

"I hope there's plenty of antioxidants," she countered.

"Antioxidants? Why?" he asked, his fork poised.

"Keeps brain cells healthy," she said.

"Very funny. I can see it's going to be interesting being married to a doctor," he said, but it didn't come out sounding like something positive. She swallowed down the feeling along with her food.

Although they had come in later, Mark and Eileen left before she and Curt. On their way out, Eileen glanced back. Terri smiled at her and she smiled back.

"Are you coming over or what?" Curt asked when he paid their check.

"I'll be there tomorrow. I'm tired," she said.

"No better rest than the rest you'll have at the farm lying in my arms," he insisted.

"Somehow, I don't think it will be just cuddling."

"So?"

"Tomorrow," she repeated with a firmness he had gotten used to knowing was rarely unhinged.

"Right. Tomorrow," he muttered.

They kissed at her car, where he tried to be softer, apologetic, and loving. She let him try and then she repeated her desire to go home and get a good night's sleep. Disappointment was masked poorly with a perfunctory smile and another quick, obligatory goodnight kiss and then he got into his Jaguar and sped into the night.

She followed out of the driveway and turned slowly toward Centerville. These rural mountain roads were quiet even during the summer months. Miles of forest was interrupted by an occasional house and lawn, but real development didn't begin until she was five miles or so from the hamlet proper.

She was driving slowly, almost totally by rote, not thinking much about the route itself. The sight of a police car's bubble lights flickering ahead brought her out of her daze. She slowed and saw the patrol car was parked behind a black Jeep Cherokee. The patrolman was on the driver's side. The door was open and he was leaning in. He turned as she pulled up beside.

"Anything wrong?" she asked. "I'm a doctor."

"A doctor? Christ," he said, "am I glad you're here!"

FIVE

The young dark-haired woman in the Cherokee was totally naked and slumped low in the driver's seat. Even her shoes and stockings were off. Her eyes were bulging and she was in a heavy sweat. She looked like she was slowly pouring onto the floor as if her body was liquefying. Terri immediately saw she was hyperventilating.

"Miss, can you talk? Can you tell us what's happening to you? Do you have any pain, any serious ailments? Are you on any medication? Why are you naked?"

Terri hated firing questions like this at the obviously distressed woman. It was like throwing everything in her repertoire against the wall and hoping something stuck, but she needed something, some helpful information to help her start a sensible protocol. From the looks of the woman, she needed it quickly.

She opened and closed her mouth without uttering a sound. She was either too weak or a mute, Terri thought. Then she smelled alcohol on her breath.

"How much did you drink?" she fired at her, sounding almost like an angry parent.

The woman shook her head.

"I just found her like this," the highway patrolman said. "Her clothes are on the rear seat and on the floor. Actually, I was off duty and heading home myself and I saw this vehicle pulled over with the lights still on," he continued, ranting. He looked very young and Terri imagined he hadn't had all that much experience.

He continued to talk as Terri went back to her car to get her bag.

"The engine was running so I pulled up to see if anything was wrong. She wouldn't speak. I don't see any blood, although she's very red."

"Did you call for an ambulance?" she fired back at him.

"Not yet."

"Do it!" she screamed.

The patrolman lunged toward his car and got on the radio.

Terri moved in on the woman and began to wrap her blood pressure cup on the woman's arm. She was gasping for breath like someone who had been under water too long.

"Jesus," Terri said when she went to feel the woman's pulse. "She's got a water hammer pulse."

"What's that?" the policeman asked, returning.

"It's pounding. You don't have to press much to feel it. I think she's going into cardiac arrest!"

Terri checked the woman's blood pressure, which revealed a high systolic and a low diastolic. Her arm felt very warm as well.

"Her heart can't keep up!" she said.

"What should we do?" the policeman asked.

"I need some more light."

The patrolman brought his flashlight and reached in and over her to flip on the interior light. The illumination highlighted all the swelling in the woman's face and neck, as well as on her chest, breasts, and stomach. She looked as if she had been attacked by a hive of bees.

"I didn't see that before," the patrolman said. "Maybe she was stung."

"Were you stung? Are you allergic to bees?" Terri asked quickly.

The young woman managed to shake her head. Her eyelids were trembling with her effort to keep them open as her gasping grew more desperate.

"He," Terri thought she whispered.

"Do you have any oxygen in your car?" Terri asked the policeman.

He nodded and hurried back to get it as well as a blanket. Terri fit the mask over the woman's face, took her pulse again and then her blood pressure. Everything was worse.

Suddenly she went into a violent convulsion. Terri moved quickly to keep her tongue from going back in her throat. The woman's body was shaking so vigorously, the vehicle seemed to be swaying.

"Holy Jesus!" the young patrolman cried and actually stepped back as if he expected the woman would explode. Terri held on, trying her best to comfort her.

A few moments later, the woman stopped convulsing and her whole body sunk in Terri's arms.

Terri felt for a pulse and then moved back slowly. The woman's head fell to her right side. She looked as if she had just fallen asleep.

Terri ripped away the blanket and began to administer CPR. She worked frantically over her, pumping, blowing air, pumping, and then, exhausted from the vain effort, stopped and sat back.

"Is she all right?" the patrolman asked.

It seemed like such a ridiculous question. Terri almost laughed.

"No. She's expired," Terri replied and closed her bag. She hated using that word. It sounded like she was talking about a parking meter and not a human being, but it was the word the medical community employed, more, in her opinion, to make it easier for themselves than the loved ones waiting for news.

"Expired? She's dead?"

"I'm afraid so," Terri said looking at her bag. Inside, she had prednisolone, specifically for serious insect stings. She could have injected it, but there had been so little time. If this woman died of an insect bite and she hadn't done that . . . her thoughts trailed off.

The patrolman stood there with his hands on his hips, looking in and shaking his head. Then, as if remembering he was a law enforcement officer, he tapped Terri gently on the shoulder.

"Better not touch anything in the car," he said. "We don't know the situation yet. It's strange, to say the least, for her to be totally naked."

Terri nodded and stepped out. The patrolman began to search around the vehicle. She watched him with a strangely detached curiosity. She was actually feeling numb, in a daze herself. Two young women had died in her presence within a week's time. One dying almost immediately after she had touched her, and now this one dying in her arms. Maybe I'm cursed, she thought.

Of course she realized this was a very small community, especially during the off-season. The chances of knowing about or confronting a serious situation were very high. This woman, too, looked familiar, but her features were distorted.

The patrolman carefully searched the glove compartment and stood back with his flashlight to read the documents.

"Who was she?"

"Kristin Martin," he said. "It's a Loch Sheldrake address."

Terri shook her head. At least she didn't know this woman personally.

"There's a paycheck stub in here from Diana's Restaurant," he added.

"I know it," she said. Great veal Parmesan, she thought,

and then shook her head at how ridiculous the mind could be at times like this.

He opened the rear door and directed his flashlight over the seat and the clothes. He shook his head at how everything was strewn about and then noted the panties were torn.

"It looks like a rape to me," he muttered loud enough for Terri to hear. "Think she had some sort of a reaction to that?"

Terri shook her head.

"No. This is too much to blame on emotional trauma. We'll have to wait to see the exact cause of death. We need to know the level of blood alcohol and what other possible poisonous element is in her."

She returned to her own vehicle and sat staring at the dead woman's SUV. She thought about calling Curt on his cell phone, but then imagined him saying something cold like she should have followed him home. Then she would not have confronted this nor been a part of it. She thought about calling Hyman, but she hated the idea of sounding as if she was in a panic, even though to be truthful she was. She was a doctor. She was supposed to be able to confront and handle situations like this and remain cool, efficient, effective. All she could think of was some idiot saying her reactions were a result of her being a woman and that's why men were better suited to the profession.

She decided to call no one.

Fifteen minutes later, another patrol car arrived and then the ambulance, its bubble light swinging like a multicolored light bulb on the end of a string, ripping through the darkness, slicing trees and bushes and waking the sleeping birds, who rose from branches and like chips of shadows dissolved into the night.

SIX

He returned to the chair facing the pond and sat quietly, relaxed. The sky was clearing. A westerly wind was pushing the low out. Tomorrow would be another spectacular day. He felt reinvigorated. He always did after a good feed. Early tomorrow, right around the rising of the sun, he would be out jogging again, filling his lungs with fresh air, feeling his blood being pumped into every extremity, restoring cells, replenishing.

These country roads were wonderful for a morning run. He had noted that as soon as he had driven into the area. As always, his senses would be heightened the morning after. He would be able to smell every plant, every wildflower and hear insects crawling as well as the flapping of bird wings. The anticipation was so great, he almost felt like doing it now.

Lately, however, the wonderful aftereffects of a good feed were not lasting as long as they used to last. He found his needs developing faster and his hunger growing more and more intense. He was far more impatient during the process than he remembered and barely went through any foreplay anymore. It was almost going right for the kill with no delicious preparations. The sexual aspects were nearly eliminated.

All this was evidenced by his choosing a victim too soon after the previous one and too close in actual proximity. He knew this was not intelligent, but there were forces at work in him now that were overpowering. He would admit it to no one, not that there was anyone to whom he could confide, but he was a little frightened of himself these days, frightened of his loss of control.

Control over everything was what gave him a sense of himself, an identity. It provided him with his radiating self-confidence, what he thought was his attractive arrogance, the magnetism that drew women to him, often despite themselves. Few that he could recall put up much resistence, and even those that had, capitulated soon enough. Suddenly he recalled a woman back in New York City, a magazine editor who almost got away. She called his romancing condescending. She distrusted compliments and began with the assumption every man was a predator. Well, of course he was. How to disguise it well or make it look insignificant was his problem to solve. In the end he pretended to agree, to confess, and to throw himself upon her mercy. She liked that, and she remained within his reach.

So many of them had been so similar in their composition. It was often like paint by numbers, but occasionally, there was a real challenge, someone like the editor who for one reason or another had the potential to escape. None had up until now. He took pride in that and it didn't seem to matter that he had no one with whom to share it. Companionship, friendship, society itself was a vague concept, a shadow that hovered out there somewhere along with all the other shadows, none so dark and distant as the one that surrounded his birth.

Once again he wondered. Did he have a birth? Did he have parents? Siblings? Was there someone else out there who was like him? Who even knew about him?

Often when his instincts were as sharp as they were after a feed, he sensed that he was being pursued, but by what or by whom he did not know. Asleep, he would waken suddenly with a jolt and lift his head from the pillow to listen. He was like a dog, disturbed by sounds no ordinary human could hear or like a wild creature alarmed by that evasive sixth sense, that mysterious animal power mankind had lost through civilization and evolution. If it was still within them, the women especially would know to run from him. Fortunately for him, it was not, or it was too dormant to ever be awoken.

Some, however, were trying to rediscover or restore it or something akin to it. He had read about and even met people who talked about positive and negative energy forces around them. It wasn't something tangible, but they claimed they could sense it. They were right of course, but they had no idea how right they were. One woman (he could no longer remember her name or even her face) told him she deliberately avoided people who were full of negativity. They were a threat to her own happiness and well-being, she said.

For a while he thought she would sense the danger to her that was in him, but she didn't have that much ability, none of them had. They were on the right track, but they had a long way to go and in his opinion, they would never reacquire what had been lost. It was too late for them. The truth was they were becoming less and less of what they were created to be. Their technologies, their artificiality, their virtual reality, all of it was quickly turning them into just another part of the machinery they were creating. Pure beings like himself would be so rare, one could search the globe and produce only a handful, he concluded with that delicious arrogance he so enjoyed.

From what well he drew all this wisdom, he did not know, and although that didn't bother him, he was becoming increasingly concerned about the loss of some memory. He used to be able to recall events that had occurred a year or so ago, and then it became less than a year, months, until now, he was having trouble bringing up vivid recollections of events that had occurred less than six months ago. It was only after a good feed, like the one tonight, that he was able to remember what he had done in the immediate past.

He gazed over the pond into the moonlit darkness that wrapped shadows about the naked trees and wondered if he was not becoming a shadow himself. Was that his final destiny, to disappear into the night and be unable to touch, to feel, to smell, taste, or hear anything? He could almost see himself looking back at himself in this chair, looking back with a deep longing, an ache that turned into a primeval howl heard only by the wildest, yet untouched creatures that roamed the rim of civilization.

Who am I? he wondered and it occurred to him that he had not wondered or cared about that very much until just recently. Who could he ask? Who would know? The answer hung out there. He sensed it.

He turned quickly and looked back to the road that led up to the tourist house, a narrow, pitted, and cracked rope of macadam that snaked through the woods, up from this hamlet of Loch Sheldrake, another little community that went into hibernation after Labor Day with most of the shop owners drawing the curtains on their front windows and the ones who remained looking like cemetery caretakers gazing vacantly at the highway of the dead.

There was a lake, of course, one with an amusing history if he was to believe some of the old timers he had met at a local bar. They told him bodies were still being discovered under the water, bodies deposited years and years ago by ruthless gangsters who had an organization notoriously known as Murder Incorporated.

What a funny idea, he thought. Did it enjoy the benefits of a corporation? He asked one of the nearly toothless balding men if it was an S-corp or a C-corp. They looked at him as if he was crazy, and then he laughed.

"Laugh all you want," one of them said angrily, "but this is a place with history."

Okay, he thought. I'll add to your history.

He continued to stare at the road that ran by the tourist house. Someone or something was coming, he thought. It was as vague a thought as usual at first, but it grew stronger, more insistent. He took a deep breath. He wouldn't be able to remain here much longer. He would have to move on to new territory. That angered him. He didn't like feeling he was the prey, he was being pursued. He didn't like running from anything. His pride was too grand for such a concept. Everything and anything should be running from him.

Yet, the instinct to survive would not be silenced and was far more muscular than his pride. Like it or not, he would eventually obey and he would move on. Defiantly, he vowed he would stay as long as he could.

He gazed back over the pond where now the moonlight turned the surface into a yellowish white layer that looked like ice. He thought that was wonderful, but then a thin, slithering gauzelike cloud slipped between the moon and the earth and cut a shadow over the jeweled water. He wanted to shake his fist at it and scare it off. He felt that powerful, but it moved on at its own pace and left him like some ingrate raging at the world he had been given.

All this was interrupted by the real sound of an automobile crunching the gravel drive that led up to the tourist house. The police car did not have its bubble light on, but it looked ominous enough to cause him to rise and move quickly into the darkness. Was this the danger he had sensed?

He watched two patrolmen and a third man in a sports jacket and tie emerge and walk to the front entrance of the tourist house. He knew the old lady was already asleep and would not be answering the door so quickly.

He watched them knock, wait, and then try the door. It was open so they entered. He drew closer to the house, close enough to look through a side window and see the lights go on in the sitting room. The old lady wearing a dull brown robe turned to the three men and listened. Then she brought her hands to her face and the one in the sports jacket put his arm around her shoulders and guided her to the sofa.

What was going on? he wondered.

SEVEN

Terri filled in a report for the police. The officers who arrived afterward wanted to know what she thought killed the woman.

"It's too soon to tell. The edema she suffered could have a number of causes, including kidney disease or some form of poisoning. It could also be the result of severe allergic reaction," she added. "We'll have to wait for the autopsy."

The hard disc in her computerlike memory suggested another probable cause, but she rejected it instantly. She was tempted to follow the ambulance to the hospital, but then thought, what for? There was nothing left to do for this woman except invade her body and search for the story of her death. Instead, she went home and decided to take a hot shower. She knew of a Jewish custom that required people who had been to funerals to wash their hands before they entered their homes. It was so silly, a superstition that suggested death was on your hands and you could bring it into your home and infect your loved ones.

And yet, she had to get the feeling off her. She had to wash away the morbid air, the memory of that cold glint that had come quickly into the young woman's eyes. Could it be that she did touch death, even for an instant? Did it pause to gloat and run itself through her just once, causing her to shudder and causing her heart to stop and then start?

You doctors, it said disdainfully, *you think you will defeat me with your chemicals and your electronics, but in the end, you will always bow your heads at the vain attempts, at the failures. I play with you. I let you think you have staved me off, driven me back, and then I return, perhaps through a different avenue, around some corner you did not anticipate, and I pluck the victory out of your hands repeatedly.*

But keep trying. I so enjoy the contest.

She shook her head at her own imagination and made herself a cup of warm milk. I'm a twenty-first century physician and I rely on my grandmother's old remedies. It made her smile and she needed to smile just now. She sat at her kitchenette and thought about her grandmother, about the nights they sat and talked when she was only a little girl. She had a way of weaving her stories, her past, into a tapestry that enthralled, educated, and at times even frightened Terri a little, especially when she described the hardships. Her grandmother had been through very difficult times when she had arrived in America at the age of only five, holding onto her widowed mother's hand.

Her mother had agreed to come to America to marry a man she had never really met, a butcher in Brooklyn who had lost his wife to breast cancer and who had three sons to raise and no patience for it. All she had done was speak to him on the phone and look at some pictures. It was a way of solving her own desperate situation, for her husband had left her nothing and times were very hard in Budapest for a woman alone with a child.

How could people have been so selfless? Terri wondered when she thought about her great-grandmother. How could they be willing to make such great sacrifices and from what well of optimism did they draw so much hope after suffering so much tragedy and turmoil? Were people stronger back then? Were we now with all our miraculous medicine and wonderful technology really a weaker species? Were we rapidly letting go of the values that gave us the power to survive spiritually as well as physically?

I hate being this heavy and philosophical, she thought. I hate it, but it always happens after something terrible like this. It's as if death was there periodically to remind us how vulnerable we were and how silly we were putting any value on anything material. Everything we owned, possessed, would belong to someone else in one form or another some day. Our homes, our clothes, our cars, even our very money. It all might take some other form, be destroyed in one way and then used to build something else, but it would not be ours forever. Even our bones would not be ours.

What was ours then?

What did we take with us?

Should a doctor be so philosophical? Was it a weakness, something that would blind her at an inopportune time? Did Hyman ever stop and have thoughts like these?

There was a time when science and religion were antagonists, when doctors were thought to be challenging the will of God. There were sects like Christian Scientists and Jehovah's Witnesses who still believed in these old ideas.

I am a doctor, she thought as if she was speaking before an assembly of such people. I have been educated and given the skills to repair and cure our bodies, not to defy God, but to do His bidding, to be a servant. Why else did He give us the ability and the desire to pursue?

In her mind, her musing, the audience was suddenly down to just two: Paige Thorndyke and this new young woman, Kristin Martin. They were sitting like corpses placed in a chair and they were staring at her with cold eyes and they were asking, "What about us?"

He heard them ask the old lady if she knew who her granddaughter had met tonight.

"Did she have a date or anything that she told you about?" the plainclothes officer asked.

"I have no idea," she said. "She never tells me anything about her love life anymore. I know she's been seeing too many different men.

"I warned her that wasn't good. I, myself, never went out with more than one man at a time for a period of time and only two before I met my husband. But young people are different nowadays. She don't listen," she concluded. She was talking about Kristin as though she were still alive and this dead thing was just a temporary, annoying condition.

The police listened politely, but from where he stood looking in, he could see their smiles behind their hands or when they turned away.

They asked her if she could come with them to identify the body.

The way she looked at them, it was clear to him that she had forgotten what they had come to tell her. No wonder she was talking like that. The realization hit her again. She faltered a moment, caught her breath, and then excused herself to get dressed.

The moment she left, they began to snoop about the room. He wondered if they had any reason to do that. Not one of them had asked her if she had any guests. His car was around back so they hadn't noticed it. They're just nosy, he concluded. Their jobs and uniforms give them the right to enter into people's lives and violate their privacy. Nothing in the old lady's world was sacred. They would explore her small intestine if they wanted. They're just like insects or rodents. No place is off limits.

Suddenly he felt like defending the old lady, like rushing in there and demanding to know who the hell gave them the right to look in drawers and in jewel boxes? He might have done just that, too, but the old lady was back from her room quicker than anyone had anticipated.

She wore what he thought was a very silly-looking hat, the brim too wide and the hat a bit too large for her head. They took her out and put her in the rear of the car. He watched them drive off and then he went inside and hurried up the stairs to his room to pack his things. He started to take his clothes off hangers and then stopped and gazed at himself in the mirror above the dresser.

What am I doing? he asked himself. Why am I running? Look at this place, these small towns. It's prime plucking, and it would be crazy for me to leave, he thought. Besides, the law enforcement here is vintage boondocks. They probably still think fingerprints are some form of mass-produced duplicated works of art.

He laughed and put the clothes back on hangers. He was in his Godself mode as he liked to call it. He always felt this way when he was restored and working on all cylinders. As confident as ever, he took a warm shower and then got into bed. A good night's sleep is what he needed and he could fall asleep at a moment's notice, if he wanted. No guilty conscience, no worries to keep him tossing and turning. He had truly forgotten what he had done. That irked him for a few moments. He recalled not knowing why the police had come to see the old lady.

It made him laugh. Then he remembered some of it, enough of it. How could I have forgotten getting into her vehicle and then running back here afterward? He questioned the darkness. He wondered if he should be worried. What difference did it make? he concluded. It's not like I am keeping a journal.

After that he did fall asleep quickly, but he also woke up when he heard a door close and footsteps on the stairway. He heard her sobbing as she ascended. He rose and went to the door, opening it first to peek out and then farther when he saw her pause at the top of the landing below to catch her breath.

"Is anything wrong, Mrs. Martin?" he called down to her.

She jerked her head his way, her eyes refocusing under the dim corridor light. From the way her mouth twisted and her eyebrows lifted, he thought she had completely forgotten about him.

"Oh," she said, "something terrible. My granddaughter . . ."

"What about her?"

"She's dead. She was found dying in her car. Someone might have raped her."

"Oh my God," he said. "That beautiful young woman?"

"Yes. My only living grandchild. I have no one now, no one I care about," she said. "I wish I could lie down and die myself," she added. "Just go to sleep and die myself."

"Yes," he said. "I don't blame you."

"The doctor at the hospital gave me some pills to take to help me rest," she said plucking a packet out of her coat pocket. "I oughta take them all at the same time."

He nodded.

"Is there anything I can do for you, Mrs. Martin?"

"No," she said shaking her head. "Nothing. Thank you."

"Please don't hesitate to call me if you need anything," he said as she started down the corridor toward her room. She shook her head and continued. He watched her until she was in her room and then he returned to his room, closed his door softly and stood there, thinking.

What a depressingly sad person. She will never have a good day from now on, he concluded. And then he thought he could help her and help himself. Vaguely, he recalled an opportunity like this in the past, although the details were as faint and cloudy as the rocks at the bottom of that murky pond at the rear of the tourist house. Struggle as much as he wanted, he would still not get a clear view of them, but that wasn't important. He had the general idea and besides, he didn't like doing the same things repeatedly. A little originality made life so much more interesting.

He waited a good hour and then he left his room in stocking feet, descending the short stairway as softly and quietly as he would if the floor were made of marshmallows. He opened her bedroom door in increments, containing the smallest squeak. She had a small nightlight on, one of those that were plugged into a socket. It threw just enough of a glow to clearly delineate everything in her bedroom. He saw her head on the large, fluffy pillow. The light made it seem as if her face was carved out of white marble. Her whole head looked like it was slowly sinking into the pillow and she would soon be gone from sight, matter of fact. She was on her back and her hands were crossed over themselves and on her stomach just the way an undertaker might have put them. How convenient and how portentous he thought and entered her room.

He stood by the side of her bed and watched her labored breathing. She was lifting her upper lip with every exhale. He couldn't imagine when, if ever, this old woman was attractive. She probably looked old when she was in her twenties, he thought. Time to start the process, he decided and tugged the big pillow out from under her head in one swift motion. Her head fell to the mattress and her eyes popped open.

"Whaaa. What are you doing in here?" she demanded.

"Helping you," he said.

He put the pillow over her face before she could reply. She started to struggle and gag and after a while, he let her breathe. She gasped eagerly, full of hope, and then he put the pillow over her face again and she fought again. Again, he let it up and again she gasped and heaved and choked for air. On and on the process continued: he bringing her to brink and she struggling, each time with less effort. What's more, each time she was free to breathe, it became more labored for her to do so.

Relentlessly, he put the pillow over her face. Her

hands were barely pushing and pulling now. She was giving it so little effort that he had to stop sooner.

"Come on now," he urged, "you can do better than that."

She gasped and choked and he did it again and again he released it until finally, while he had the pillow up, she waved her hand, fought for breath, and died.

She died of heart failure, not asphyxiation.

It was his design. Someday soon after he was gone, she would be discovered and that was what they would believe. That was what the coroner would determine. Again, how he knew all this, he couldn't say, but he knew it. What difference did the how make after all?

He brushed down her face to be sure there were no traumas, no evidence of anything against her skin, no pressure, no blows. The pillow had been wonderful.

"Good choice," he told the corpse. "Soft, downy. I kind of like it. Do you mind if I use it tonight?"

He laughed.

Why not? He'll return it to her in the morning, and she won't complain.

She won't complain about anything anymore and she had him to thank for that.

Why couldn't they send thank-you cards back from the afterlife? he wondered. If they could, he would cover a wall.

EIGHT

Terri overslept.

She had not set her alarm clock either. It was the phone that woke her and thankfully so, she thought when she opened her eyes and saw the clock. She threw off her blanket and sprung up like a jack in the box.

"Dr. Barnard," she said swinging her legs over the bed after she had seized the receiver.

"Terri, forgive me for calling so early," she heard Will Dennis say. She knew it was he before he added, "It's Will Dennis." He had that distinct a voice.

"Oh. No, it's fine. Actually, I'm glad you called. I forgot to set my alarm."

Will Dennis laughed.

"Even doctors oversleep, huh?"

"Especially doctors. How can I help you?" she followed, trying not to sound impatient. She would have to shower and dress in twenty minutes and like a character on a television commercial, grab some breakfast bar on her way out and to the office. Grandma Gussie's single-story Queen Anne–style house was just outside Centerville, so fortunately there wasn't that long a commute to the office. When she was little, she called it the Gingerbread House because of the color of the shingles and the shutters.

"One of my ADA's was summoned to a situation regarding a Kristin Martin from Loch Sheldrake last night. The on-the-scene officer's report has your name on it. How did you come to be the one attending to the victim?"

The sheer coincidence of it was obviously not lost on Will Dennis, whose voice sounded full of wild suspicions.

"I was on my way home from dinner when I saw the patrol car and the vehicle. The officer asked me to look at her when I told him I was a physician."

"So you had time to examine her?"

"Barely. She went into a convulsion quickly. I can't tell you what happened to her except to say it was probably heart failure. What caused it is another . . ."

"Well, there is evidence of sexual intercourse," he said quickly, "so considering the condition she was in when she was discovered, we would have to consider an assault, but the report from the autopsy I was just given over the phone has thrown me for a loop, as they say."

"Oh. What was it?"

"The official diagnosis is going to be an extreme case of wet beriberi."

She could feel herself holding her breath involuntarily. That diagnosis had lingered like a persistent itch she refused to scratch or acknowledge.

"Wet beriberi," she repeated as though she had to say it to confirm that she had heard it.

"Correct me if I'm wrong, Doctor, but isn't that caused by a vitamin deficiency?"

"B_1, thiamine," she said.

"The report claims not a trace of it in her body," Will Dennis said. "Isn't that very unusual?"

"Not a trace? Yes. A very low level would be common in the Third World, a chronic alcoholic, breast-fed babies, but not a trace?"

"That's what they're telling me, which was basically what was on Paige Thorndyke's autopsy report, not a trace of vitamin C in that case. Can you offer any sort of explanation, Doctor?"

"I'm not any sort of expert for this, Mr. Dennis. I just know what any family physician would know."

"I realize that. I'm calling you solely because of the coincidence of your being an attending physician on both these bizarre cases. I wanted you to know about it, first, and then, maybe later, we can talk."

For a second or two, she couldn't speak and then her voice returned.

"Yes, of course. I'm on until five today and then I'm going to the hospital to do rounds," she said.

"You have a worse schedule than I have," he kidded. He was silent a moment. "I really don't know what to make of all this. That's why I'm reaching everywhere. I mean, if someone dies because of malnutrition, I don't see how I can indict anyone unless it was a child and a parent situation involving criminal neglect. And yet, as you pointed out, this sort of phenomenon is too unusual in a highly developed country. We're out here a ways and some people think we're still hicks, but two otherwise healthy young women dying of vitamin deficiencies within a week's time. . . ."

"I understand your concern," she said. "If I were you, I'd have the same and start to bring in some real medical experts," she said. It sounded too much like she was trying to get him off her back, however. "Of course, I'll be glad to add anything I can to any investigation."

"Thank you. What time do you actually begin at the hospital?"

"As I said, I'll leave the office about five and grab a quick bite in the hospital cafeteria before starting my rounds about seven."

"Okay, I'll stop by the hospital and catch you at dinner. The way this is going it might be my only chance to grab dinner tonight, too. Even hospital food has some nutrition in it, right?" he added.

"Right. Although I'm beginning to wonder if it matters all that much where we eat," she quipped.

He grunted.

"If you have a quiet moment, give some thought to what you saw last night, what if anything the girl managed to say, that sort of thing."

"She didn't say . . ."

"For now, Doctor, I would appreciate it if you would keep what I have told you confidential," he interjected before she could finish. "I have no idea where I'm going with this or what I'm looking for and that makes me a very nervous man," he concluded, thanked her, and hung up.

Makes you nervous, she thought. What do you think it does to me?

She had just backed out of her driveway when her cell phone rang. She had it on speaker and flipped the lid.

"Dr. Barnard," she said.

"Say Doc, you make house calls?" Curt asked.

"Not today," she said dryly. They often had humorous conversations before either of them said anything remotely serious, but she was far from that mood. He heard it in her voice.

"I was hoping to hear from you this morning," he said, a little more irritation in his voice than she expected.

"I overslept. I'm actually rushing to get to the office."

"Oh. Hope it wasn't something I said or did. I did think I would hear from you before you turned in, remember?"

"No. I had a problem last night on the way home, Curt."

"What? What happened?"

"I came upon a woman in trouble. A police car was on the scene and I tried to administer medical aid, but she died shortly after I had arrived."

"Holy shit! What happened to her? Who was she?" he asked rapidly.

She thought about Will Dennis's request to keep the information confidential.

"She had heart failure," she replied. That was at least partially the cause. "Her name is Kristin Martin and she's from Loch Sheldrake."

"Loch Sheldrake? Yeah, I know of a Martin family there. They have a tourist house, one of the last remaining old-time borscht belt properties," he said. "A bed and breakfast type."

"Did you know the young woman?"

"No. Dad did something for the family years ago. I think there was a dispute over a submersible well or something. Heart failure. Jesus. Was she very fat or something?"

"No, Curt," she said. "I don't know the exact cause yet," she said, deciding not to tell him what she already knew. It was still too bizarre and inexplicable.

"Will I see you today?" he asked. "I'm in the office all morning and then I'm off to court, but I have time for lunch, I think."

"I have a full day, Curt, and tonight's my night for hospital rounds, remember?"

"No, but I hope I won't have to get sick to see my wife," he quipped.

"And I hope I don't have to sue anyone to see my husband," she fired back.

He laughed, but it was forced.

"You should have come home with me," he finally said. She had been counting the seconds.

"If I follow that logic, I shouldn't come out of the house, period," she replied.

"Okay, okay. What about meeting for a quick dinner, then? I'll even eat in the hospital cafeteria with you."

"I have to meet with the district attorney about then. He's coming to the hospital."

"Will Dennis? Why?"

"He wants to talk to me about the situation I confronted last night, Curt," she said. She realized half truths made it all even stranger. Curt was far from dense when it came to things like this, she thought. He was silent for a moment.

"Why?" he demanded. "Were there signs of foul play?"

"The woman was totally naked and probably raped."

"What?" He thought a moment. "I don't like the sound of any of this, and I especially don't like you talking to Will Dennis without my being present," he said.

"Huh?" She smiled and froze a laugh. "Why not?"

"I just don't like it. First, maybe an undercover detective, maybe not, and now this."

"You're sounding a little paranoid, aren't you?" she quipped.

"It's my job to be that way, especially when it comes to law enforcement officers who look for the easiest way out, and," he added before she could comment, "who are political creatures."

She stifled any reply. Was he right?

"I have to speak to him, Curt. It would look worse if I didn't. I'll call you right afterward."

"No, you won't, but I'll call you," he said. "Maybe you should have become a paramedic."

"Maybe you should have become a court stenographer," she retorted.

"Right," he said, his voice full of controlled anger.

She flipped the phone closed and concentrated on what she knew she had at the office, hoping she would be able to do just that: focus on her patients, but news of any death in the township traveled fast, even before it made the local radio news.

"Did you hear about Kristin Martin?" Elaine Wolf asked Terri the moment she entered the lobby.

Apparently Elaine Wolf, her one-woman news team, did not have much detail yet and didn't even know Terri's involvement. Will Dennis was keeping the lid tight on this one for as long as he could, she thought, but she knew Elaine would feel betrayed if Terri didn't tell her something.

"I came upon the scene last night and attended her myself," she replied.

"Oh. I didn't hear that. My God, poor you. Well, what happened to her? All I heard was she had a heart attack. A girl that young?"

"We'll have to wait to see," Terri said quickly, trying to make it seem as routine as possible. Before Elaine could ask anything else, Terri continued into the offices. She went directly to Hyman's.

He was on the phone talking to the radiologist at the hospital about Marvin Kaplan's fractured femur. The sixty-year-old plumber had fallen from a ladder in his own home, screaming how he could crawl through sewers, swing on rafters, and lug two hundred pound pipes and not get hurt, but do something for himself . . . . Hyman had his hands full with him when he was brought to the office and then sent on to the hospital.

"We'll have to chain him to the bed," he concluded after hearing the full report. "That man hasn't taken a day off for forty-five years. Weekends to him just mean time and a half."

Hyman nodded at Terri and held up his hand for her to wait.

"Thanks, Fred. I'll see you at two thirty."

He hung up and turned his chair around.

"One of my spies at the hospital called me ten minutes ago and told me something on the Q.T. It seems we have another very bizarre fatality in the county."

She sank into the chair in front of his desk.

"You don't know that I was the attending physician on the scene last night?"

He sat back, his mouth slightly open, his eyebrows raised.

"You're kidding."

"Believe me, I wish I was," she said and reviewed

what she had discovered and what she had done. "It all happened so fast," she concluded. "You know how rapid and dramatic the response to flooding doses of thiamine hydrochloride in patients suffering with wet beriberi can be. A diuresis starts between 4 and 48 hours with visible resolution of most of the edema within four to eight hours. It's all gone in two days!" she added with frustration turning her eyes into Ping-Pong balls.

"I'm beginning to sound like a broken record, but I've never seen this serious a case of wet beriberi, even during my internship. No trace of thiamine in the blood!" He paused and considered her. "No one could possibly blame you in any way."

She shook her head.

"I'm not even thinking about that," she said. "We didn't have time to get her to the hospital for blood tests so we could start a protocol."

He nodded and leaned forward, putting his elbows on the desk and pressing his two forefingers into the bottom of his jaw, a habitual posture for him.

"It's a maddening sort of déjà vu."

He nodded.

"Yes, but I would even go as far as saying there are some diseases so rare in the modern world, many physicians wouldn't recognize them or consider their possibility when they confronted the symptoms," he said. She knew he was just trying to help her feel better about it.

"I really considered that diagnosis, Hyman, but I shook

it out of my head. I was concentrating on an allergy," she said, hating the sound of her voice, the whining. "The policeman got me thinking about a bee sting."

"Logical. You had the hyperventilating, the racing heartbeat, edema."

"I also smelled alcohol on her breath and a whole series of other possibilities flew by."

"A-huh," Hyman said. "Well, I can't tell you any of it makes sense to me."

"The district attorney feels the same way."

"Oh? How do you know that?"

"He was my first call this morning. He wants to see me so much he's coming to the hospital to meet me in the cafeteria before I begin my rounds."

"Oh." Hyman's forehead went into folds. "Why? He has his own medical experts to call upon. No offense, but I would think he would contact an expert on nutrition, not a family physician still green around the gills."

"I agree, and I think Curt does too, although I didn't tell Curt about Kristin's beriberi. Will Dennis wants it kept as quiet as possible for now."

"Oh?"

"Dennis's request to see me confused Curt or worried him. He was upset about it and chided me for agreeing to talk to Dennis like this, but I was the attending physician on both cases, Hyman, and for some reason Will Dennis thinks I might know something or help him understand the deaths of these two women. Kristin

Martin, like Paige Thorndyke, was in no condition to provide valuable details. She mouthed something, but I made no sense of it."

He stared at her for a moment and then sat back shaking his head.

"I admit Curt has me feeling a little paranoid," she confessed.

"This is all just coincidence," Hyman said. "We live in a small town. There's no reason to make any more of it."

"I hope so," she replied. "I hope that's the way the district attorney sees it, too."

"Well," he said starting to laugh, "what else could it be? You're not some sort of medical serial killer, are you?"

It was on the tip of her tongue to tell him it was some mystical or fated force at work, a dark force that had decided to attach itself to her, something her grandmother would believe as strongly as she believed in the Evil Eye, but Hyman would call that a *bubbe meise,* an old-wives' tale.

He was reading it in her eyes.

"You're not going to go all funny on me now, are you, Terri?" he asked, half-jesting, "and talk about Fate and some curse or something. Are you?"

"No," she said rising. "But please, give me colds, allergies, even diabetes today and leave the bizarre outside our door."

He laughed and she went to set up for her first patient of the day.

NINE

He didn't do anything with the body. Just leave her in bed, he thought. Keep the door closed and the window open a little to help contain the stench and forget about her. She wasn't going anywhere. It never occurred to him that she might have relatives or friends or even that someone like him might come along and ask for a room.

Up at the first sign of light, he put on his running shoes and did what he had planned. He ran a good two and a half miles, barely feeling an ache in his legs or feet. At times he thought he was literally Mercury, off the ground, actually gliding over the macadam. His breathing was wonderfully regular and easy. Actually, he could have gone five miles, but he was hungry this morning and was looking forward to a big breakfast.

The house had a very large kitchen, which during the heyday of the Catskill resort era was probably justified and well used. Now, the old lady had turned off all but a small refrigerator. Fortunately, she, or perhaps Kristin, had gone shopping recently. There were fresh eggs, milk, coffee, bread, and a bag of oranges. He loved fresh orange juice even though all the nutrition passed through him along with the waste. He loved everything that was full of good food value. He was never fond of fast foods or greasy foods. In fact, if anyone could pose as the poster boy for good eating habits, it was he. How ironic.

But this was not a morning to waste over disappointments or problems. This was a morning full of rejoicing. He would continue his celebration by buying himself some new clothes. He never wore again what he had worn during a feeding. It wasn't some imaginative or superstitious thing either. He could smell the scent of them, especially after a feeding when his senses were so heightened and no amount of dry cleaning, no washing, no cologne, nothing could remove or disguise it.

It occurred to him in a truly vague way that there was a thin line of remorse streaming through his conscience. Only a surgical removal such as the old lady upstairs in bed didn't bother him at all, not that he was actually troubled enough to consider anything a bother. It was just something that gave him a moment's pause. He wished there was some way he could draw what he needed and not leave them so fatally depleted, but alas, in the end it was always either they or he, and frankly he wasn't in the altruism business. He always had to protect himself and never pass up an opportunity.

I have such insecurity, he thought shaking his head. That's the one thing he had yet to overcome and conquer: this terrible sense of fear that he would find himself on some desert or suddenly lose the ability to draw nectar from the flowers. He had that fear since it all began.

Actually, that memory, the memory of the first time, was still vivid. He liked to compare it to a woman losing her virginity. Even at the point of Alzheimer's disease, she would remember that, he thought.

It all happened purely accidentally, this entirely new existence, this grand life. Some nerd of an assistant got himself stoned and forgot to feed him through his IV. He nearly died, but fortunately Doctor Toby . . . yes, that was her name . . . Toby . . . stopped by after she had attended some social event. The ordinary-looking woman with her dull brown hair and pockmarked cheeks had actually gone to a beauty salon and had her hair styled and colored. What's more, she was wearing makeup. The pallid complexion was well hidden and even her pockmarks were diminished. She had a firm bosom. So many times she had pressed it to him or he had brushed across her breasts and realized that although she wasn't wearing a bra, she held her form. In the eyes of others he saw the thought that her voluptuous figure, most of the time well hidden under her lab robe, was a waste. Not only didn't she have the face it deserved, but she didn't radiate any sexual energy or interest.

This particular evening, the evening he was to break his cherry, she came flying through the special living quarters surprisingly still laughing over something funny that had been told to her or had happened to her, her eyes still full of tiny explosions, which he imagined to be the aftermath of her drinking champagne and dancing and being romanced by someone she fancied. He heard her giggle again when she entered his bedroom. She didn't check the clipboards, which was her fatal mistake. If she had, she would have corrected the error and all would have gone on as it was. Not that it was much of a life, any of a life, in fact. Her blunder was his blessing actually.

When he set eyes on her, he was lying in bed, naked, struggling to breathe actually, just like some of his recent victims. Her eyes, on the other hand, were so full of fantasy, she was blinded to his problem. He saw the way her bosom rose and fell beneath the low-cut black dress, and he felt himself aroused with such speed and intensity, he was actually frightened for a moment. Later he would compare it to accelerating in an automobile and realizing he was going far too fast to negotiate the upcoming turn. He understood that panic could disable him and he fought it back and beat it down in time to take control.

That was what he had done this time. She drew closer, intending to give him a quick examination. What happened was beyond his own expectations and far beyond his control. His arms, his hands, and his legs— every part of him moved as if it had its own mind.

Whatever he wanted back in the command center made absolutely no difference.

When she reached out to touch his forehead, finally becoming concerned at his pallor, he seized her wrist and drew her down to him. She tried to resist, but he was driven now by a force hitherto undiscovered deep within him, so asleep not even he had ever realized its existence.

She cried out and tried to pull away, but he was all over her, tearing away her dress, twisting and turning her so he could get on top of her and suck on her mouth, drawing the very air out of her lungs. He could actually see them in his mind's eye, both of them like balloons collapsing. Her eyes had become neon bulbs brightening with such fear they were close to bursting. He wondered if she could feel or even see the life being drawn out of her. His prick was more like a beak, drawing the nectar. Every part of his body had become a portal ingesting, a sponge soaking her up. He was illuminated with the power of it. She was literally being absorbed into him.

Her final cries were so thin and low, only someone or something with his acute sense of hearing could know she had uttered any sound at all. Her eyes, once full of light, began to dim and then grow dark and icy. Once he was satiated, her body looked nauseating, like the rotting skin of a banana. Even flies would avoid it.

He stepped away and then dressed himself. What he realized was he was stronger, more full of energy than he had ever been. Not the shots, not the pills, not the IVs, nothing made him feel as good as this had, and like some lion cub that had been given its first taste of meat, he lunged forward on the unsuspecting world that to him had suddenly become a grand feast, a table of delectable delights.

How could he ever forget that? Even now, reliving it in his thoughts, he felt himself aroused. Eat a good breakfast, go get some exciting new clothes, and go forth to seek a new sexual encounter, if not to feed, than to enjoy, for every sense in his body needed to be satiated. He wanted to hear wonderful music, eat delicious foods, smell the aroma from a beautiful woman's skin and hair and feel the softness of her breasts and the promise between her thighs and especially see the enjoyment in her face, too, for when he was like this, he was capable of giving them so much pleasure it even made him jealous and wonder if he was getting as much as he was giving.

Whoever the lucky woman was today, she would never forget him, he thought and laughed.

He started to prepare his eggs when the phone rang. He stared at it on the kitchen wall while it rang and then he decided he had better answer it.

"May I speak with Mrs. Martin, please," he was asked by a very official, dry-sounding man.

"She is unable to come to the phone," he replied. "She can't talk to anyone."

It was all true, he thought smiling.

"Oh, well, of course. This is Dr. Anderson. I wanted to let her know she could have Kristin's body moved to the funeral parlor today."

"Right, right. I'm her nephew," he said. He always thought well and quickly on his feet after a feed. "I'll see to that immediately."

"Thank you. I'm sorry," the doctor added.

"Aren't we all?" he replied. It was something the doctor obviously hadn't been prepared to hear. He was silent a moment and then said good-bye.

Now what to do? he thought gazing around the kitchen. He really would like to remain here a while longer. It was so convenient and comfortable. He started to rifle through drawers until he found the phone book and flipped to the Yellow Pages. Thanks to the GPS system in his car, he had a very good concept of the area and its surrounding hamlets. He located a funeral parlor in a place nearby called Woodbourne and phoned. When the gentleman who took such great care to make his consonants crisp and his vowels full answered, he introduced himself to the man as Stanley Martin, a nephew and only mature and living close relative of the deceased Kristin Martin. Not surprisingly, the undertaker already knew of the death. Next to the deceased, he was probably the first to know. After all, it was his business to know death, to tap in on its calls like some FBI agent plugged into a suspect's phone lines.

"We'll take care of her immediately," the undertaker

said and assured him everything would be handled properly and with the most possible respect.

"My aunt will be eternally grateful," he told him. She was already in eternity. The gratitude would follow. "I'll be by to discuss the arrangements as soon as possible."

"We understand," the undertaker said.

Was there anyone more understanding than an undertaker? His role, his objectives were crystal clear. He made no value judgements after he tried to get the bereaved to buy as expensive a funeral as he could, but even that he did subtly, never implying any choice was wrong or disrespectful.

In a way he's like me, he thought.

He sucks the living as much as he can and then he leaves them alone and moves on to the next customer.

He turned on the old radio in a wooden casing, found a station with soft but upbeat music, and sat at the kitchen table to enjoy his breakfast.

He took a deep breath and then gazed out the windows facing the east. The sun had already begun to paste itself on the grass and flowers.

He couldn't wait to wallow in its falling rays and have it paste itself on his smile and his heart as well.

The third time Curt heard someone at the law office make reference to Terri and her being on the scene of another young woman's death, he felt a fist of anger in his chest opening and closing with the regularity of a second heart. The rage was inexplicable, even illogical, but nevertheless made its presence clearly known through his snappy replies and the furious way he went at his work. No matter how hard he tried, his eyes would not stay on the pages of the brief before him. His gaze kept wandering toward the framed picture of Terri after her medical school graduation. His father had bought her the new stethoscope and had presented it to her that day. She wore it in the picture. His father's camera had caught the sunlight glittering off it, making it look like a halo at rest.

He recalled being as petulant as a jealous sibling. His parents hadn't made as much of a big deal over his graduation from law school, he thought. Thanks to the O. J. Simpson so-called Dream Team, lawyers, who never enjoyed great popularity, were now the most notorious subjects of derogatory humor ever created. There were probably more lawyer jokes flowing through cyberspace than anything else. He had no tolerance for them anymore and either forced a smile or looked away and changed the subject. Everyone telling the jokes with him in hearing range usually said something like "Present company excluded of course."

Teachers hated it when people in their presence said "Those who can, do and those who can't, teach," didn't they? Yet some of the teachers he knew wouldn't hesitate to tell the latest lawyer joke.

"They hate us until they need us and then they hate

us even more," Howard Sages told him a few days ago when a new lawyer joke was being circulated at the county courthouse. Some lawyers were just as responsible for passing the jokes around. To him they were like black people who used the word *nigger* freely.

There were jokes about doctors, for sure, jokes about their penurious ways, their greed, but Howard's remark about people hating lawyers even more when they needed them didn't apply to doctors. People worshipped their doctors, looked upon them as true miracle workers, saviors who had the skill and the wisdom to frustrate and defeat Death. If a lawyer did a good job, it was understood somehow that he or she did it because he or she was well tuned into the corrupt system. They knew how to play the game and they did it with every available trick or method, regardless of the underlying sense of unfairness.

For example, if his client was sued by someone, he would recommend a countersuit, knowing that the legal costs would injure them both and both lawyers would then try to convince the clients to settle and endure less pain. Right and wrong had little to do with it. Use the system to defeat the opponent: prolong, delay, work every convolution until the injured party relented and settled. What was true in civil law was just as true in criminal law. Wear down the prosecutors and the courts and get your client off with the least punishment possible, no matter what he or she had done.

Maybe he should have become a doctor, too, Curt thought, and then he thought how much such a pursuit would have been beyond him. He almost failed chemistry in high school, and he was never fond of the sight of blood. He even fainted once when he had blood taken, something no one knew, not even Terri. And then, the whole idea of touching and cutting and exploring a human corpse was revolting to him. It turned his stomach just to think about it.

Sometimes lately, although he would never dare say anything, he thought about Terri examining sick people and he wondered if she could inadvertently transmit something to him. He tried convincing himself that it was such a ridiculous thought, he shouldn't even permit himself to think it, but he couldn't help it. He had even had a nightmare about himself wearing a surgical mask and surgical gloves while he made love to her and in the nightmare, she turned out to be a corpse. That was when he literally jumped up and nearly fell out of his bed. He was so nauseated afterward, too. He had to take something before he could get back to sleep and when he did, he was afraid to close his eyes, afraid the nightmare still stuck like honey to the inside of his eyelids.

Another thing he had never told her.

A knock on his opened door snapped him out of his musings. He looked up at one of his partners, Bill Kleckner. Since Curt's father left the firm, he and the lanky, six-feet-four former high school and college basketball star had taken over most of the litigation. Bill had that troubled expression on his face that usually blossomed at the realization of a critical problem. His light brown hair was short on the sides, but fell over his forehead to the point of covering his eyes. He had the habitual habit of running his fingers through the strands in a repeated motion while talking, even in court, which drove Curt crazy and surely annoyed some judges. Bill's eyes were narrow, dark, and full of concern at the moment as well.

"What's up?"

"You know Dawn Kotein, Dick's wife."

Dick Kotein had been on the same high school basketball team and had gone on to play college ball, too, although not as impressively as Bill had. Now Dick was an architect working out of a Monticello office and building a great reputation. He had thrown some work their way lately.

"So?"

"You know she works at Community General."

"I know all this, Bill. Is there a point?"

He sat, folded his hands and pressed them against his long, flat chest upon which he wore a loose white shirt and an out of style wide tie.

"She works for Dr. Stern in pathology."

"I love it when you come in here and interrupt me and give me pages and pages of information I know. It reinforces my belief in tape replays in sports."

"She told Melanie something a few minutes ago."

"Why didn't you say she told your wife Melanie? You left out something I know."

"Which," Bill said ignoring him, "she claimed no one knows yet, but soon will, about the Martin woman whom Terri tried to save last night."

Curt stopped smiling. He put the pages down on his desk and sat back in his chair.

"And what would that be, Bill?"

"She said she died of an extreme case of beriberi, which is a disease caused by a vitamin deficiency. One of the B's, I think."

Curt stared at him.

"Why didn't you tell me?" Bill asked. "I mean, why is it a secret?"

Curt swallowed.

That fist of anger was opening and closing again, growing, too. He put his right palm over his chest as if he thought Bill would soon be able to see it palpitating.

"I didn't know. She didn't tell me that," he said.

Bill nodded and then shrugged.

"Maybe she didn't know either. Anyway, it's going to cause a stir around here, don't you think? Two young women die of vitamin deficiency diseases within a week of each other?"

Curt nodded.

"Maybe."

"And here's our Terri right in the middle of it all or

unfortunately at the wrong places at the wrong time, huh?"

"Unfortunately. I don't think we need to lose any sleep over it," Curt said. "I've got to get back to this," he said tapping the brief. "I'm in court this afternoon."

"Right. Just thought you'd like to know. You going to Roary's for lunch?"

"I'm not going to have time," he said.

"Don't work harder than I do. It makes me look bad," Bill joked, pretended to flip a basketball at a net, and left the office.

Curt stared after him.

Trust, he thought.

Trust is more important than love in a relationship.

The fist beating in his heart thumped on.

TEN

"Am I a suspect of some kind?" Terri asked Will Dennis, who was waiting for her at the nurse's station. She had gotten to the hospital a little early and had seen Sally Peters, a fifty-four-year-old widow who suffered serious hypertension.

Will Dennis raised his eyebrows in surprise. She had barely acknowledged him before asking. Perhaps it was her medical training or just being under the sign of Sagittarius that made Terri the type of person who was so direct and to the point. It was to think about all of this while she was attending patients, but all day at the office she found herself slipping into it. Her eyes drifted from charts and her thoughts fell back to the bizarre deaths of both young women, especially Kristin Martin because, as short as it was, she did attempt some therapy.

"Why would you think that, Doctor?" Will responded.

She looked at the nurse on duty and then started away without answering him. Will Dennis walked alongside her. She paused at the elevator and turned to him.

"I don't have any satisfactory medical explanations for

you. I told you that you would have to seek out more learned people," she began.

Although Will Dennis's eyes were full of interest and curiosity, he didn't really look at her with suspicion and accusation. Of course, she attributed most of that to his skills at questioning witnesses and suspects, but she also wondered about her own paranoia, something she could lay at Curt's feet for sure.

"We are doing just that, and we're not getting answers that help us along. No one we've spoken with yet, and we've even gone to the Centers for Disease Control in Atlanta, can offer anything that even comes close to a logical, noncriminal cause for all this. It's possible that something you saw, something you remember, might just lead us in a sensible direction."

The elevator door opened.

She nodded.

"You're right. I'm sorry," she said. "It's been a long day and especially made longer by a horrid night."

"I understand," Will said after they stepped into the elevator.

"Well," she began. "As I said, I tried to get her to speak, to tell me if the cause of her difficulties might be an allergy, perhaps to a bee sting. She mouthed something that sounded like '*he*.' "

"*He*? That's it? *He*?"

"And I can't even swear to that," she added quickly. "Don't hold me to it."

"No, no, of course not," he said thoughtfully.

"I'm sure pathology has already told you about any suspicious-looking traumas."

Will nodded. The elevator door opened and they walked out and toward the cafeteria.

"What is especially puzzling to me," Terri continued, "is the selectivity of the deficiency. One woman lacking vitamin C and another lacking B and of course the speed with which they each went into the deficiency ailments."

"Yes," Will said. "I had detectives question Kristin Martin's grandmother last night and according to her, the girl showed no signs of illness, and today, questioning her employer, fellow employees, we've come up with the same sort of puzzling description we had when we spoke to the people who knew Paige Thorndyke: she was full of energy, healthy looking, no complaints of pains or any of the other symptoms."

Terri listened and nodded. They went to the counter and began to choose their dinner.

"Let me get this," he offered at the cashier. "Expense budget."

She smiled and went to a table far enough away from nurses and doctors having their dinners. Some recognized the district attorney immediately. Will Dennis sat across from her.

"Someone has already suggested terrorism, you know," he mentioned as he shook his lemonade container.

"Terrorism? Here? Why?"

He shrugged.

"They've got to start somewhere and make an example so they can throw the country into a panic like they did with anthrax."

Terri smirked.

"We've become a nation of paranoids." She started to eat and then thought of something. "Do you know if Paige Thorndyke knew Kristin Martin?"

"We're working on that, but at the moment it appears they did not have any sort of friendship or relationship, nor did they frequent the same places, although Kristin did go to the dance club Paige went to the night she died. Kristin was there more frequently."

"I see. I would hope you might find something, some connection that would help us all understand any of this. Nothing at either crime scene?" she asked.

"No, nothing yet."

"I even feel funny calling them crime scenes. You haven't established any crime was committed, right? I mean, it looks like Kristin Martin might have been raped, I suppose, but unless Paige Thorndyke was kidnaped and brought to that motel forcibly, a woman having sex is not a crime in this country, at least not yet," she added.

Will Dennis smiled and began to eat. She pecked at her own food.

"Once this comes out, you will probably see a run on vitamins," Terri said.

"Maybe the vitamin companies or a company is behind it then, huh?"

She paused and looked at him. He was half serious, she thought. Talk about rampant paranoia.

"Look," she said leaning back, a little more frustrated and confused by this meeting. "I'm like what's-her-name in *Silence of the Lambs* here, practically a trainee called upon to help solve something experts are struggling to understand."

"Well," Dennis said, holding his smile, "maybe you'll have the same success she did."

"That was a novel, Mr. Dennis. This is real life."

"Doesn't feel like it," he said gazing around.

Terri stopped eating and studied the district attorney a little harder.

"You didn't come here to see if there was some little tidbit I had left out of my report, did you, Mr. Dennis? You have something else in mind, don't you?" she asked him.

For a moment it looked like he wasn't going to reply. He even looked like he might just get up and walk away, Terri thought. There was a debate raging in his own mind. He smiled and leaned forward.

"There is some information no one else has in this county, in your township especially," he said, "and very few have within the state, in fact."

"Am I going to be told this information?"

"I've been deciding that as we speak," he said. "It's

not that I don't trust you with it; it's what I want to ask you to do about it."

"I see," she said. "Actually, I don't see," she continued, shaking her head and holding a smile of confusion.

"What would you say if I told you that the two young women who died so unusually here were two of now ten across eight states who have died in similar fashion?"

She shook her head.

"I wouldn't know what to say."

"When we had the diagnosis on Paige Thorndyke, it sent up a flare. The FBI contacted me and we all sort of stepped back and waited to see if the second shoe would drop. It did with Kristin Martin.

"This FBI investigation is a little over a year old, and they have not made any significant headway. They are excited about our situation because this is the first time a second death of similar causes has occurred within the same area. The previous deaths, which we will now call murders, were spread over considerable distance. Whoever is causing these deaths was careful about proximity. This doesn't seem to be a concern any longer and because of that, they believe whoever is doing this is still here. In short, they are expecting another fatality to occur within our county.

"What their serial killer division has concluded is that the time period between killings has gradually been dwindling."

Terri shook her head.

"So you and others believe these are murders? I can't imagine how someone can kill people this way," she said.

"Well, that's another thing, Doctor. He is not killing people. He's killing only relatively young women, women about your age."

Terri's smile seemed to freeze on her face.

"If we're dealing with such a fantastic situation, how do you know it's a he?" she asked.

"In all the cases, ours included, the victims had recently had sexual intercourse. The DNA they have been able to capture is identical, too. Whatever is going on, the same man is at each death scene."

"My God, what is this?" she asked, her heart pounding.

"We have a description of a man seen with Kristin Martin at Diana's Restaurant. It's a better description than the one we got from the bartender at the Underground or anyone else there, but not really detailed enough to get a good police sketch artist involved yet."

"Weren't there any witnesses involved with the previous deaths in other states?"

"Nothing concrete. Somehow, he manages to stay shadowy."

"I see. So this man I said came to question me and claimed to be a BCI investigator . . . he was FBI. I just got that wrong? My fiancé thought an undercover investigation might be under way and you were pretending not to know about it," she said quickly.

"No. I was doing nothing of the kind, Doctor. We don't

know who that man is. No one from any agency was assigned to interview you, however," he added, his words hanging for a moment in the air between them, "in some of the other instances, a similar thing occurred . . . there was a man who matches your description of the man who came to see you, and he did the same sort of thing."

"How weird. I thought he was at the funeral, but when I went to check, he was gone. It's all very strange."

"Very, but there is something else I have to tell you which will make it even stranger, I'm afraid."

She held her breath.

"What?"

"The description you gave me of the phoney investigator who had come to your office . . ."

"Yes?"

"He could very well be the man seen with both Paige Thorndyke and Kristin Martin."

"What?"

"Blond hair and cleft chin in each case."

If Terri didn't fully appreciate what a patient hyperventilating felt like before, she did now.

"So you're saying the killer for some sick reason is pretending to be investigating himself?"

"He might just be seeing how much is known about his activities and about him, although I will tell you the forensic psychiatrists and profilers working for the FBI suggest even weirder explanations."

"Such as?"

"Such as a true schizophrenic who kills as one personality and investigates as another."

"This still doesn't make an iota of scientific sense to me," she said. "How do you kill someone this way, and more importantly perhaps, why?"

"Why might follow how or vice versa. I don't know. What I do know," he said slowly, "is that you spent some quality time with this man. You're observant, doctor observant, and as you said, you thought you had seen him at the funeral."

"In other words, you want me to sit down with a police artist?"

"No, not yet. They don't want to spook him if he's still here and send him fleeing. Not just yet."

"I know I can recognize him quickly if I see him again," she said.

"Precisely," Will Dennis said. "The FBI agents working on the case wanted to come see you themselves, but I suggested they let me talk to you first."

She stared at him and then looked up when one of the interns said hello in passing. He paused after she responded.

"Are you looking in on Mr. Kaplan tonight? He's raising hell up there."

"Yes, I am," she said smiling.

"Great. See you later," he said and walked on. She saw him join Mark Lester, the nurse who had been with Paige Thorndyke's friend Eileen Okun at the restaurant. They spoke and looked her way.

"Why did they want to talk to me? Were they going to tell me all this, too?"

"Perhaps not as much," Will Dennis said. "But enough, I suppose, before they asked you to do something."

"Something you're now going to ask me to do?"

"Yes," he said. He smiled. "I think we should keep all this close to home. It's our territory to protect, our people," he added.

"I thought the FBI works for all of us."

"They do, but it's only natural that the people who will look after you the best are the people who know you the best," he replied.

"Look after me? Why would they have to do that? Does this man come back to the people he questions? Is that the piece of information you're waiting to tell me?"

"Not as far as I know," Will Dennis said.

She smirked.

"I don't like that sort of answer. It sounds too much like 'To the best of my recollection' or the like."

"I can't tell you any more than they tell me," he said.

"So then, what . . ."

"What I thought, what they thought once they heard about you and the man who came to see you, was you might go out, on any evening you can, of course, and . . ."

"Look for him? You mean, in dance clubs and bars?"

"We'll have someone there at all times, of course, but if you spotted this man and pointed him out . . . well, you might prevent another tragic death here."

She shook her head slowly.

"I don't know. My fiancé won't be too happy about doing that sort of thing, going to those places. He feels he's outgrown it, calls them meat markets, sex pits . . ."

"We were thinking of you going more in the guise of a single woman," Will Dennis said.

For a moment all the sounds in the cafeteria, the other conversations, the cling and clatter of dishes and glasses disappeared.

She took a deep breath and like someone emerging from under water, released it.

"You mean, be bait, try to attract him?"

"There's probably no other young, very attractive woman within a thousand miles who is also capable of recognizing medical problems or health threats and indeed knowing how to treat them, as well as recognizing the individual who might be responsible for all this," he replied in a single breath. "That's it, all my cards on the table."

"All?"

"Well, there is one more small thing," he said.

"Give me the whole dosage, Will," she told him.

He smiled.

"If you agree to do this, help us, even for a night or two," he said, "you'll have to keep it to yourself for obvious reasons. You'll have to keep everything to yourself. In other words, don't trust anyone, even someone else who might come to you and identify himself as a law enforcement officer of some kind, especially that sort of person. Don't accept any proof and don't talk to him. Just call me," he emphasized.

"You make it sound like there's more than one of them out there."

"At this point, who knows?" he said.

She stared and then shook her head.

"I'd have to tell my fiancé about this idea of my going to local clubs," she said.

"I wouldn't. What if he decides it's too dangerous and comes after you, assuming you still wanted to go forward?"

She thought a moment.

"I don't know," she said. She glanced at her watch. "I have to get moving. My rounds."

"Okay."

"Let me think about it," she said.

"Of course."

"Maybe he's gone."

"Maybe," Will Dennis said. "It will be someone else's problem then, but until then, please remember my admonitions, Doc. Don't talk to anyone but me."

She stood looking at him. He smiled and turned back to his food.

"I think I'll finish this," he said nodding at his plate. "It was better than I expected."

She smiled.

"I'll call you," she said.

"Here," he said quickly reaching into his pocket and producing a card. "It has my personal numbers on it. Call anytime."

"Okay."

She left him, but it wasn't until she was actually at the first patient's bedside, that she stopped thinking about all he had told her and all he wanted her to do.

ELEVEN

Even though he was prepared to deal with it, it was encouraging to him that the phone did not ring all day. Aside from the undertaker, no one apparently had any interest in the old lady's well-being. Where were her contemporaries, her friends? Weren't there any relatives who by now would have found out Kristin was dead and would call to offer their condolences and their assistance? What about Kristin's friends? Didn't she have any? He couldn't remember anything he had said to her or she had said to him, so he didn't recall any mention of a girlfriend. If there were any, maybe they didn't like the old lady and didn't want to call her now, especially now.

Death, he realized, quarantined the survivors. People ignored or procrastinated as long as they could so they could avoid the sorrow, but more than that, he thought, so they could ignore their own mortality. Every death was a severe reminder that yours was waiting, patiently or impatiently, and no one wanted to be reminded of that, least of all, himself. There was a ruthless determination to keep his body alive and well, perhaps more so than the others, as he had come to call them, for there was he, unique, a wonder, and there were they, the prey, the food source. He thought of the old lady upstairs, no longer involved in the daily struggle to exist.

He went up to the bedroom and looked in on the corpse, still to him lying contentedly, comfortably in the bed.

"I guess you really have been a loner, Grandma," he said. "No gossips coming over for tea and cookies? No cousins, no sisters-in-law, no one?"

Families intrigued him, however. Was it simply because he could recall no one in his own? Vaguely, he thought there were people related to him, but his memory problem had become severe lately. All of the images he had been able to draw up from the well of his past experiences came to him like underexposed film full of shadows, silhouettes, faces with no distinct characteristics, voices garbled like something recorded and played at speeds far too slowly. Even his dreams had become colorless streams of obscure, wispy shapes.

All he had, he concluded, was the present, and of course, the future. Just like the body's nutritional wealth that he was unable to store, so were the events that made up his own history. It sort of made sense to him. Things passed through him. Nothing stayed. He felt loose, primed, and ready for anything, almost virginal.

Maybe not almost, he thought. I am virginal today. I can remember no lovemaking, and just like that, the momentary sense of emptiness, being lost and alone, floating in space, left him. It was replaced instantly with this youthful excitement, the wonder of something new that was about to happen. He was going to go out on his first hot date. Everything about sex and women was back to being mysterious and fresh.

On the other hand, the old lady looked stale. Her memories were squeezed and shoved into every available closet in that yellow brain now rotting away. No wonder she had been so bitter. If people had no memory, they would never feel they had lived too long, nothing would be tired and nothing would be anticipated, no result expected. Every day would be a birthday. Who needs a past? The hell with trying to remember, he told himself.

"I don't want to look at your family albums, read any of your correspondence, or even see your heirlooms. If I could, I'd put it all in the grave with you. It belongs with death," he told her.

Of course, she didn't move, didn't acknowledge anything.

He stepped back and closed the door, and then he went to his room and he changed into a pair of jeans, a black silk short-sleeve shirt that fit him snugly and clearly revealed his buff body, and scooped up his blue sports jacket. He checked his hair, the smoothness of his face and patted it down with some aftershave lotion.

Like some teenager who had been given permission to take the family car for the first night ever, he bounced gleefully down the stairs and hurried out and around to his vehicle. He got in, started the engine, taking pleasure in the sound of its power when he pressed down on the accelerator. Then he turned on the radio, found a station that played upbeat music and, again like some teenager, revved up the volume. The music poured out the open windows and trailed behind him as he shot down the driveway just a little too fast for the turn at the end. The tires squealed their complaint and he laughed.

I'm alive, he thought.

And I'm on the prowl.

Terri nearly turned to run back to the hospital entrance when the car door of the vehicle beside hers opened and a man stood up. The car had been parked beside hers a while. She had seen it as she had left the hospital after completing her rounds. None of the car lights were on. She had not expected to see anyone still in it. He was obviously sitting and waiting for someone or something and here she was.

He moved into the rim of illumination spread by the parking lot lights and her heart did stop and start with a pounding that made her feel her very bones vibrate. It was the blond-haired man, the man who had come to the office impersonating a BCI investigator.

"Dr. Barnard," he said.

She backed up a few steps and looked toward the hospital entrance. There was no one in sight. She could run for it, but there was too much parking lot to cross. He should be able to catch up to her and out here, alone, she would be relatively defenseless. A shout might bring some help, but too late.

He continued around the rear of her vehicle, walking toward her. He was dressed the way he had been the day she had seen him. He smiled.

"Remember me?" he asked.

"Yes," she said. "What do you want?"

"I have just a few more questions," he said.

The question in her mind was should she confront him with what she knew or should she pretend not to know he wasn't a BCI investigator? If she did the latter, would he come at her? Would he come at her anyway?

Sometimes, being a doctor, especially a family physician who confronted not only the patient, but the parents of the patient or the children of the patient, required her to utilize psychological skills as much as medical. It was important to relieve anxiety, calm people down—in short, have a good bedside manner. That was still a raging debate in medical school: How important was it to treat the patient as a person, treat the whole person, and not just the ailment? Mental turmoil could prevent healing or complicate it. Doing this required her to be a little bit of a liar at times or at minimum having a convincingly confident demeanor without crossing the line into what Hyman called medical arrogance.

"Oh," she said struggling to give off a sense of relaxation. "Detective Clark Kent. I'm sorry. I didn't recognize you in the poor lighting."

He stared at her without softening his lips into a friendly smile.

"Yes, well, I'm sorry about that. I called your office and was told you were at the hospital. I didn't mean to startle you. I just thought it was more convenient if I met you out here and left you to your duties and responsibilities in there. I'm sure you had enough to capture your full attention and concentration with your patients' problems."

"No question about that," she said, holding her smile and moving slowly toward her car. "So? What brings you to see me so urgently? I really don't have any more information about Paige Thorndyke than anyone else, especially the police."

"I'm not here to talk about Paige. I wanted to ask you about Kristin Martin."

"Oh?"

She stood at her driver's side door. Her left hand was in her bag, fumbling for the key. When she found it, she held it.

"What a remarkable and yet unfortunate coincidence that you had to confront another, shall we say, unusual fatality involving a young woman," he said smiling now.

"Please, don't remind me. Even doctors get nightmares," she said and inserted the car key into the door.

He stepped closer, close enough to prevent her from opening the door and getting into the car. It was a very subtle threatening gesture.

"What I really wanted to know is, did the young woman say anything to you?" he asked. "Was she able to describe what happened to her, give you any information at all?" he added, his normally calm sounding, friendly voice turning impatient.

She started to shake her head.

"A name of a man, anything?"

"No, you don't understand," she said. "By the time I had arrived, she was too far gone. She was barely conscious."

"So she was conscious," he said leaping on her words.

"Yes, but . . ."

He moved closer.

"It's important you tell me everything, very important. I might be the only one who can prevent this from happening to anyone else," he said, his voice now full of desperation.

"Oh?" She battled the panic that was trying to take hold inside her. "Well, why is that, Detective? You weren't even sure any crime had been committed in relation to Paige Thorndyke."

He stared coldly at her.

"Another death complicates the matter," he said.

"Surely there are more investigators on this then."

"I'm the most familiar with the M.O.," he said. "Who else have you spoken to about it?"

He's going to find out I know he's not who he says he is, she thought.

"Actually," she said now opening her car door and forcing him to step back, "I was surprised that no one has contacted me. I couldn't do much for the poor woman and I gave as much medical information as I had to the paramedics, but she was gone by the time they arrived. My first concern was I hadn't correctly diagnosed a serious reaction to bee stings. Many people are highly allergic to that, you know."

He studied her.

He knows I'm fudging it, she thought.

"I see. What did you learn about the cause of death?"

"I didn't learn everything. As I said, I merely happened onto the scene and . . ."

"You're a very intelligent woman, a scientist. You know this is far from an ordinary medical situation. I'm a specialist in these matters, too. If you confide in me . . . ."

"I told you. I don't know anything more."

"This is a mistake. It's not being handled correctly. You're going to regret it," he said. "Let's begin with . . ."

A car came into the parking lot, its headlights washing over them. To her surprise and delight, she recognized it to be Curt. He pulled up right behind her.

"Oh, my fiancé," she declared, seeing the concerned, truly angry look in the man's face. "I'm afraid he's having a hard time adjusting to a doctor's schedule," she added to lighten the moment.

Curt got out of his car.

"Terri?"

"Yes, I'm here," she said.

"I'll catch you another time," the so-called Detective Clark Kent said. "Think about what I said to you and how important all this could be," he added and moved quickly to his own vehicle as Curt came around the front of his car and approached Terri. He watched the man get in and start his engine.

"Who's that?"

Everything Will Dennis had told her earlier came rushing back in like a dam that had collapsed. As a doctor she was used to making decisions on the instant, of course, and it didn't escape her that this one could be just as life or death.

"A state police detective," she decided to say. Something told her to keep Curt as away from all this as she could.

Clark Kent, as it were, backed out and pulled away quickly, his tires squealing.

"He's in a hurry. What did you tell him?"

"Actually nothing he probably didn't already know," she replied, the possible irony of that answer not lost on her. "What are you doing here?" she asked Curt.

He smirked and leaned against her car.

"I thought we might go somewhere and have a drink," he said.

"Oh. Well, why didn't you just call or page me?"

"I was nearby," he said, "and took a chance I might catch you coming out of the hospital. I knew you were coming out about now. See, I do pay attention to your horrific work schedule," he added.

She smiled.

"Okay."

"First, I have something to ask."

"Oh?"

"When you and I spoke this morning and you told me about Kristin Martin, you already knew she had died of some bizarre vitamin deficiency, just like Paige Thorndyke, didn't you? You knew it wasn't just a heart attack," he followed with a cross-examiner's speed and intensity.

"I don't understand, Curt. What if I did? Why are you so upset?"

"Why am I so upset? The whole world knows something weird is going on and my fiancée, who is right in the middle of it, doesn't tell me. I have to learn it from that schmuck Bill Kleckner. I told you how he's been looking over my shoulder, gloating over every one of his successes or any one of my failures."

"That's what this is about?" she said, astonished. "Competition with your partner?"

"No, that's not what it's about, Terri. It's about trust, about confiding in each other."

"First," she said, "I wasn't sure about this diagnosis, Curt. There are other tests that have to be run. Even as of now, I don't know the full extent of the woman's illness. I knew she had died of heart failure. That was certain, but there are a number of possible causes for it. Besides, I have to have some concern about patient confidentiality. You do for your clients, don't you?"

"Some confidentiality. Bill Kleckner gets to know it all before I do."

He sounded like a little boy whining, and after what she had just experienced and the things she had seen in the hospital during her rounds, she had little patience for it.

"I don't believe this, Curt. I don't believe you're complaining about this. Look, I'm really very tired. I had a day and a half. I think I'll just go home, take a hot bath, and go to bed."

"I think we should talk more," he insisted.

"Get over it," she snapped and got into her car. He stepped back in surprise as she started the engine and began to back out of her spot.

"Hey!" he yelled.

She hit the brake and had the window roll down.

"What?"

"That's it? I'm dismissed?"

"I'm tired, Curt. You're overreacting to everything. You need a good night's rest too."

"Is that the doctor talking or my fiancée?" he asked disdainfully.

"Your psychiatrist," she replied, rolled up the window, and drove away. She didn't look into the rearview mirror. She was afraid of what she would see.

But the moment she was off the hospital grounds, she reached for her phone and fumbled for the card Will Dennis had given her. She read his number and called as she drove. She could see Curt's headlights closing behind her.

"Will Dennis," she heard.

"Mr. Dennis," she began, but it was his way of starting his answering machine.

"I'm not available at the moment, but please leave a message and it will get to me immediately."

"It's Terri Barnard," she said. "He was there in the parking lot waiting for me, the infamous Detective Clark Kent. I didn't let on what I knew about him, and my fiancé appeared. Our detective left quickly, but I have the feeling, not for good," she said. "I'm on my way home."

She hung up and continued driving. Watching Curt's headlights in her mirror now, she expected he was going to follow her home. A part of her wanted him, too. She didn't like parting the way they had. Everyone was on edge these days. When she came to a traffic light and it turned red, she stopped and thought she would step out and say something soft to him, perhaps even invite him to her house for the night.

She glanced into the side mirror as she put her hand on the door handle and then she stopped cold.

It wasn't Curt.

It was Clark Kent.

TWELVE

Darlene Stone lifted the glass of beer up and swiped under it with her bar-top rag. Jimmy Hummel not only had spilled more than half of his glass, he dropped half his roll-your-own cigarette tobacco into the puddle of foam, and if there was one thing that Darlene couldn't stand, it was a messy bar counter when she was working the Old Hasbrouck Inn. It was her five nights a week job to support herself and her two children and compensate for marrying and divorcing Jack Stone, poster boy for deadbeat dads.

"Can't you watch what the hell you're doin'?" she snapped at Jimmy. "I don't need extra work."

The forty-nine-year-old mechanic raised his untrimmed, bushy eyebrows under the heavy folds of rust-spotted skin hanging on his forehead and wiped his thick, bruised lips with the back of his grease- and oil-laden hand. His lower lip was still bruised from the ten-second fight he had with Charlie Weinberg in the parking lot three days ago. The 240-pound hotel chef barely had extended his Popeye-like arm, but it was enough to catch Jimmy in the middle of another insult, driving him back into the front entrance and cracking the window pane with Jimmy's balding head. He shuddered and then slid down to a sitting position. It brought the whole crowd of barflies to the doorway where they teased Jimmy and gave reviews of the short-lived event that at least added some iota of excitement to their otherwise routine existence.

At least, that was the way Darlene thought of it. The truth was she had little or no respect for any of the inn's regular customers. They were almost all blue collar laborers who alternated unemployment checks with temporary work projects. To Darlene most of them were monotonous, boring, and uninspired people who had almost no ambition. Their sole objective seemed to be to meet the week's basic needs and have money to piss away at a place like the Old Hasbrouck Inn.

Tonight, a weekend evening, they had a local trio to entertain them, two men and a woman who called themselves the Outlaws. The woman, Paula Gilbert, was only twenty-four. Darlene knew this for a fact because she knew Paula from her high school days at Tri-Valley. She was in the ninth grade when Darlene was a senior. However, Paula looked like a woman in her forties. More than fourteen years of smoking gave her a hard, dark complexion, especially around her eyes. She wasn't really overweight, but her body was already shifting, putting more than it had to into her thighs and around her waist. Her once button nose, soft mouth, and crystal turquoise-green eyes framed in long auburn hair could no longer provide that innocent, sweetness to compensate for her used-furniture look. Her voice was throaty, hoarse at times, and the whiskey and drugs she used to keep herself going were stapling shadows into her face. However, there was still just enough sexiness about her, most of it hovering in the well-exposed cleavage of her Dolly Parton bosom, to keep the goats and monkeys howling when she turned a shoulder or batted her eyelashes. Someone somewhere taught her how to work the microphone stand in a suggestive manner, too, and that was really what gave the Outlaws its cachet, for the voices of the two men, Jack Dawkins and Tag Counsel, were just a shade more than ordinary, as was their guitar, harmonica, and electric keyboard playing.

"Who the hell are you to tell me what I should watch and what I shouldn't?" Jimmy snapped back at Darlene. "I pay for everything I spill, don't I?"

"I doubt she was hired to clean up after you," the new customer, a total stranger, commented as he slid effortlessly onto the bar stool beside Jimmy.

How such a handsome, strikingly good-looking man had come into the inn without Darlene noticing immediately confused her for a moment. He seemed to have just materialized. She stood there like a star-struck teenager, her mouth half open, and stared. He smiled in return, friendly, full of sincerity, a diamond sitting in rock salt.

"Huh? Who the hell are you?" Jimmy said, breaking the magical moment.

"Shut up," she told him, "or get out."

"Hey!" he moaned.

There was enough noise from the music and the chatter around them to keep most people from hearing the exchange.

"Don't pay him any attention," she said to the stranger. "What can I get for you?"

With his beautiful blue eyes, he panned the whiskey and hard liquor display behind her. She just continued to stare at him. Someone shouted for a beer down the bar, but she didn't move. He shouted again.

"Hold your water!" she screamed back. "I have another customer here."

"Well, what's he doin', givin' birth?"

There was some laughter.

Darlene smirked.

"Sorry," she said in as soft a voice as she could manage. "What did you want?"

"I'll take that Jack Daniel's on the rocks, thanks," he said nodding.

"And I'll have another beer," Jimmy said belligerently.

Darlene scowled at him, turned, and got the Jack Daniel's.

"I'm dying of thirst down here," the man at the end of the counter cried.

"You're dying of more than thirst," Darlene yelled back and there was more laughter.

She found the cleanest, nicest glass and dropped in some ice cubes. Then she poured a good shot of Jack Daniel's and, with a coaster under it, she put it on the bar in front of the stranger.

"How come I don't get no coaster with my beer?" Jimmy whined when she put the bottle down hard in front of him. "I spend a lot more money here than this guy's gonna spend."

"Why would a man your age be such a pussy?" the stranger asked him. He turned, leaned toward him, and considered him the way someone might consider a contradiction.

Jimmy's eyes nearly bulged with rage. He swung his arm around to push the stranger back threateningly, but the stranger caught his hand in midair and held it there with such little effort, Jimmy felt a surge of absolute terror shoot up his spine. Even Charlie Weinberg didn't have this sort of power. He relaxed, expecting the man to release his hand, but he didn't. He squeezed it harder, the pain surging down his wrist and into his elbow.

He groaned.

"Why don't you go to the bathroom and wash your face? You're turning my stomach, and you're surely bothering our bartender," the stranger told him, his eyes not shifting, the intensity of them burning a hole in Jimmy's head.

Then he released Jimmy's hand.

He looked at his reddened palm, up at the stranger, and slipped off his stool.

"Thanks," Darlene said. "I wanted to do something like that all night. Actually, all year."

"No problem."

"Hey, already!" the man at the end screamed. He held out his hands, palms up.

Darlene excused herself, poured a new draft beer, and brought it down to the end of the bar. She collected the money and hurried back as if she was afraid the stranger would get up and go before she had returned.

He sat there, comfortably, smiling at her and then turning to look at Paula. Darlene saw the way he concentrated on the singer and inexplicably, she felt a wave of jealousy roll through her.

"She used to be good," she said.

"Oh?" he turned and smiled again.

"Drugs, alcohol, you know. She might have gone somewhere. Who knows?"

"She got here," he said.

Darlene laughed.

"Here? Here is nowhere."

"Is that what you think?" he asked, sounding surprised.

He looked around the old tavern. The building was nearly two hundred years old. Sections had been added on over the years until it had the dance floor, the modernized kitchen, the upstairs apartments, and the expanded storage and refrigeration room in the rear. It had a fieldstone foundation and had been built at what was once the crossroads of two old pioneer trails that had been turned into county highways. Behind it ran a creek that trailed off the Neversink river, now controlled by a dam that provided drinking water to New York City.

"Why not?" she replied.

"I was told this was practically a historical site," the stranger said. "Wasn't there some kind of famous murder in here in the early 1800s?"

Darlene laughed.

"Who told you that?"

"This elderly lady who runs the tourist house I'm at. She's old enough to remember, I think," he said and Darlene laughed.

"That's a legend the owners and previous owners of this property have used to boost up its value for as long as I can remember," she said.

"Sometimes legends are more valuable than facts," he replied.

There were more demands for service now that the Outlaws paused to take a break and reluctantly, Darlene had to get back to work. Every once in a while, she glanced back at the handsome stranger and caught him watching her, smiling softly with those perfect, strong lips. The slight cleft in his chin reminded her of a young

Kirk Douglas. His eyes followed her every move. Sensing his full attention on her, she moved faster than usual so she could return to him as soon as possible.

"So," she said catching her breath. "You're not researching local history or something, are you?"

"No," he said laughing lightly, "hardly."

"What are you doing here then?" she asked. She asked it with such forcefulness and surprise in her voice, he stared at her a moment, his smile frozen. She realized how she sounded. "I mean, the Old Hasbrouck Inn isn't exactly on the tourist tour these days."

"Oh, I'm just passing through and wanted to get out for a while. The old lady said there was music here so I thought, why not? It's always more interesting to see what the locals do anyplace, anyway. At least, it is to me."

"What are you, a salesman or something?"

"I'm into computers, networking. What I do is set up systems for mid-to-large companies. I'm on my way to Ohio, actually, after completing a job nearby. You live here all your life?"

"All my twenty-eight years, yes," she said.

"You're kidding me. You're twenty-eight? I had you pegged for twenty at the most."

"Thanks, but that's just the poor lighting," she said and went to serve two other customers, thinking to herself, what would he think if he knew I had a three-year-old boy and a two-year-old girl back home with my mother? Would he be more impressed or would he make like the wind and blow? He could be full of what makes the grass grow, too, she mused. It had been so long since she was in a conversation with anyone more sophisticated than a chimpanzee.

Jimmy Hummel walked by, eying the stranger but keeping his distance.

He finished his Jack Daniel's.

"You want another?" Darlene asked quickly, the note of hope hardly unrecognized.

"Yes, please," he said. "I think I'd like to hear another round of that music. The singer has a flash or two of something, but you're right," he added quickly, "she's gone about as far as she will."

Darlene nodded.

"Local kid, too," she said reaching for the Jack Daniel's. "Back about four years behind me in high school."

"She is?" He looked at Paula sitting at a table with two men, the smoke pouring out of her nostrils like a dragon as she downed a beer. "I would have thought it the other way around: she was four years ahead of you."

"Like I said, booze and drugs and cigarettes."

"You don't drink or smoke?"

"When you work behind a bar, you get a first-hand look of what it does, so no, I don't drink much. I hate smoke and wouldn't be working here if I didn't have to, and as far as drugs. . . ."

"Yes?" he said smiling.

"I won't even take an aspirin unless I'm force-fed."

He laughed.

"I thought you looked too healthy for this sort of life," he told her.

She blushed.

"I do what I can to take care of myself."

"It's paid off," he said.

She glanced at him quickly, her neck warming with a blush, and then she went down the bar again. A little more than ten minutes later, the Outlaws began to perform. More people came into the Inn, and it became a great deal noisier, at times the laughter and the loud conversations really competing with the singing. None of the three members of the group seemed to care or even realize. Darlene was working constantly, barely having a moment to say a word to the stranger who ordered another drink and immediately turned away this time to face the trio.

She was disappointed. For whatever reason, he was losing interest in her, and despite the negative comments they had both made about Paula, he was fixated on her. As she sang, Paula's eyes seemed to gaze above the crowd and not at it, but finally, her attention was drawn to the handsome man at the bar, dressed in a nearly electric black tank top and blue sports jacket. She could feel his eyes were on her and her alone and without realizing it, she began to direct all her energy and her singing at him.

It wasn't lost on Darlene, who slammed glasses down harder on the counter and whipped insults at any of the customers who so much as breathed too heavily in her direction.

"I've only got two hands!" she screamed at one poor young man who had asked twice for a beer only because he thought she hadn't heard him the first time.

"Well, use them then," Jimmy Hummel shouted from behind the young man.

"Go fuck yourself, Jimmy," she shouted back at him over the din.

"If I did, you'd be jealous," he replied with unusual quick wit. It brought a wave of laughter that seemed to wash over the bar and drown Darlene in her sudden sense of misery.

She glanced at the stranger to see if he had heard the exchange, but he hadn't turned from his concentration on Paula.

"I hate this job," she muttered when she was close to him. She was looking for any way possible to restart what to her was the most interesting conversation of the night with the most interesting person. However, if he had heard her, he didn't care to acknowledge. His continued interest in Paula Gilbert convinced her he was just another dickhead, just one better dressed and with better manners.

Despondently, she returned to the end of the bar where her sometimes boyfriend Dave Taylor and two of his fellow carpenters sat. Every once in a while, she looked toward the stranger. He nursed his drink and avoided conversing with anyone around him. When the Outlaws took another break, he slipped off his stool and walked over to Paula, who seemed to be expecting it. Darlene watched them converse and saw Paula's eyes light up with interest as she laughed at something he had said.

The break in music produced another run at the bar, so she didn't have much time to watch the stranger in action, but when she looked at Paula a while later, she was surprised to see her sitting with the other members of the trio and the stranger gone. She stopped and looked around the Inn. He wasn't anywhere to be seen. Maybe he had gone to the bathroom, she thought and watched for him, but he didn't appear and the Outlaws began their final set for the evening.

"What the hell? I knew he was too good to be true," she muttered to herself, smiled, shook her head, and returned to heed the call of another customer.

Terri pulled into her driveway slowly, her eyes more on her rearview mirror than her garage door. Since she had made a turn off Highway 17, she no longer saw Clark Kent's car behind her. Maybe, she thought, I just imagined it was that man. She decided to stop at a 7-Eleven to get some fresh milk for the morning. After she emerged from the store and started for home again, she watched for him, studying every vehicle behind her or coming toward her. Although she didn't see him and kept telling herself it had really only been her imagination after all, her anxiety level didn't diminish.

Still concentrating on the rearview mirror, she studied the road in front of her home carefully as the garage door rose. Remembering a documentary on self-protection she had seen recently, she did not get out of her automobile when she had driven into the garage, and kept the car locked until the garage door was fully descended and locked in place.

She could hear her phone ringing inside and hurried out of the car and into the house, seizing the receiver in the kitchen so forcefully and quickly, she nearly ripped the phone off the wall.

"Doctor Barnard," she said.

"Terri, Will Dennis. I got your message and I have a sheriff's patrol car on the way to your home. Are you all right?"

"Yes. I thought he was following me for a while back there, but . . ."

"But what?"

"But I'm not positive it was the same man."

"Someone was following you, though?"

"No, I don't know. No," she concluded. "I'm not thinking like a rational person at the moment."

"Just sit tight anyway. Keep every door and window closed until the officer arrives. Did this man threaten you in any way at the hospital?"

"I felt he was trying to intimidate me. He was certainly more demanding than he was the first time we met at my office."

"What did he want from you exactly?"

"He was very interested in whatever I might have learned from Kristin Martin. He seemed so positive I had something. I didn't let on that I knew he wasn't really a law enforcement officer, but he said one strange thing, I thought. Among many, I guess."

"What was that?"

"He said he was the only one who could prevent this from happening to someone else. When I asked him why, weren't there other police officers on it, he said he was most familiar with the M.O."

"That might be very true, but not for the reasons he's implying."

The light from the headlights of a car turning into her driveway washed over the wall.

"Someone's here!" she said.

"Check to see if it's the sheriff's car. I'll hold on," Will Dennis said.

She went to the front window and breathed relief when she saw the sheriff's logo and the bubble light on the roof. Then she returned to the phone.

"It's the sheriff's car."

"Good. Tell him what happened and let him look around. He'll check everything for you and help you feel more comfortable. I'll call again in twenty minutes."

"Okay," she said and hung up.

The door bell rang, and she went to greet the officer.

"Dr. Barnard?"

"Yes," she said, "please come in."

"The district attorney contacted our dispatcher, who got to me just a while ago. Someone threatened you at the hospital parking lot?"

"He didn't exactly threaten me, but, well, didn't they give you any more information?"

"I was just told to get here quickly and make sure you were all right, Doctor," he replied dryly.

This police officer has a really robotic military demeanor about him, she thought. He stood firm, straight at six feet two and looked at her with a stern face of granite, his features sharp. Normally, she would not appreciate him, but at the moment, he gave her a sense of security, and that she did appreciate. Combining her spat with Curt with her terrifying moments, she felt drained of any energy and resistance. It was good to have someone else upon whom she could lean.

"I just spoke with the district attorney. There's a man going about impersonating a state investigator. He came to my office and he just confronted me in the hospital parking lot. He didn't attempt to harm me in any way there, but I thought I saw him following me when I left."

"Can you describe the vehicle driven by the man following you?" he asked.

"Actually, no," she said, a bit ashamed and disappointed in herself for being so distracted by her own fears. "I mean, it was a dark color, but I didn't take note of the make or model."

He nodded, not showing any disapproval.

"Perhaps I should check around the house first," he said. "Just precautionary."

"Yes, of course," she said. It had never occurred to her that the man impersonating a state police investigator would not need to follow her home to know where she lived. That added a new dimension of terror to the situation.

"That stairway goes . . ."

"To the bedrooms," she said. "Downstairs is the living room you see here on my right. The dining room is straight ahead and after that is the kitchen and pantry. There's a bathroom just before the kitchen."

"Backdoor?"

"Through the pantry. It's an old house. It was my grandmother's," she added.

He finally broke into a smile.

"I like these older homes. They have character," he said.

"A character living in one," she muttered to herself as he walked on through.

She brought the milk into the kitchen and then thought about making some herbal tea.

When the rear door opened, she nearly jumped over the table, but it was only the police officer. She had thought he had gone directly upstairs.

"It's quiet out back," he said. "I'll look through the bedrooms and closets upstairs. Is there an attic?"

"Yes, but you have to pull down one of those ladders to get to it."

"Yes, I understand."

"Would you like something to drink? I'm making myself some tea," she said.

"No thank you."

He went to the stairway. She made the tea and sat with her hands around the cup, watching the steam rise out of it. She almost didn't hear him return.

"Everything looks fine, Dr. Barnard. You should just lock up. Is there an alarm system?"

"No," she said. "I haven't gotten around to adding that yet. My grandparents never even considered having one."

"I understand. Well, I'll have another patrol car make a sweep by here tonight and of course, if you hear anything or for any reason want us to return, please don't hesitate to call."

"Thank you."

"My pleasure," he said. "I imagine the district attorney has his eyes on this. He's a good man."

"Yes, he is," she said.

She followed him to the front door and locked up after him. A moment or so later, the phone rang. It was Will Dennis.

"Everything is quiet. I'm sure I just imagined that man behind me," she told him.

"Still, he had the nerve to come looking for you at the hospital. He's arrogant in his madness. You have your regular office hours tomorrow?"

"Yes, an easy day, just a nine to five. About what you proposed at the hospital earlier," she started to say.

"Let's not talk about that. I think it's a little more complicated now than I had anticipated."

"You mean that he came after me again?"

"Something like that. Just be a doctor," he told her.

"Why is it that suddenly sounds easy?" she quipped and he laughed.

She put away the teacup and then went up to her bedroom. First, she decided to take a warm bath. Then, she would try to sleep. If a dozen or so medical files didn't parade through her brain, and if the events of the last few days didn't return in vivid replay, and if she didn't think about the spat she and Curt had in the hospital parking lot, she might actually get some.

A warm soak never felt as good as it does this moment, she thought after she lowered herself through the bubbles generated by her bath oils. She closed her eyes and took a deep breath. She was almost asleep in the tub when she heard it, a distinct rap on her front door downstairs. She listened and then she heard it again and sat up quickly.

Should I ignore it or get out, put on a robe, and see who it was? Or, maybe I should just call for the sheriff's patrol. She was expecting no one. That was for sure.

She heard the door knocker again. There was no

doubt about it. The sound reverberated through the house as if it could travel through the very foundation and frame. She made a quick decision to ignore it and to make that phone call to the sheriff's patrol.

Still dripping wet, she was at the phone in her bedroom. The dispatcher knew who she was immediately and assured her a car would be in her driveway in less than ten minutes. All the lights were off downstairs, but anyone could see her bedroom light was still on, she thought. She turned it off and, still wrapped in only a large bath towel, went to the front window and parted the curtain. She saw an automobile in the driveway. Unfortunately, out here, there were no street lights and she didn't have a light on the outside of the house. Still, as her eyes grew more accustomed to the shadows and the clouds parted a bit to permit more starlight, she realized it was Curt's car.

"Oh no," she muttered, realizing she had just contacted the police to investigate her own fiancé. This was going to be hard to explain to him. Maybe it was time to tell him everything, she thought. He was right, after all. They should be sharing this problem.

She wiped herself as dry as she could as quickly as she could and put on her robe and soft leather slippers. Then she flipped on the lights in the hallway and hurried down the stairs, wondering why Curt hadn't continued to knock. His car was still there. She turned on lights as she moved toward the front door. As fast as she

could, she unlatched it and opened it, realizing it was
practically pushing itself open.

It was easy to understand why.

Curt's limp body was against it, falling in as she
opened the door.

Paula Gilbert lingered in the parking lot. They had
played the night's final set, and although the Inn would
remain open another hour or so, they had all decided to
leave. Jack and Tag got into their cars, complaining to
her about the lousy money they were both making and
wondering aloud if they shouldn't just chuck it all. It
wasn't the first time, and like all the other times, she
didn't put up any vigorous arguments. She wasn't going
to stop singing and if they wanted to end the group,
fine. She would easily find two other men, or maybe she
would hook up with the Boggs Trio. They were always
suggesting she should. What else would she do? She had
no intention of ever becoming someone's secretary or
take any of those boring nine-to-five jobs her friends
had, even working for the post office.

All they talked about was their benefits, benefits. As
far as Paula was concerned, they had traded their freedom and their chance to enjoy life for the security of
medical insurance. Just don't get sick, she told them
with a laugh. What are you going to do, work for retirement and hope that by the time you collect your pen-

sion, you'll still be healthy and young enough to enjoy life? Not me. I'm still having fun, like always.

They nodded and smirked, but in her heart she knew they were envious. They wished they could be as carefree and as independent as she was. No worries. Jack and Tag quit? So what?

"Don't let worrying about it all keep you up boys," she told them.

They, too, shook their heads at her and left her. Good riddance, she thought. She looked around. She was disappointed. That handsome guy disappointed her. He was supposed to be out here, and they were supposed to go for a late-night drink in a place where people didn't have fertilizer on their shoes. So much for that, she thought, tossing off the expectation like a piece of gum that had lost its flavor.

She walked toward her own vehicle, a present from her brother, one of his leftovers. It was a beat-up Chevy Impala, but it still ran and he did take care of its maintenance for her. Just as she reached it, the handsome stranger came around from the rear of the car.

"Where the hell did you come from?" she asked, after gasping and stepping back. "I just about gave up on you."

"I was standing here in the shadows watching you say good night to your partners. I didn't want to intrude, and I wanted to be sure you didn't have other plans that included one or even both of them," he replied.

She laughed.

"Hardly. It's enough I work with those stump jumpers."

"Stump jumpers?" he said laughing.

"Hillbillies, rednecks. Their idea of a good time is a game of darts over at the Old Mill."

"I see. Well, if you're not too tired," he continued.

"Tired? The night's just beginning for me," she said smiling.

"I'm happy to hear that. Can you leave your car here?" he followed.

"Sure," she said shrugging. "Who'd steal it?"

He laughed and they started walking toward the front where the customers parked.

"I'm right over here," he said indicating they go to their right.

She saw the black Lincoln Town Car, a late model, and smiled. It glittered in the illumination of the Inn's neon lights.

"Nice wheels," she said.

"I like a lot of steel around me," he said. "And soft leather seats."

"I won't turn that down either," she replied when he opened the door for her. When was the last time any man ever did that for her? she wondered and got in.

He walked around and did the same.

"Here we go," he said starting the engine. "Hold on to your seat."

She laughed.

"Where are we going?" she asked when he turned left

instead of right, which would have taken them into Woodbourne and then onto Route 52, which she had described to him earlier in the Inn.

"I was told I shouldn't leave this area until I've seen that dam and lake where they store water for New York City. It's just a little ways," he said smiling at her, "and with the clouds parting and those stars tonight, it could be quite a beautiful site, don't you think?"

She smiled to herself. It wouldn't be the first time she had parked with a man up there, but she hadn't done it since she was in high school. That titillated her. Neck in a car? With the music playing? Maybe it wasn't as sophisticated an experience as she was anticipating, but this guy was like someone who had walked out of a soap opera and it all did make her feel like a teenager again.

Afterward, they could go for that cocktail somewhere.

"America has so many beautiful places to visit," he said. "There is nothing like traveling and traveling and suddenly being surprised by a breathtaking sight. You know that expression, stop to smell the roses?"

"No," she said. It suggested something to do at a cemetery to her.

"Well, it means taking the time to appreciate the beautiful things, Paula. You should think about that more. You should stop to smell the roses, too."

She laughed. She didn't know why exactly, but there was a new tone in his voice that actually stung her with a little trepidation.

"Most people never do and one day they wake up and realize it, but they also realize it's too late. It's all passed them by, understand?"

"Sorta," she said. That was her philosophy in a roundabout way, wasn't it, she thought.

"I knew you would understand. Anyone who can sing like you do, who can feel words and music, has to be able to understand what is and what isn't important in life. You're an artist," he continued. "Artists are by nature more sensitive."

She liked that. No one ever called her an artist.

"Look at these houses out here," he said as they drove on. "Each one has a sizable piece of land around it. They look so peaceful, too, don't they? You feel the contentment, the quiet bliss. With that sky opening up, those homes silhouetted look like they're on the edge of the world. In them, people are sleeping snugly, fathers and mothers are embracing each other, their children are feeling secure, safe, dreaming about bubbles and balloons and tinsel."

"Are you a poet?" she asked him.

"No," he said smiling, "I'm just poetic."

"Same thing to me," she said.

"Maybe it is," he said nodding.

"I don't understand what you do, this networking thing."

"Oh, it's boring work compared to what you do, Paula. You're out there with people, all sorts of people, personalities, and you have the music that can carry you above it all. I watched you carefully. You're not bothered by the noise or anything. You're in your own little world, aren't you?"

"Yes," she said. "That's it."

"Of course that's it," he replied.

They made another turn and climbed a hill and moments later, there was the dam and the lake and the starlight playing on the water. He found a dirt road that turned in and off the highway and drove in as far as he could, switching off the lights.

"Just look at that," he said. "Breathtaking."

She looked at it as if for the first time, too.

"Yes," she said.

He sat there so still and so unmoving that for a few minutes she thought this was going to be it. He wasn't even going to try to kiss her.

Finally, he turned to her.

"I can't help it," he said. "I get so stirred up by beauty. Forgive me," he added.

She raised her eyebrows.

"For what?"

"For wanting you so intensely," he said and leaned toward her to kiss her, softly at first and then harder.

She pulled back as if she was angry.

"I'm sorry," he said. "I . . ."

She put her finger on his lips and smiled.

"Wouldn't it be better in the rear seat?" she suggested.

How wonderful it was to have one so eager, he thought. It filled him with new confidence, not that he needed any boost in that department.

"You took the words right out of my mouth," he said, only he said it as if she literally had, as if when their tongues met, the words that were in his brain and transmitted to his tongue, were then conveyed to her.

They got out of the car and opened the rear doors and met on the wide leather bench seat. In moments, his lips were on her neck and his hands were moving over her breasts.

This is just like high school days, she thought and moaned with pleasure. Despite the darkness, she could see his eyes, luminous above her. She let him undo her belt buckle. He undressed her slowly, never moving much without kissing her somewhere. She was contented to just lie there and let him do all the work, serve her as it were, deliver the ecstasy. When she was totally naked, he lifted her breasts with his palms as if he was weighing them.

"Magnificent," he said and lowered himself to her.

He entered her with the same gracefulness he had with his every move, the same assurance and confidence. She accepted him as she would accept any necessity of life itself, as if sex were nourishment and could ensure her own well-being. Every part of her was full of wanting and welcoming. Vaguely, she felt he was drawing new strength from her compliance. He was moving deeper and deeper into her. He seemed to have no limit, to grow to enormous length, like some kind of a snake, moving through her very organs, into her intestines and on to her very heart where he wrapped himself and squeezed until she found it harder and harder to breathe. It wasn't a dream; it was literally true. She started to gag, to plead for an easing, a moment or two of respite, but he was relentless and soon she felt her eyes go back. Moments later, she blacked out.

THIRTEEN

Terri had just pulled Curt fully into the house when the sheriff's patrol car turned into her driveway. She saw the head trauma immediately. Whatever had been used as a weapon, had split open the front of his skull just under the hairline and the flow of blood down his temples and over the bridge of his nose made it look horrible. She turned him on his back and leaped up to get her doctor's bag. When she returned, the patrolman was already there, kneeling at Curt's side.

"What happened?" he asked.

She shook her head and went to work, checking his pulse, cleaning the wound, and evaluating what had to be done. As she spoke, she cut away some of his hair.

"I heard a knocking at the door, but I was in the tub," she began. "I had no idea he would be at my door, of course."

"Who is he?" the patrolman asked.

"My fiancé, Curt Levitt. By the time I got downstairs, this had all obviously happened. I opened the door because I saw his car in the driveway and this is how I found him," she continued, deciding he needed stitches immediately. "I want to stop this bleeding and then we'll need to get an ambulance and get him to the hospital to see what sort of injury he's obtained."

The patrolman nodded and returned to his vehicle to make the call for the ambulance.

"They're on the way," he told her coming back.

"Thanks."

"Do you have any idea how this happened?"

She shook her head.

"I didn't see anyone else or even hear another car," she said.

Curt was still unconscious. She felt her heart tighten, and her breath quicken. Suddenly, she was not the doctor anymore; she was a very concerned loved one.

"I'll look around," the police officer said. She barely heard or acknowledged him.

"Curt," she said. "C'mon honey."

His eyelids fluttered. When he opened them, she could see immediately that the pupils were enlarged. He had been hit very hard. All the complications paraded before her.

"Whaaa," he said.

"Don't move. What happened, Curt? If you can, tell me. There's a policeman here."

The patrolman returned.

"Nothing," he said and noticed Curt's eyes were opened. "What's he say?"

"Curt, can you tell us what happened?"

"Hit me," he said. "He was . . . at your . . . door . . . hit me," he finished and closed his eyes again.

"Try to stay awake, Curt. Who hit you? Did you recognize him? Curt?" She shook him gently.

"Man . . . at the hospital," he said in a voice barely above a whisper.

She looked up at the patrolman.

"Get in touch with District Attorney Dennis. Tell him to meet us at the hospital," she said. "Stay with Curt. I'm running upstairs to throw something on. Stay with him."

"What should I do first?" the patrolman asked, confused by her list of commands.

She looked at Curt, his eyes closed again.

"Call Dennis first," she screamed and ran up the stairs.

The ambulance was there moments after she returned, and the paramedics had Curt on a stretcher in seconds. They kept track of his vitals all the way to the hospital. Terri followed in her own car, the sheriff's deputy leading the way.

She knew the doctor on duty at the emergency room, of course, Steve Battie, who was only a few years older than she was and working out of his cousin's practice in Liberty. The protocol for Curt's situation was cut and dried. They immediately determined he had a concussion, slight, but significant enough to hospitalize him and keep him under observation.

Will Dennis appeared at the hospital only twenty minutes after she had. She described as much of what happened as she could and then, after Curt had been through X-ray, they both went to his bedside.

"Curt, Will Dennis is here," she said and Curt opened his eyes slowly.

"She did it," he said. "Book her."

Everyone laughed.

"What really happened, Curt?" Will asked.

Curt turned to look at Terri before speaking.

"Terri and I had a lovers' spat earlier in the evening. I was feeling miserable about it and decided to go to her house to apologize. I wouldn't have gotten much sleep anyway. When I pulled into the driveway, there was a man at the door. He was kneeling down and obviously doing something to trigger the lock and open it.

"He stood up quickly when I drove in and I guess I was a little too much Mr. Superman. I wasn't thinking sensibly. I charged out of the car toward him, yelling, 'What the hell are you doing? Who are you?' As I drew closer, I recognized him. He was the same man Terri had been talking to in the hospital parking lot. She said he was a state policeman," he added looking accusingly at her. He turned back to Will Dennis. "He stood his ground, but when I stepped up to him, he lashed out with the handle of a pistol . . . looked like a .45-caliber pistol to me, and caught me in the head so sharply, my lights went out.

"The rest," he said after a deep breath, "you guys know."

Will Dennis nodded, looked at Terri and then turned back to Curt.

"Did you notice a car in front of the house? I imagine you would have seen one in the driveway," he said.

"There wasn't any in the driveway, but I vaguely recall passing a car parked on the side of the road, right by the house."

"Anything you remember about the car?"

Curt started to shake his head and closed his eyes. He was still having some pain.

"Sorry. All I can tell you is it was probably black and probably a full sedan."

"Okay," Will Dennis said turning to Terri. "I'll be in touch."

"Who was that guy? What's going on?" Curt asked, showing more agitation.

"I'll tell you, Curt. Just relax. Let me just see Will out," she said and followed the district attorney into the hallway. "What should I tell him?" she asked when they were beyond Curt's hearing.

"It doesn't look like he's going anywhere for a while. You can tell him all you know, if you like. Ask him to keep it to himself. He's earned it," Will Dennis said. "Not that it's anything he would want to earn, I'm sure," he added.

"Do you want me to meet with the police sketch artist? I'm no law enforcement officer, but I think it's about time."

"Yes, probably. We'll talk about it tomorrow," he said.

"Okay, but as a physician, I'm advising you to go

home and get some sleep. One of us has to be fresh in the morning and I know it's not going to be me," she said.

"Should I alert your patients?" he asked jokingly.

"Hey, this won't be the first time I go to work on a few hours of sleep, if any. You should try interning."

"Thanks, but I have my own internship going at the moment," he replied, wished Curt well and left.

She returned to Curt's room. For a few moments, she thought he would doze off now and she could put off telling him anything, but as if he could sense her decision, his eyes popped open.

"Hey," he said. "What the hell am I doing here?"

"You said it yourself, big shot. You decided to be Superman."

"Okay," he said reaching for her hand. "I don't have the strength for cross-examination, so just give me your testimony straight."

She smiled.

"Where do I begin?" she asked rhetorically, and then proceeded to tell him all she knew. His reactions moved from incredulity to abject terror.

"No one knows how he's doing these terrible crimes?"

"Nor can they say with certainty apparently that he is doing them at all. It's a mystery that just grows deeper and now, more complicated for me," she said examining his wound again.

"You're not going home now, are you?"

"I don't know. I didn't think about it."

"I'd feel a lot better if you would go to my house instead, Terri, or to your parents."

"Right. Go to my parents and we'll have panic in the streets," she said.

"Then go to my house. Our house," he added. She nodded. "Promise?"

"On my Hippocratic oath."

Two hours later, after Curt was resting comfortably, she got into the elevator and walked down the corridor to exit the hospital through the emergency room.

That was when she knew not only wouldn't she go to Curt's house; she wouldn't get even an hour's sleep.

Darlene Stone finished cleaning up and shut down the lights behind the bar. Griffy asked the last two hangers-on to leave, telling them as he usually did, to get a life. She and he had no doubt they would stay until morning if Griffy didn't shove them off. He was the current owner of the Inn and lived with his wife in a small apartment above the bar and restaurant. She did most, if not all, of the cooking, not that they had that much of a food crowd here. Burgers, fries, meatloaf twice a week, and roast beef sandwiches were the heart of their small menu.

"All and all a pretty good night," Griffy told her after quickly reviewing their receipts. "I guess we'll keep the Outlaws on another month for sure."

"Sometimes I think you could have my grandparents up there howling and it wouldn't matter," she said.

"And they probably wouldn't charge as much," Griffy said laughing.

She gave him a hug, said goodnight, and left the Inn. She was halfway to her car in the rear parking lot where the help parked when she noticed Paula Gilbert's automobile still in the lot. It gave her pause. She smirked and nodded to herself, imagining the handsome stranger had been waiting for her and taken her off to some rendezvous. Envy boiled in her heart. It could have been me, she thought. It should have been me.

She continued to walk, gazing back at Paula's car. Suddenly something caught her eye and she stopped again. The clouds had shifted and some starlight moved a shadow just enough to reveal what looked like someone silhouetted in the front seat behind the steering wheel.

Who was that? Paula? Why would she be just sitting there in her automobile this late in the evening?

Curious, Darlene changed direction and headed toward the car. As she drew closer, the sight before her became clearer and clearer and stopped her in her steps, practically gluing the soles of her feet to the tarred surface. Were her eyes playing tricks on her? She actually wiped them with her balled fists and looked again.

Paula Gilbert was naked. Her bare bosom could not be mistaken. The two mounds of white flesh capped by those large areolas were too impressive. She hurried over to the car and then, just before she reached out to knock on the window, gasped, and stepped back quickly. The sight brought up the little she had eaten and the small amount of beer she had drunk to wash it down. She shook her head to deny what she had seen and then she turned and ran back to the Inn.

Griffy had already locked the door behind her and put out the lights. She shook the handle and then pounded the door and shouted for him. Almost three full minutes later the light went on in the kitchen, and he appeared, moving cautiously with surprise toward the rear entrance. He was in just his pants.

"What's wrong, Darlene?" he asked opening the door.

She started to speak, but turned instead and pointed at Paula Gilbert's car.

"What is it?"

"Go . . . look," she said.

"I ain't got my shoes on," he complained.

"Go look!" she screamed and he jumped and then started out and across the lot to Paula Gilbert's car. Darlene followed slowly but remained back a good twenty or so yards. Griffy slowed down as he approached the car, stopped, and then slowly opened the door.

"Jesus!" he shouted. "Get in there and call for an ambulance."

"Yes," she said, realizing that should have been the first thing she had done.

In a panic she punched out 911 and gasped her

words. The dispatcher needed her to repeat it all and she did, fighting the hysteria in herself to slow down and be sensible.

"They're on her way!" she shouted to Griffy. He was standing back. The car door was open, and he was just gaping at Paula Gilbert as if he was terrified of touching her or talking to her.

"You better see to her," he said.

"What's going on?" Darlene heard from behind. Griffy's wife Dorothy was there in her bathrobe. "What are you two doing? What's all the shouting for? What's happening?" she followed, delivering her questions in shotgun fashion.

"Paula Gilbert," Darlene said nodding at the car.

She walked to it slowly and joined Griffy to look in.

"Oh my God," she cried, but unlike Darlene and Griffy, she went forward and tried to rouse Paula. Her eyelids fluttered.

"She's alive!" she screamed. "Did you call for help?"

"They're on the way."

"Go get a blanket for her," she ordered Griffy, and he turned, happy to have a reason to get away from the scene. He charged past Darlene and into the restaurant.

Now feeling ashamed at her own response, especially in light of how quickly Dorothy had moved into action, Darlene joined her and they both looked in on Paula Gilbert.

"What happened to you, Paula?" Darlene asked her.

She opened and closed her eyes and moved her lips. Reluctantly, still feeling as if she was getting too close to a leper, she lowered her head to turn her ear like a cup catching the soft, nearly inaudible words.

Darlene's eyes widened as she listened to her speak, gasping out her incredible tale.

"What happened to her? What is she saying?" Dorothy asked.

Darlene shook her head.

"She must be delirious," she said. "She's making no sense."

"God only knows what really happened to her," Dorothy said, "but whatever it was, I hope to hell it's not catching."

He was in an unusually disturbed state of mind. He had set out this evening believing he was in a vigorous, healthy state, never feeling more energized and contented. That was why he was so charming in that saloon and why he was so poetic and philosophical with Paula. He had really intended to have a simple romantic evening, make love, and bring her back as contented as he was. Despite some of the disturbing things that had recently happened, he still harbored the belief that he could transfer wonderful things to women when he didn't have to take what he needed from them. In a sense he was truly the world's greatest lover. Not only did women have difficulty turning him away, but they were ruined for other men, always dissatisfied afterward since none could come up to his level of satisfaction. It was a delicious sort of arrogance that put vigor in his strut and power in his eyes.

But something very unexpected happened when he began to make love to Paula Gilbert. He had a need he had been unaware of until he was actually making love to her. Usually, this was a feeling he experienced before he went looking for prey. Something in his body always first sent signals to his brain to tell him to go on a hunt. He hadn't had any such signal all night. What was going on? Why were his periods of contentment getting shorter and shorter? At this rate, he'd be hunting day and night and never have a rest. It was like those batteries running cell phones and the like, he thought. After time, they held a charge for less periods of time and had to be recharged so often, it was cheaper or easier to throw them away and start with a new one.

But how was he to do that? He couldn't throw away his body and start with a new one, could he?

Or could he?

Something was rising toward the surface of his memory. He sat in the dark and waited patiently for it to break out. It was coming, coming up out of his past. Something to do with his body. What?

It stopped coming up.

He grimaced as if he could squeeze his brain like an orange and force the memories to drip out.

It was sinking again, going deeper and deeper into the blackness. Wait, he wanted to shout. Don't give up. Come back to me.

Tell me who I am.

Exhausted with the effort, he finally gave up and started the engine of his vehicle. Paula was still in the rear seat, breathing with such great difficulty, he could hear her gasps clearly. The sound was haunting him.

"Stop it!" he screamed at her. "Just die quietly like the others."

It occurred to him that he had never spent this much time with a woman afterward. He would take what he needed and leave them. It was his own fault now, of course. He had taken her in his car. He could have left her on the side of the road, he realized, left her in the bushes by the lake if she had begun to die immediately.

For a while he was surprised by what happened but she didn't show signs of anything detrimental, so he told her to dress and he would take her back to her car. She was quiet, but he interpreted that simply as her sense of contentment. Let her savor the lovemaking, he thought proudly.

Then he looked into the rearview mirror and saw she basically hadn't moved.

"Get dressed. We'll be back at the tavern soon," he ordered. She didn't respond so he pulled over to the side of the road and leaned over the front seat. He flipped on the overhead light and saw what was happening.

"Damn it," he shouted at her as if it was entirely her fault.

Cars whizzed by, even at this hour. He was back on a busy highway. A few hundred yards down was the first of those houses he had pointed out to her on the way to the dam. So he turned around, shifted into drive, and shot forward, now speeding toward the tavern. When he arrived, he saw a pickup truck with three men crowded in the cab pulling out of the lot. He waited until they were gone and then he drove in, pulled alongside her car, and deposited her in the front seat. He flung her clothes into the rear of her car, got back into his, and drove off thinking maybe no one would find her until morning at least and by then it would be far too late. She would be unable to tell anyone about him, not that anyone would believe her if she did.

When he pulled into the driveway of the rooming house, he hesitated before driving around back. There was something stuck in the front door, a piece of paper. It waved gently in the breeze. He looked around cautiously, his sixth sense triggered like the instinct of a wild animal. He could practically smell the presence of someone else. It was faint. Whoever it was had been here and gone.

He got out of his car, leaving the engine running, and went to the door to pull the sheet out from between the screen door and the front door.

It was from the minister, a Reverend Dobson.

Dear Mrs. Martin,

I hope you are all right. I came by to comfort you and discuss the funeral to see if there was anything special you would like me to do.

Please call me as soon as you can.

God Bless,
Reverend Dobson

He had forgotten about that; he had forgotten there would be a funeral. How stupid of him. He was taking too much pleasure in all this and making too many mistakes. Of course, he would have to leave this place now. There was no doubt anymore. He really was enjoying the area, the peacefulness, the easy pickings. He had been feeling like a fox in a rabbit warren. All he had to do when he was hungry was reach out.

After he parked his car behind the house, he went in through the backdoor and up the stairs. He went to the old lady's bedroom and looked in on her corpse again almost as if he had expected she had moved.

"Thanks," he said. "Now I have to go."

Blaming her made him feel better even though he knew how ridiculous it was. He felt drunk, intoxicated. The evening had been full of ups and downs and it left him giddy. He might even have trouble sleeping, he thought. He was too wired.

He went to his room and packed his bag reluctantly. This place was really very comfortable and he had so looked forward to the morning, to sitting by the lake. It had been so relaxing. The more he thought about it, the angrier he became. It was the old lady's fault. If she hadn't been so pathetic, he wouldn't have killed her.

Of course you would have, he told himself. She would have pointed you out. You had to be sure she couldn't do that.

He continued to argue with himself, even considering remaining one more day, and then, suddenly, it began as always, a slight ringing in his ear. He went to the window and looked into the night.

It was out there . . . something threatening. It was coming in this direction. He couldn't stay here any longer, no matter what he wanted.

He hurried now and then he rushed out and started down the stairs, still regretting his quick exit. He paused at the foot of the stairs. An idea occurred to him. Confuse the trail, keep whatever it was from following his scent. He went into the kitchen and looked around. The old gas stove was perfect, he thought.

Carefully, he prepared the flammable oils and put them in a frying pan. He started the fire and then he let it spread to the molding on the floor. He watched the fire, fascinated with how quickly it invaded the heart of the old wood and crept in behind the walls. He could hear the crackle and the small explosions. The home was as brittle as old bones.

He was saddened by it all as he walked away. By the

time he got into his car, he could see the hot illumination in some of the windows. It wouldn't be long, he thought. The fire was ravenous.

He drove away slowly, looking back when either a gas pipe or the heating oil set off an explosion. The flames were crawling out the windows and up the sides of the house now. What a parasite fire is, he thought.

It never occurred to him that he was one too.

FOURTEEN

"Hey," Steve Battie called to Terri as she was going through the corridor and the emergency room. He was in an examination room. "You've got to stop and see this."

"What do you have?" she asked stepping into the room.

The sight before her stopped her cold. Her first thought was it looked like a patient who had overdosed on Coumadin, an anticoagulant drug to help prevent the formation of blood clots in the blood vessels or dissolve them by decreasing the blood's ability to clump together. Because they prevent clotting, they can, if poorly managed, cause severe bleeding.

Terri had never seen a case like this, even in her textbooks. Two lines of blood trickled out of the young woman's eyes like red tears. The trauma appeared all over her body. It looked like an explosion of arteries and veins. There was no question she had intracranial bleeding as well.

"She expired about ten minutes ago."

"Was she a hemophiliac?" Terri asked.

"Don't know yet. She has been in the hospital before, so we're tracking down her medical history, but if ever I saw an example of a congenital or Acquired Factor II deficiency, this is it," Battie replied.

Terri nodded. She knew, of course, that normal blood coagulation was a complex process involving as many as twenty different plasma proteins, or blood coagulation factors. The complex chemical reactions using these factors took place rapidly in a healthy person to form an insoluble protein called fibrin that stops bleeding. To be congenital, the woman would have inherited it from both parents. What triggered alarms in her mind, however, was that acquired Factor II deficiency resulted from one of three possibilities: a severe liver disease, the mismanagement of the anticoagulant drug, or a vitamin K deficiency.

A nurse came into the room and handed Battie a file.

"Hold on," he said to Terri. She watched him read. He flipped a page. "She was brought in here for an appendectomy. No history of bleeding, a normal blood workup. She wasn't put on any anticoagulant for any reason here."

"How long ago?"

He looked up again.

"Just three months."

"My God," she whispered. "I've got to get to a phone." She went out to the desk and called Will Dennis.

"Sorry," she said, "neither of us are getting any sleep tonight," she began, and then told him what she feared.

"No, you go get some sleep, Doctor," he told her. "I'll

call you at your office tomorrow, or should I say, today, as soon as I have anything definitive."

She agreed. There really wasn't anything more she could do here anyway.

She debated going to her own home, but the memories of Curt collapsed at her door were still too vivid. Why the police impersonator would be coming for her, she did not know. In his madness, he was convinced perhaps that she wasn't telling him something she knew. The chances of a so-called normal villain returning to her home after having a confrontation with someone like Curt were probably very slim, but they weren't dealing with anything like a normal villain here, so when the cross streets came up at which a right turn would take her back home or a left would take her to Curt's, she turned left.

The key was under the flowerpot to the right of the front door as usual. She let herself in and then paused. Being here now with Curt hurt and in a hospital room suddenly brought tears to her eyes. Maybe if she had been more forthcoming at the hospital parking lot, they wouldn't have argued and he wouldn't have felt it necessary to come to her house to patch things up. She should have been less the doctor, and more the fiancée, she concluded.

Curling up in his bed gave her a sense of security and contentment, however. The scent of his cologne and hair dressing was there and it was something she welcomed. She had crawled in naked too. Pretending they had just made love, she turned over and closed her eyes. She hadn't realized just how exhausted she was until that moment. It took only seconds, it seemed, for her to fall asleep.

Sometime before morning, she woke with a start. Whether it was a nightmare or what, she wasn't sure, but the echo of what sounded like someone at a window remained in her ears. She shuddered and then slowly sat up and listened hard. If he found her home, why wouldn't he be able to find Curt's, knowing he was her fiancé?

Why didn't she consider this and go to a motel?

She reached for the phone. Call the police to her aid again? She was feeling so stupid. I'm behaving like a hysterical person, she thought.

She knew where Curt kept his pistol and went to the drawer. It was there and it was loaded. He had insisted they take target practice together.

"I'm sworn to do all I can to save lives," she told him. "How can I fire a pistol at someone?"

"If that someone is going to take your life, you're going to let it happen because of your Hippocratic oath? What will you be able to do for your patients when you're dead?" he reasoned.

"All I'm saying is I can practice with you, but I don't know if I can ever fire the gun at someone."

"You'll know," he said with a smile of cold confidence. "If the occasion should ever arise, you'll know."

She grasped the pistol and, after taking a deep breath, walked slowly out of the bedroom and listened again in the hallway. A squeak at a window in the den sent a hot chill down her spine. Heart pounding, she walked to the door of the den and peered in.

The window was up. She couldn't move. Had Curt left it up? Can't call him to find out now, she thought.

Instead, she backed up, returned to the bedroom and closed the door. As much as she hated to do it, she called the sheriff's office again and related her message to the dispatcher. The woman of course knew exactly who she was.

Then she got into bed, sat up with the pistol in her hand, and waited for either the door to open or the patrolman to arrive.

He was well on his way to somewhere when he suddenly slowed down. What am I doing? he wondered. Why do I have to run off like this? I'm starting to act like them.

Them?

Funny, he thought, he rarely differentiated between himself and the women he mined for nutrition and life-giving compounds, except to remind himself how superior to them he really was, and especially superior to their men.

He had a big night, too, and where was he going? A nice fatigue was setting in him, nice as compared to the fatigues he felt when he was in need. Nothing ached. There was just this sense of deep relaxation settling in his body. The prospect of lying in a bed and lowering his head to the pillow was looking better and better. In the morning he could reconsider everything and make decisions. Morning wasn't all that far off anyway.

The flicking bulb on a motel sign ahead seemed to be beckoning him. He smiled, slowed down, and pulled into the lot and parked by the office. This late in the evening, there was no one visible, but the door was open and there was a bell on the counter to summon someone.

The night manager was actually asleep in an oversized easy chair. He was dressed in a thin, yellowing T-shirt and a pair of jeans held up with suspenders. Under the weakened neon ceiling fixture's illumination, his face looked as if it consisted of old wax. The sick pallor of his complexion was emphasized by his obviously unprofessionally colored black thinning hair. He looked like someone who had dumped a bottle of ink on his head.

For a moment he stood there watching the manager breathe. He reminded him of a fish. His large nostrils moving in and out like gills. His face spotted with patches of reddened skin and a mole on the right side of his nearly indistinguishable chin.

The man is ugly enough to kill, he thought and for a moment actually considered doing just that. He grunted with the thought.

The manager's large round eyes opened as if they had

two tiny springs on the lids. He looked up with an expression of utter astonishment at the sight of someone staring at him so intensely.

"Whaaa . . ." he said and scrubbed his face vigorously with his dry palms to bring some blood into it and maybe into his brain. He sat up, realized he had a customer, and immediately stood. His potbelly seemed to roll down and settle itself just under his waist as he rose to his feet. He actually looked like a pregnant woman in her ninth month.

"Sorry," he said. "We rarely get any customers this time of night."

"Why? It's on the road. Doesn't anyone travel on this road?" he asked with an unexpectedly aggressive tone.

"Oh, sure, sure. It's just not a main highway anymore," the manager said defensively. "Since they built the bypass. My parents left me the place just about the time it all went to pot." He shrugged to indicate there was nothing he could do about his fate. "I don't need much. I'm by myself here. So, you want a room for the night?"

"Maybe two nights," he said and the motel owner's eyebrows went up as if he had won the lottery.

"Oh, sure. Well, as I said we have lots of rooms available."

"Give me one as far from the highway as possible. I want it to be as quiet as possible," he said.

"Gotcha." He turned the sign-in book to him and stepped back to choose a room key.

Who am I tonight? he wondered as he lifted the pen to sign. He decided he would be Rip Winkleman. After all, he was going to sleep and he felt confident this excuse for a man wouldn't get the irony and humor. He was paying with cash so there was no name to check on a credit card.

"Thirty-eight fifty a night," the motel owner told him, and he gave him a hundred-dollar bill.

The owner went under the counter to get a cash box out and the change, which he gave him with the key.

"It's the last room on the end, as far from the entrance as I have."

"Perfect."

He spun around and started for the door.

"Where you headed?"

He turned to him, at first annoyed at his curiosity and then realizing that wasn't the best reaction to have, smiled.

"I've got to make my way to a business meeting in Newark eventually. Just taking my time. Enjoying the trip. Stopping to smell the roses, know what I mean?"

"Sure," the motel owner said, although it was clear from the look in his face that he had no idea what "smell the roses" meant. "If you need anything, just pick up the phone. It rings automatically in here."

"Thank you."

He went out to the car and looked back to see the ugly, overweight man settling himself in the chair, looking as if he was sinking into his own body. He couldn't help wondering if this sort of man had any sexual energy whatsoever. His sex seemed to have dissolved into his fat. Who could be attracted to such a creature anyway? He looked like a personified wart. Who would mourn its death?

And then he thought, who would mourn mine? Did that matter? Should it matter? When you're dead, how do you know you've been mourned at all? Or in what spirit and with what pomp and circumstance?

These sorts of philosophical concerns only complicated life, he decided. They distract, depress, disturb. The only thing that was important was the moment, now. The past was the past. It couldn't be changed. And the future was unknown except for one thing. There was an end out there, a place where it all stopped, where the light inside you went dark. It seemed to him there was only one thing to concentrate on, one thing to have as your priority therefore, and that was to do everything possible to keep the light burning for as long as possible. Everything else was just a distraction.

It occurred to him that he was very much like any other creature out there. Like any of them, he spent his day working on keeping himself alive. There was a time, he thought, however, when he had more time for the distractions, when they weren't as detrimental or harmful to that effort. Vaguely at first, but suddenly getting more vivid in his mind, was the realization that the periods of time he could afford for such things was diminishing to the point where they were almost gone entirely.

He had no doubt, for example, that when he woke in the morning, he would feel the early signs of an oncoming need to hunt, and this, after just doing so the night before. Again, he concluded. This wasn't good.

The imagery of that rabbit's warren returned. What he might have to do, he thought, was find a central location and stock it with prey, gather up a half dozen or so and have them there for harvesting when he required and as he required. Not a bad idea, he thought and now regretted having set fire to the rooming house. It might have served him in that purpose. On the other hand, someone like that minister, was bound to come by and make things difficult. He'd have to go somewhere else.

After he brought his suitcase into the room and prepared for bed, he rested his head on the pillow and gazed into the darkness, still thinking about this great idea. What a wonderful fantasy. It would be like a fish with an endless supply of worms at the bottom of the bowl. Hungry? Just dip down and pluck one. It brought a smile to his lips.

Gather them, keep them in one place, and stop this endless traveling, he told himself. It was a real project to consider, a purpose, something with a beneficial objective, a new reason to be. How wonderful. He closed his eyes, turned in the bed, and snuggled comfortably under the blanket and against the pillow.

I might live forever yet, he thought, and fell asleep on the fluffy cloud of that enormous possibility.

FIFTEEN

"It's all clear, Dr. Barnard," the patrolman said. "No evidence of anyone breaking in or attempting to," he said. He was holding a walkie-talkie and conferring with another officer who had been searching around the house. This patrolman had inspected every inch of Curt's home and reported there was nothing of any concern inside as well.

"When I came back here tonight, I guess I didn't notice my fiancé had left the window open in there," she said. "I'm sorry I bothered you guys."

"No problem, Doctor. That's why they pay us the big bucks. Especially after what happened at your home. Why don't we hang around a bit out there just to be sure you're safe?" he said.

She was about to tell him it wasn't necessary when she could hear a little voice inside her say, "Don't be a big shot. Take their protection."

"Thank you." She looked at the clock. "Almost doesn't pay to go back to sleep," she said. She had called her service this time and left Curt's number, asking them to be sure to give her a wake-up call.

"I know what you mean, Doctor," the patrolman said smiling. He tipped his hat and started out. It wasn't until she was in bed and under the blanket again that she truly appreciated the patrolman's offer. The sense of security it gave her helped her to relax enough to fall asleep. She was sleeping so deeply that it took three rings to wake her.

"Good morning, Dr. Barnard," she heard.

"Thank you," she said and rose like a zombie to stumble her way into the bathroom and shower. If she could, she would have stood under the water for twenty minutes, she thought. She went to the phone right after drying her hair and called the hospital to find out how Curt was doing. The nurse on duty told her he was resting comfortably and he had a good night.

Better than mine for sure, she thought and amusingly wished she had been the one in the hospital.

"Please tell him I called and I'll be up later when I do rounds," she told her and hung up.

She had a great deal to do this morning. Both Curt's parents and hers had to be told something. She had no idea how she would begin to explain these events to them without putting them all into a panic. For sure, her parents were going to rant and rave about her staying by herself at Curt's house.

To put off the inevitable a little longer, she prepared some breakfast first. She turned on the television set to watch some news while she ate. The local station began with the story of the fire at the Martin tourist house. A reporter on the scene questioned the fire chief, who revealed Tilly Martin's death and an investigation that was considering the possibility of arson. He made it sound as if the fire might have been started by Tilly Martin herself to collect insurance on a building that was no longer providing enough income.

It was the reporter who then spoke of the depth of this family's tragedy by pointing out that Tilly Martin's granddaughter, the only person living with her, had recently died, too, and from all reports, a totally unexpected death.

"More reason to consider the possibility of arson," the fire chief said dryly, even more encouraged to project his theory. The implication that it might have been a suicide resulting from deep grief was clear.

"That's ridiculous," Terri shouted at the screen. "Why would someone burn a house down to kill herself? And besides, it's a painful death."

She went to the phone to try to contact Will Dennis. It took a while for her to be passed through to his cell phone.

"Yes, terrible coincidence," he said. "But arson? No one in my office has given out any information like that," he said. "There wasn't much left of the old lady. You'd need a psychic forensic expert to come to any conclusion this early in the investigation. All we know at the moment, as I understand it from the people I have in the field, is that the old lady was found away from where the fire actually had begun."

"Maybe it wasn't such a coincidence, Will. Could the families of these women be in some danger too?"

"Now, don't get wild on me, Doc. Expanding it into some fantastic sort of psychotic conspiracy won't do anyone any good," he said. "We'll panic the Thorndykes, to say the least."

"Of course, I don't want to do anything like that, but . . ."

"Anyway, Doc, we have other problems, more pressing," he interrupted. "Our fears last night were confirmed very early this morning for me: Paula Gilbert had zero traces of what she needed to clot blood. Our vitamin vampire took all of her K," he concluded.

"I had no doubt. This is an incredible nightmare."

"Who sleeps long enough to have nightmares?" he replied. "One good thing came out of it all last night," he continued. "We've acquired a fairly good detailed description from Darlene Stone, the bartender at the Old Hasbrouck Inn. It matches with what you gave me. I've already had a police artist draw a facsimile of the man Darlene claimed showed great interest in Paula Gilbert. The chief characteristics match our guy and the descriptions you've given. We got it completed in time to make the front page of the local newspaper."

"Good. About time," she added. She was not unhappy

if Will Dennis took it as a bit of criticism. If he did, however, he ignored it.

"The FBI is here in more strength, convinced our man is still in our backyard. Their profiler is with them and she says the speed at which he is adding victims now and the fact that he has done so within the same vicinity indicates a major change in his M.O. In other words he is keeping himself here for one reason or another. I was going to call you at your office today and fill you in on all this, Doc. We might consider having an officer near you, considering all that's happened to you and Curt."

"What happened to the idea of my being bait?" she asked. "If we have a policeman on my tail, our guy won't return, will he?"

"Far, far too dangerous for you to think of doing that now. As you know better than anyone, we don't know how he does this, why, or if he really does anything? All we know at this point is young women are dying from these deficiencies and our suspect is either with them or around them at the time. Even if we catch this guy, can you imagine what it will be like trying to convict him of anything?"

"No," she said. "It might be easier to be a doctor than a lawyer after all."

He laughed.

"The only solid thing I have is what he did with you, impersonate a policeman. This might be a form of biological terror, but no one I've spoken with at CDC or the FBI or anywhere can explain how any compound would deprive people of their vitamin stores and selectively to boot!" he exclaimed. It was the first time he sounded on the verge of hysterical frustration. Gone was the possibility of local law enforcement solving any crime. If anything, the bizarre nature of all of it made it far too complicated, even for the Feds.

"I understand," she said.

"I'm glad you do. I don't. Look, I'll just have a patrolman at your offices today and one will follow you about and be close by should you spot our guy or should he try to contact you again, okay? They won't be in your way. I promise."

"Okay," she said. With the way she was calling the sheriff's office, it almost amounted to the same thing anyway, she thought.

She looked at the time.

"I've got to get moving. I'm going to the office soon, but first I have to call my in-laws and then my own parents and tell them about Curt."

"I'd love to tap those calls, just so I hear how you explain it. In any case reassure them we're providing protection."

"Thanks," she said, smiling for the first time this morning. "If I come up with something good, I'll send it over to you."

He laughed and they concluded their conversation.

After a moment to catch her breath, she called Curt's parents. His father answered.

"Good morning, Pop," she said. She had been calling Curt's father "Pop" ever since Curt had given her the engagement ring. Then she began to relate the events as close to any form of logic she could compose.

"What's that?" he asked after every revelation, partly because he really needed it repeated as a result of his faulty hearing, which he stubbornly refused to correct with an aid, and second because he needed to confirm he really understood what she was saying. "Why didn't you call us last night?" he demanded at the end of her attempt at any explanations. The best she could come up with was some sort of psychotic schizophrenic was out and about their hometown and Curt had intercepted him trying to break into her home.

"It was very late by the time I left the hospital. Curt was out of any danger," she explained.

"None of this makes any sense to me. I've been reading about these deaths that involve some sort of deficiency or another, but I still don't understand how you are involved," Bill Levitt said.

"Neither do I, Pop."

"Terri. I don't like being left out of the loop," he added sternly.

"You're not, believe me. There isn't much of a loop at the moment."

"Makes no sense," he repeated. "We'll head over to

the hospital. You should have called us last night," he repeated, obviously disturbed.

"I'm sorry. I thought I was being sensible."

"I might be retired," he said, "but I'm not dead."

"I'm sorry," she chanted.

"What?"

"I'm sorry," she practically shouted.

"I'll see you later," he concluded.

Now, feeling worse, she punched out her parents' phone number, dreading their reaction even more. Everything she expected resulted: her mother's hysterical panic, her father's deep concern.

Somehow, her mother found a way to blame it on her delaying her marriage to Curt.

"A woman can't be alone in today's world," she declared with a formality and portentous air that made it sound like the title of an Oprah show. "You might be a doctor, but you're still a woman. Poor Curt," she followed. "We'll go right up there."

Terri was going to discourage that or at least have them go later, but then she thought, the more Curt is occupied, the less he will be worrying about her.

"You'll come home tonight, won't you, Terri?" her mother asked.

"I'll see, Ma."

"I'll fix your old room. You'll be safe," she insisted.

Here she was a physician responsible for the health and lives of hundreds of people and her mother wanted her home, sleeping in her old room, surrounded by her stuffed animals. Maybe, she thought, maybe I really did make a mistake coming back here to practice medicine.

Hyman warned me in so many ways. 'You can't be a prophet in your own land.'

If depression fell like raindrops, she was leaving the house in the midst of a torrential downpour.

SIXTEEN

He was never a late sleeper, especially after he had fed and felt invigorated the night before. Sometimes, immediately after he awoke, he would literally fall to the floor and do dozens of push-ups, hundreds of sit-ups before going for his jog. He was like that today, exploding with energy. He had gotten a wonderful rest. The room had proven to be as quiet as the ugly motel owner had predicted. The highway itself was lightly traveled and his room was a good distance from the road.

First, I'll go for my run, he thought, and then I'll find out from the motel owner where I could go for breakfast close by. It would be a big breakfast today. Maybe even steak and eggs. He got into his sweats, put on his running shoes, and opened the door.

It was a much cooler morning than he had anticipated. He could actually see his breath. The sky was clear and a darker shade of blue. Across the way the branches of trees denuded of their leaves turned the scene into a field of skeletons, bones growing out of tree trunks, scarecrows picked clean by oncoming winter, nature's vulture. The bark of many of the trees looked streaked with dried blood. A pair of crows seemed to be looking his way, nervously lifting and dropping their wings as if they were churning up energy for a quick get-away should it be required.

"Hey!" he screamed at them.

One flew off and then the other, after a moment of courage, followed quickly. They circled and disappeared to the right.

He laughed and then stepped completely out of the room. When he looked down the railroad car–designed motel building, he saw his was the only vehicle. He had been the only customer last night. The owner had been right about the drop-off of his business. How the hell did this guy exist? he wondered.

He could see the light was on in the office. Walking at a brisk pace to warm up, he started in that direction. When he reached it, he glanced at the newspaper machine at the front door and stopped instantly. The resemblance between him and the drawing on the front page was very clear, very sharp. So much so, it was as if he was looking into a mirror that reflected only one's high-lights, but enough of them to make it clear that one was looking at oneself. He read that the police were looking for this man for questioning about the death of Paula Gilbert, a country singer who had performed at the Old Hasbrouck Inn. There were no other details about the man they were looking for, but what he had read and the picture drawn was enough to disturb him deeply. This was the first time such a thing had occurred, and he hated the idea of being the hunted.

That's what I do. That's my purpose, he wanted to shout.

His eyes lifted from the machine to the window of the office door. Through it he could see the motel owner staring down at the front page of the paper. He seemed to sense his presence and lifted his eyes, too. They confronted each other. Panic rose to the surface of the owner's face, coming out of it like a thick, red blotch. His eyes brightened like two tiny lights warning outsiders not to enter his thoughts, recording was taking place within.

Without hesitation, he lunged at the door and stepped into the office. The motel owner backed away from the counter.

"Good . . . morning . . ." he said, practically choking on each syllable. "How was, was your room?"

"Full of snakes," he replied.

"Whaaa."

"Snakes!" he shouted. "Snakes, everywhere. You put me in a den of snakes!"

The owner shook his head vigorously and continued to back up.

"What are you talking about? What snakes?"

In response, he moved quickly, practically leaping over the counter until he was at him, his hands grasping the man at the neck and practically lifting him off the floor as he drove him back into his living quarters, smashing the door open and pushing him in until he stumbled and fell to the floor, carrying him over with him as he went down.

The man struggled to break free and was doing well, his panic giving him unusual strength. Quickly, realizing the motel owner might break loose, he drove his knee onto the man's Adam's apple and pressed all of his weight there.

The motel owner's face began to explode with terror. His eyes bulged, rising like hard-boiled eggs being squeezed in the middle. His mouth contorted, the lips losing all their shape, and the blood that rose to the surface of his face seemed to jell and clog in the pores of his skin. His choking grew more and more intense. He clawed and swung and tried to buck like a wild horse so he could throw his aggressor off, but nothing worked. He began to lose consciousness. His tongue edged its way out from under his clenched teeth and peered about like a desperate thick-headed snake. It trembled along with the rest of him until he gasped a final time and then sunk into himself, dropping into his death like a rock sinking in water.

Still he pressed his knee into the dead man's throat as if he had to put a stamp of success on this kill. This sort of battle and killing wasn't something he liked doing. Killing the old lady was one thing. That was nearly effortless on his part. This was a whole different scene, a victim who put up real resistance, so much in fact that he was surprised himself at how successful he had been.

Producing death in the women he was with for sexual and feeding reasons came subtly at first and then with an ecstatic easiness that gave him pleasure. This sort of struggle with a man who could offer some opposition required a much bigger physical effort and was therefore far uglier to him. For one thing there was no sexual enjoyment, and for another it made him feel dirtier. The man's sweat was on his hands and the stench of his death, imagined or otherwise, was already rising up to his nostrils.

He stepped back and looked down at him.

Drool ran out of the sides of the man's mouth and down his chin. It was revolting. He hated him even more in death than he had in life.

"You know," he said, "when I first set eyes on you, I knew I was going to have to stamp you out. You're too ugly to live. And what kind of a life did you have anyway, huh?" he shouted at him, waiting as if he expected the corpse would smile and nod and agree he had no reason to be. He would be as grateful as the old lady had been. Or at least, he should be.

"This place . . . it's a world of death. You should have put yourself to sleep in one of the empty rooms.

"No, instead you were going to do me harm, weren't you? Me, who has ten times the reason to live than you do. You're . . . you're . . . an ant, a bug," he said and stepped on the man's swollen abdomen. The mushy feeling disgusted him.

He gazed around the pathetic-looking apartment. The furniture looked as if it had all been rejected by a thrift shop. Not even a charity would accept it. The rug was worn so thin, he could see floorboard beneath it in spots, and the sofa dripped stuffing and showed broken springs beneath. The room actually stunk with staleness.

"This putrid life you led, it disgusts me," he muttered. He seized the man's right ankle and pulled the body along the carpet, his head bobbing and turning as though he was saying, "NO! Stop!"

He deposited the corpse in a corner so no one could look through the door and see it lying there. He even sat him up, leaning him against the wall so there would be less of his legs in sight. His head fell forward and he stared down at the owner's coal-black hair, bald spots now quite visible.

"So much for your stupid dye job," he muttered.

Then, he stepped back and tried to remember what he was going to do before all this had exploded in his face.

Oh yes, jog, he thought and started out. When he looked at the paper on the counter again, he stopped. His gaze went from the drawing to the door and then back to the drawing. He couldn't go out there now. Not with that picture plastered everywhere. Someone was sure to spot him.

He backed away as if someone was coming to the door. It was as quiet and deserted looking as it had been, but this situation was no good. Get in the car and drive away, he thought. Go where people won't see the picture and read the description.

"Maybe we should reconsider when you take your vacation, Terri," Hyman Templeman said. She and her mentor met first thing every morning to go over what they knew to be the day's expected events. "As soon as Curt can travel, take him and disappear for a while."

"You know that will be a while anyway, Hyman. Curt needs to be kept calm."

"Go sneak him away to my cabin in Willowemac then," he suggested. "He likes to fish, doesn't he? You'd be out of it and yet not so far you couldn't get back here in a short time if you needed to for any reason. You could go up there tomorrow."

She started to shake her head.

"You're not going to be much good to your patients like this, Terri. You think you can put it all out of your mind and for a while in your examination room here, you might, but every quiet moment, every pause in the action, you will be thinking about Curt, the attack on him, your fears, this madness.

"Are you going to be happy with a policeman parked in front of your home, in front of this office, following you everywhere you go? I know your mother," he added with a smile. "I'm surprised she's not camped out on our front lawn this morning."

"Give her a chance," Terri said and they both laughed. "I don't know, Hyman. Let me see how it goes, okay? And thanks."

He lifted his hands, palms up, and shrugged.

"Every time you think you've lived long enough to have seen everything, there's something new waiting around the corner."

"See," she said, "you have good reason to live forever."

He laughed again and then they broke to begin to see the first patients of the day. Her lunch hour was cut short because Mrs. Mogolowitz kept coming up with new pains and aches extending her visit a good fifteen minutes. Hyman had wanted her to join him and Estelle at Willy's Luncheonette, the small village's one and only place for lunch, but she had decided to use her time to take a quick ride up to the hospital and visit with Curt. She still had a good two hours before she had to see her next patient. She wasn't all that hungry anyway, and she knew Hyman would just have Estelle join him in a ganging up on her to persuade her to take him up on his invitation.

Because her last morning examination had cut into her time, she wanted to drive faster. Having a police car on her tail was intimidating, however, and she stayed just a hair or so over the speed limit. When she arrived at the hospital, Curt's parents had just left. She considered that good fortune.

Her fiancé looked tired and very upset when she entered his room.

"Dad showed me the newspaper," he said as soon as she kissed him and stepped back. "I don't like Will Dennis releasing your name and the event at your office like that. I think it puts you in even more danger. Dad agrees and your mother called me this morning. She's going to come after you with handcuffs," he added.

"If you lie here worrying about everything, you won't recuperate as quickly, Curt. You won't sleep well and you will be laid up longer," she threatened.

"Don't change the subject. What are you going to do tonight?"

"I have police protection, Curt, round-the-clock."

"It's not enough," he insisted.

She sighed deeply.

"What do you want me to do?"

"Stay with either my parents or your own," he replied. "Until I'm out of here."

"Okay," she said quickly. He raised his eyebrows suspiciously.

"I'll call," he threatened.

"I'll stay with my parents. I promise, swear," she said raising her right hand. "You'll be able to tell. You'll see the aggravation in my forehead the next day."

He finally smiled.

"I want to go home. They're not doing much for me here anyway," he complained, now appealing to her as a doctor.

"It will take a while for the bruising and swelling to go down."

"So? It can go down outside as well as inside the hospital."

"We'll see," she said, noncommittal.

"Who is this guy? How is he doing these things, Terri?"

"I don't know. According to Will the FBI is here in what he calls significant numbers." She paused, wondering if she should add anything more substantial. Despite his condition, he sensed it.

"What?" he asked.

"They think he's definitely still in the area, something about a major change in his M.O., whatever that is. They don't tell me everything, of course. Maybe they know a lot more."

"I wish we were on our honeymoon," Curt said, closing his eyes and shaking his head.

"Maybe we will be," she told him, thinking of Hyman's offer. "Or, at least, a test run."

He looked up sharply.

"Really?"

"Hyman offered us his cabin for a few days, maybe a week."

"You'd do that?"

"Let me think about it a little more," she said. "I'll be back tonight."

She kissed him again and then went to speak with the nurse on duty to review his chart. Satisfied he was doing as well as he should, she left the hospital. He could be released tomorrow, she thought.

Her patrolman escort was parked right beside her car. He's not very subtle about it all, she thought, but then again, such protection wasn't meant to be subtle. She just waved at him and then got into her own vehicle.

When she turned the key, nothing happened. Surprised, she did it again and still, the engine didn't start. It was as if there was no engine, not a sound, nothing.

"What the . . ."

She did it again and again and then slapped the dashboard as if the car was a disobedient child. Checking her watch, she realized she didn't have time to wait for AAA. Now, she was happy she had a police escort.

She got out of her car and opened the passengers' door of his vehicle.

"My car won't start. You have to get me back to the office," she said. "I have patients lined up to the street."

She slipped in and he put his transmission into reverse and backed out without saying a word. She thought he took off rather quickly, too.

"It's all right. We have a little time," she said.

"Oh, I know," he replied. He turned and looked at her. "We have lots of time now."

Her heart seemed to fold up inside her chest the moment she saw the cleft chin.

He practically tore the man's bathroom apart, throwing things behind him—pill bottles, cough syrup, deodorants—until he found what he thought he could use. He hated being a scavenger, but he hated being on the run even more. He would need everything and anything to keep himself strong, protected.

Searching the closets he found some sweaters he could wear. On the floor of one closet, he discovered a coffee can stuffed with twenties and fifties, too.

Every time he passed through the living room, he paused to thank the corpse.

"Very thoughtful of you to keep cash on hand," he told it.

Pictures of what must have been the owner's family were in an album on a shelf of a side table in the living room. Curious, he flipped through it.

"Your parents weren't much better looking," he told the corpse. "Looks like you were an only child, huh? Lucky for the world. It limited the ugly."

He laughed at his own cleverness and then, for a moment or two, he considered how much in common he had with this dead man. They were both loners. He actually felt sorry for him, for the motel owner had none of the power he had. He was trapped in this life.

What sort of a legacy was this for his parents to have left him?

"Inconsiderate bastards!"

He hated them and began tearing their pictures out of the album and scattering the pieces over the living room floor. The rage took him over for a while and then, suddenly, the sound of a bell froze him. He listened and the bell sounded once more.

"What is that?" he asked the corpse.

Then he rose and peered through the door at the motel office lobby.

He saw a tall, dark-haired woman with a far shorter, elderly lady standing there. The woman had short hair and a comely face, with just a light shade of lipstick to give it any brightness. She wore what he thought was a much too heavy dark brown coat. The old lady looked a bit distressed.

He gazed at the corpse as if he expected it would be resurrected at the sound of that bell and go and do its duty. Then, he moved out to the motel lobby slowly.

"Oh, hi," the woman said. She smiled. Her teeth were the best part of her face, he thought, very white, very straight.

"Hi."

"We need a room. We started out a little too early this morning and I'm afraid we got a bit lost. My mother is tired. We need to just have a good day's rest before continuing."

"Where are you going?" he asked. He was really curious about it.

"Oh, we're heading for Raleigh, North Carolina. My mother's older sister is very sick and I promised to take her to see her. I had some vacation due me and took it," she added.

The speed and ease with which she revealed personal information impressed him. First, it was nice to have personal information, and second, it was nice to see someone so trusting, so expecting of compassion and sympathy.

"Sure," he said moving with more enthusiasm now. He looked at the old lady. "You need to rest, Mom," he said as if he had known her all his life. She didn't smile. She was one of those elderly people who resented people who became too personal too quickly. He could see that, but he ignored it.

He turned the sign-in book around and the young woman opened her purse.

"How much is a room?" she asked.

"Thirty-eight fifty," he replied.

She nodded and opened a wallet to take out four tens, which she counted carefully.

"Mom hates credit cards," she whispered. "She thinks it makes people spend way above their means. Is cash all right?"

"Oh, absolutely," he said. "Just sign in and I'll give you the keys to . . ." He looked at the board of keys and saw the room next to his. "Unit 12. Next to the very end. It will be quiet there for you."

"Oh thank you," she said. "We need to get some rest before we go for some dinner. Are there good places nearby?"

"Oh, absolutely," he said. "When you're ready, just let me know and I'll point you in the right direction."

"Thank you very much."

He turned the book around and saw she had written Erna Walker. Her address was in Rochester, New York.

"What time did you two start out, Erna?" he asked.

"A little before four in the morning. I guess we were a bit too enthusiastic, but this is the longest trip I've taken in a car, and certainly the longest for my mother," she said.

"Well I'm sure you two will get some rest. Do you need help with your luggage?" he asked.

"Oh no. Thank you," she said taking the key.

The old lady had been looking around and he could see she wasn't pleased with the lobby. The walls were too dull and the baseboard was dirty. The floor needed a good vacuuming and washing and the windows needed washing, too. She smirked at him, showing her disapproval.

Old people can be so critical, he thought. They expect everyone to be just like they are.

He watched them return to their car and then drive down to the room. Erna took two small suitcases out of the trunk of her car and then opened the door of the unit. She entered and her mother followed very tentatively. He expected them to come charging out, the old lady complaining about cobwebs or something, but they didn't.

"That's good," he muttered. And then, suddenly, he had an epiphany, an incredibly explosive and wonderful revelation.

That woman was choice. She had a virginal aura about her. Everything in her was fresh and high quality. He could mine her, draw everything he needed, and she had come to him!

In fact, he thought, gazing around, this is what I was thinking of, the fish bowl, my feeding ground. They'll come here. I'll have something in every room. I'll never be without.

He rubbed his hands together. He no longer wanted to jog. The struggle with the motel owner had taken too much of his energy. That troubled him for a few moments. He wasn't usually this tired this fast after something physical.

But he rejected all negative and troubling thoughts in light of the good luck he had somehow stumbled upon here. I'll grow very strong and then, when I'm ready, I'll go on.

And on.

And on, forever. . . .

He returned to the living room to thank the corpse.

In a real sense, he should thank all the corpses that trailed behind him.

It amused him.

I'll send thank-you cards to cemeteries, he thought, and laughing, felt more like his old self.

Whoever and whatever that was.

SEVENTEEN

"I need your help," he began. "Don't panic. Please."

During the few moments that had passed between her realizing who he was and the moment he began to speak, a parade of deficiency diseases and illnesses marched through her mind. The three young women she had seen degenerate right before her eyes were sharing the Grand Marshal position, waving their dead hands in warning.

"Who are you?" she asked.

"You knew I wasn't really a state detective when I met you at the hospital the other day, right? I sensed that, but I was hoping you would be cooperative anyway.

"I'm not picking on you, Doctor. I had to visit you after the first death to be certain I was on the right track, that the M.O. fit, and I had to see just how much you really knew and understood.

"I'm sorry about frightening you before, and I'm sorry about your fiancé, but I don't have much time to waste, and now that the rather good rendition of his face and mine is on the front page of the newspaper and undoubtedly being broadcast periodically on television stations, there is even more urgency. He'll become more dangerous, more like a cornered rat.

"He's very smart, very intelligent, and he will find a way to avoid detection. He will go on and he will, as I fear he has already, find new victims at a geometric level of activity. He's obviously growing more desperate. Something is happening to him. He might die or he might kill at a rate that will create panic in the streets . . . literally," he concluded and turned down a side road that degenerated into a gravel one.

He stopped the car and turned off the engine.

"Where is the policeman who was with me?" she asked.

"He's in the trunk," he replied. "Don't worry. He's still alive, only sedated."

She reached back, behind herself to fumble for the door knob.

"Don't," he said quickly realizing what she was doing. "Where are you going to run to anyway? And don't you think I could catch you? Settle down, Dr. Barnard. You are a very intelligent young woman, my best hope so far. I need to know what you do know, what that second victim told you before she expired. I need to know his whereabouts or anything that might lead me to him. I need to find him before anyone else does and I need to destroy him before anyone discovers what he is," he continued.

"What are you telling me?" Terri asked realizing what he had said about the picture on the front pages of the newspaper. "That he's your twin brother?"

"Not in the traditional sense, no," he replied. "And I'm not a schizophrenic. I assure you. He is a separate entity. I'll tell you what I can, if you tell me everything you know about him. I'm sure he's said something I can use. He's very arrogant. He would not hesitate to tell one of his victims things about himself so he most probably revealed important information to the woman you began to examine.

"He has anticipated my every move so far and is always a step or two ahead of me. Part of his brilliance, you see. He possesses qualities we cannot fathom."

"How do you know so much about him?" she asked. She had found the door knob, but she was drawn to remain both out of curiosity and fear he was right—she would not be able to get away.

"I created him," he replied. "I'm Dr. Garret Stanley. I work for a research corporation that is hidden within layers and layers of legal detours, so sophisticated even the CIA would have trouble getting to the heart of it." He smiled. "There's that arrogance showing, I'm afraid. He shares my best and worst qualities."

She narrowed her eyes.

"Are you telling me . . . are you saying, he's a clone of you?"

"Precisely," he replied. He put up his hands. "I know, I know. Cloning human beings has been outlawed by our government, but believe me, there are people in our government who are not only aware of my work, they find ways to support it."

"How do I know you are not simply a madman, a schizophrenic?"

"If I were, I would have killed you by now," he said, "especially if you consider how quickly he's accumulating new victims."

"Why is he doing that?"

"What can you tell me, Doctor?" he asked instead of replying.

"I wasn't lying to you. That young woman I examined, Kristin Martin, was unable to speak intelligibly. She went into cardiac arrest almost immediately. She mouthed something that sounded like he, and that's it."

"He?"

"I think she was trying to tell me her situation wasn't caused by any allergy or the like. He . . . whoever he is . . . caused it, but how, why?" she asked.

He looked pensive.

"Maybe she was trying to tell me her grandmother was in danger. The tourist house they owned burned down and she died in the fire. That's all I can tell you. That's it."

His face grew gray with disappointment, but she also recognized a fury in those penetrating eyes. Despite what he was telling her, was he really a schizophrenic? He looks capable of violent rage, she thought.

"The FBI is here," she said, making it sound like a warning.

"I would expect so. They were in Pennsylvania, too.

There were only two killings in the whole state, so you see what I mean. He's already killed three here in this New York county and by now, I fear a fourth and maybe even a fifth. Whoever dies after today might very well be on your conscience, Doctor."

"They might have his fingerprints on a glass," she warned. "Which, if you're telling me the truth, would be your fingerprints too," she said, still hoping to make him back off.

He smiled.

"Fingerprints from what? The bar at that tavern? Well? Are you saying the bartender didn't wash the glasses before she left for the night? Well?"

She sucked in her breath. Of course he would know about the story in the papers.

"You were there already?"

"No. Forensic evidence is a waste of time. Forget about that. What else were you told about the events at the tavern?"

"Nothing. I'm not part of a police team. I'm just . . ."

He shook his head.

"Doctor, you're wasting precious time. There is a significant witness you're protecting." He smiled. "This drawing in the paper wasn't done only from your description of me in the office. I know he spent significant time with that bartender and I know her name, Darlene Stone. She knows more than she has told the police at this point. I'm sure of that. They're incompetent, especially when it comes to something like this. Only I can find him."

She was afraid to say another word. Stall him, she thought.

"I don't understand how he causes deaths through vitamin deficiencies," she said. And then she added, "I don't trust you, trust what you're telling me."

He looked away, took a deep breath, and looked back at her.

"Okay," he said, "this is what happened."

Despite how drawn she was to what he was saying, as he spoke it occurred to her that if he was telling the truth, if he was this research scientist and if he did indeed work for a powerful, clandestine corporation, she would now be in a different sort of danger, but one perhaps just as potentially fatal.

"I'm sure you know that toward the end of the twentieth century, there were basically three types of cloning: embryo cloning in which one or more cells are removed from a fertilized embryo and encouraged to develop into one or more duplicate embryos; adult DNA cloning, cell nuclear replacement producing a duplicate of an existing animal; and therapeutic cloning in which the stem cells are removed from the embryo with the intent of producing tissue or a whole organ for transplant.

"My work centers around adult DNA cloning, but the production of an identical twin without the use of sperm, although successful, had one drawback: time. It took too much time before the twin would develop into a mature adult, capable of utilizing all the talents and knowledge of its host. By the time it reached that capacity, what it knew could not only be obsolete, but what is more important, not further developed, not benefiting from that time, understand? I mean, reproducing Einstein at the point when he made his important discoveries, but having that reproduction spend years to get to that point, makes no sense. What I have been working on is speeding up the growth, accelerating the development of the duplicate.

"Of course, none of this is perfected and in the process of my experimentation, I did succeed in creating a duplication of myself and bring its development to approximately my age in a matter of months, but an unusual disorder developed almost immediately: my second self, as I like to refer to him, was unable to store most necessary vitamins and minerals. They are passed through his digestive tract and not broken down and carried by the blood, and so I had to put him on an intense vitamin and mineral therapy program to keep him alive while I tried to determine what exactly was malformed.

"One of our assistants basically screwed up and missed a treatment and that was, unfortunately, when we discovered a second unusual disorder, a true threat to others. My research partner was killed. Like a bee drawing pollen from a flower, my second self appears to have the ability to draw what he needs at the moment from another human source, mine it, so to speak, vacuum the blood. I'm not absolutely sure of how he processes the material, but it bypasses the digestive breakdown somehow and provides what he needs. In a true sense of the word, I have inadvertently created a monstrous parasite, but a parasite, however, that also possesses a high degree of intelligence, charm, wit, in short, *moi*, yours truly. That's why I know he's arrogant," Garret Stanley said.

Terri continued to stare at him.

"Don't tell me you are one of those who have some religious objection to human cloning, one who believes there will be no soul in the new individual if he or she is created without the use of sperm?" Garret asked with some disdain.

"No, I'm not, but what I am is one of those who believes in strict observance of research guidelines to prevent exactly what you've done," she replied.

"If we followed the guidelines, as you call them, we wouldn't be doing this at all and the human race would lose a golden opportunity to end disease and aging. As far as our puritanical and fundamentalist religious influences go, all they have done is permitted groups in other countries to move ahead of us. Including the Raelians. You have heard of them, I assume?"

Terri shook her head.

"They are a religious sect that believes, among other things, that human beings were created in laboratories by extraterrestrials, and that the resurrection of Jesus was a cloning procedure. You would be shocked to know who belongs to the sect and how much money they have already invested in their research. Recently, I saw a list of women, surrogate mothers, who have paid close to a half million dollars to be part of their experiments.

"No, Dr. Barnard, I am not some mad scientist running amok, but they are out there who are mad and they are working. I am, in fact, our best hope to seize the initiative and capture the patents and processes which will one day recreate the world, vastly improve on the current model, so to speak, for in my world, you will see no human misery, no starvation, and every beautiful thing, every wonderful talent will be truly immortalized, so don't try to make me feel in the least bit guilty about all this."

"Is that what you will tell the parents of Paige Thorndyke, the families of Kristin Martin and Paula Gilbert, not to mention all the others he's destroyed on his way here?"

"Every great stride in history, in progress came at some cost," Garret said. "I regret what he's done of course, and that's why I'm pleading with you to help me find him so we can stop it."

"You just don't want anyone to know what you've created and what responsibility you bear," she told him, her eyes narrow and steely.

"All right. Let's say that's my motive. The result will

be the same, won't it? He'll be brought to an end before he does any more damage. For Christ sakes, woman, you're a doctor. You're supposed to care about people."

She turned away from him.

"I don't know that much. I'm not holding back," she said after a moment. "I told you exactly what Kristin Martin was unable to say. The bartender at the Hasbrouck Tavern was able to give the police a more detailed description. That's all I know," she practically spit at him.

"Putting that picture in the paper was a big mistake. It will drive him off. He might be gone already and I won't know where to go until he takes another victim."

"How do you find out so quickly?" she asked.

He looked at her.

"That's not important. We've got to go see this bartender. I told you. The police won't know what else to ask her, what to look for," he said.

"If you try to speak with her, she will think you're him, it, whatever," Terri pointed out.

"That's right." He smiled. "That's why I need your help. And don't ask me something stupid like why don't I just go to the police. You know the reason why I can't do that. Will you help me or won't you?"

Terri looked at her watch.

"I'm already seriously late for my office visits thanks to you."

"You'll find a way to explain it. Look, surely you realize this is more important than treating some flu and arthritis problems."

She sat thinking a moment.

"When are you going to let that policeman out of the trunk?" she asked.

"We'll go back, get your car, and let him wake up in his uniform," he promised.

"Get me back to my car," she said. "I need to use my phone."

He studied her face.

"If you betray me, I'll disappear and believe me, no one will believe a word you say and no one will be able to track me down or my work. All you do is permit him to take more lives. You'll attend more funerals."

"All right," she said. "I said I would help you. I'll help you. Drive."

He started the engine and turned the car around.

"Someone who has decided to devote her life to medicine, to helping people, shouldn't be so unsympathetic," he muttered.

"Oh, I'm sure you have only altruistic motives for your research, Dr. Stanley," she replied dryly.

"If in the end the result is we benefit mankind, what difference will that make?" he fired back. "Yes, I have to compromise to get the necessary funding and protection, and I have to promise great profits to these people, but it would be naive to think that hasn't been the story since the first cave man corporation invested in a new and better wheel.

"You more than anyone know how opportunistic and profit-driven our best pharmaceutical companies are, and last I heard, doctors don't take jars of peaches for their services any longer."

"Whatever," she said. "The time for philosophical debating is long over apparently."

"Precisely," he said.

Hyman got on the phone himself when she called in from her car. While she spoke, Garret Stanley went behind the building to free the patrolman. When he returned, the policeman was dozing in the front seat and back in his uniform. Garret was back in his own clothes as well.

"I'm sorry, Hyman," she told him, "but it's not something I can prevent."

"What are you doing, Terri?"

"I don't have time to explain it all, Hyman, and frankly, I don't know if I can. I'll call you as soon as I am able to do so," she said. "I promise and I'm sorry, really. You'll just have to trust me."

"All right. I'll cover for you here, but please, please be careful."

Garret Stanley brought his vehicle next to hers. When she hesitated, he turned his hands palms up and nodded at the police car.

She got out and into his car.

"Do people at this tavern know who you are?" he asked.

"They might."

"I thought so. That will help enormously," he said and she drove out of the hospital parking lot, looking back once in a rearview mirror toward Curt's floor, imagining to herself just how wild he would become if he had even an inkling of what she was doing.

He was able to remember a time when anticipation was a sweet thing. It was almost as if a bell went off inside him then and a clock began ticking. As vague as time was, he realized that it wasn't very long ago when it was always that way. There was a signal to go hunting, but without the intensified urgency he now experienced. Or should he say, suffered, because he didn't enjoy it, not at all. He felt like an addict in withdrawal, writhing in agony, ready to claw up the walls in fact.

Something within him was clawing up his walls now. In his imagination, he saw an ugly, rodent with sharp talons stripping away his flesh, leaping from side to side and crying with a piercing shrill metallic sound that reverberated through his bones and into his head. He actually put his hands over his ears and pressed as hard as he could to stop it. That didn't work. Only one thing would work.

Every living thing enjoyed some pleasure when it fed as long as it wasn't in the midst of starvation where gorging of food and nutrition took place. Once, he had participated in a sweet sexual fine dining. Now, he was like a ravaging beast who would eat away its own body.

He blamed it all on the amount of energy he had expended killing the ugly motel owner. The intensity of that struggle drained him of more than he had imagined. That realization added anger to lust and he returned to the corpse to deliver a revengeful kick at the dead man's jaw. It looked as if it cracked. Of course, that wasn't enough to satisfy him. He had to go elsewhere for what he really needed.

He went back out front and gazed at the motel units. The plain-looking woman and her mother had not emerged from their room yet. They were still resting before dinner. Well that was a pleasure he couldn't have. He couldn't rest before his dinner. He envied them for their calmness, their toleration. To be able to sleep and put off feeding was a wonderful thing. His envy quickly turned into resentment. Why should they have this power, for that was what it really was: a power?

The most skillful and effective hunters were the ones that had the strength to restrain themselves, to take their time, to study and wait and pounce when it was most advantageous to do so. Look how tigers and lions, even household cats, quietly stalked their prey, every part of them poised and strung, their bodies loaded and ready to fire, but their power to restrain keeping them from pulling their own triggers.

It frightened him to realize he was losing that. For the first time since he had escaped, he was afraid, and not of something out there, something hunting him. No, he was afraid of himself, of betraying himself, of making serious mistakes. He wanted to take time to think and plan and do this with intelligence, but that damn beast inside him wouldn't give him a moment of quiet.

He nearly ripped the motel office door off its hinges when he opened it and stepped out. Fall evenings fell faster. They were into daylight saving time. Stars had already appeared to put periods on every sentence of daylight left. Nocturnal creatures were stirring. Birds stopped their aerial gymnastics and went wherever birds went when the sun dipped below the horizon. The lights of the motel, on a sensor, began to flicker and go on. He could feel all living things turning, some on their backs, some on their stomachs. The prey of night predators scurried for cover. Little hearts pounded. Fear, like some thick syrup, began to flow in alongside the shadows that crept over the highway, under trees, and around the motel structure itself.

As Shakespeare had written, *Graveyards yawned.*

He was ready.

Whether he liked it or not, he was ready.

Full of resolve, he started toward the unit, the little beast within him at least pausing with that damnable anticipation.

• • •

Erna Walker awoke from her nap and was up. She went to the bathroom and debated taking a quick, hot shower. The unit was adequate, but far from the quality of bedding and furniture she and her mother were accustomed to enjoying. In fact, it took a great deal of consoling and extra effort to get her mother to calm down and take a nap once she was confronted with this room. Erna had to take off the faded pillow case on her mother's bed and wrap one of her clean white blouses around it. Her mother refused to undress.

"I don't want these dirty sheets and this dirty blanket touching my skin," she said. "Look at the grime around the baseboards and on the windowsills. Was this room ever cleaned? And that bathroom, Erna. . . . I'm sorry I have to pee. Uggh," she said shaking herself as if merely talking about it all gave her a terrific chill.

The room reeked of cigarette smoke, too. It was embedded in the walls and the faded, worn carpet. She chided herself for not continuing on until they had come upon a more well-known motel chain, but she had taken a wrong turn here and a wrong road there, and she was very lost. She should never have listened to that gas station attendant who had assured her the detours and shortcut would save them hours and hours. Not wanting to let her mother know just how lost they were, she had thought it better to pull into a place for the night, rest, and have a good dinner. In the morning the world would look brighter and they would both have renewed energy.

Her mother carried on so much about the poor quality and the lack of cleanliness of this unit that Erna did some of the same things: wrap a blouse around her pillow and sleep in her bra, panties, and nightgown. She had managed to get some good rest, however, and now concluded that a quick, hot shower would probably restore her spirits even more. Mom was still fast asleep. Why not do it?

The unit didn't have a separate shower stall. She had to manipulate the faucet on the tub to get the water to come out of the shower head. The pipes groaned and then the water began to trickle out faster and faster. It took a while to get it warm enough, however.

After it was, she undressed and stepped gingerly into the yellow stained tub, shivering, but finally enjoying the warm water over her shoulders, down her back, and then over her breasts and stomach. She used her own soap. Mother wouldn't travel without her own soaps and shampoos, and for once, Erna thought she had been right about that sort of detail.

She wasn't under the shower long, but it was enough to satisfy her. Stepping out carefully, she reached for the bath towel. It smelled as if it had been hanging on the rack for months, but she was soaked and had no choice. After she dried herself, she thought she would need another shower as soon as possible but in a cleaner motel or hotel.

Just as she reached for her panties, the bathroom door

opened. Expecting her mother, of course, she turned slowly and confronted the motel manager, naked, his penis erect, pointing up at her like a purple finger of accusation. The sight was so startling and shocking, she couldn't manage a sound. Her throat closed, and then a sort of croaking finally emerged.

He put his right forefinger up.

"Don't scream or I'll go out there and smother your mother to death," he threatened.

She was frozen. Neither of her arms would move.

"Down," he said pointing at the floor. "Down," he repeated.

He seemed to rise above her, to expand and grow wider every moment.

She whimpered like a terrified puppy and did as he ordered, folding her legs and sitting on the cold, cracked white tile. Then he walked around behind her and knelt. She had the towel pressed against her breasts, her hands clenched so tightly, she could feel her fingernails cutting into her palms, even through the towel.

He brought his arms around her and took hold of her wrists, pulling her arms down. She started to resist and he said, "I will. I'll smother her."

She relaxed her forearms and her arms were straightened. Immediately, he cupped her breasts and pulled her back against him. She heard him breathe deeply, suck in air through her hair, his mouth on her head now. In small increments, he lowered her farther and farther until she was on her back between his legs and looking up at that pulsating penis. She closed her eyes.

He seemed to whimper himself, but more like something that had been overwhelmed with its good fortune. She felt him move over her, turn, and then lift her legs. She didn't want to open her eyes. She wanted to keep them shut the whole time and will this not to be happening. She thought if she looked at him, if she captured an image, it would haunt her forever. Perhaps if she kept still, kept herself apart from all this, it wouldn't become a redundant nightmare and it wouldn't destroy her.

He entered her in one swift, driving motion and for a long moment, he didn't move. She even hoped that was all he wanted to do and now he would withdraw and go, but suddenly she felt herself being drawn to her own sex, being pulled down as if she were going to be absorbed into his penis and be gone. It was a terrifying, unexpected, and unnatural feeling, not anything like she had ever been able to envision, nor anything like she had read. All of the pains and feelings common to mankind were registered somewhere in her brain. She knew what it was like to be stuck with a pin, cut, bruised, punched, kicked, scraped, chaffed, all of it, but this came from a place beyond human experience. That was her only thought, because soon after, she felt herself falling and spiraling downward into a darkness that was again unlike any she had known. She made a small, ineffective effort to extricate herself, and then she surrendered quietly to her own inevitable death.

On the way out, he paused at the old lady's bedside. She groaned and turned with discomfort. When she opened her eyes, she saw him standing there, but he was like a vague, gray shadow. It confused her and she scrubbed her cheeks with her hands for a few moments. He hadn't moved.

"What is it?" she cried.

"Something is wrong with your pillow," he said. "It's alive. There's something inside it, some creature or creatures inside it."

She couldn't move.

This dirty pillow?

He reached down and pulled it slowly out from under her head. She started to call for Erna when he flipped the pillow in his hands and put it over her face. Unlike the Martin lady, she didn't struggle as much as she flailed about and he didn't toy with her as he had with the tourist house owner. He had no reason to and no patience for it. This old lady died quickly, and then he threw the pillow aside and walked out, closing the unit door behind him.

He felt okay, but not as perfect as he was accustomed to feeling after a feed. It bothered him and it angered him. This wasn't going right. Something was wrong. It wasn't fair. He walked back to the motel office and paced for a while. He wasn't even hungry and he knew he should be that. His juices should be flowing.

I'm dying, he suddenly thought. I need something more. I need it now.

I'm out of control.

And for the first time that he could ever remember, he was in as much panic as all of his victims had been.

The crowd at the Old Hasbrouck Inn usually began to build by late afternoon as it was. Paula Gilbert's horrible death stirred far more interest in the tavern than usual, however, so by the time Terri and Dr. Garret Stanley turned into the lot for the restaurant, the bar was full and there were a half dozen tables already occupied. Darlene was working as hard as she did on a weekend night and she was very annoyed about it.

When he saw the number of cars there, Garret Stanley drove around the building and parked in the rear.

"You'd better go in there and bring her out here," he told Terri.

"And how am I supposed to do that?"

He reached into his pocket and peeled seven one-hundred dollar bills off his fold.

"Offer her this. I'm sure it's more than she's making weekly in there. Tell her I'm a private detective. Tell her anything," he said sternly, "but get her out here."

Terri hesitated a moment. His penchant for rage rang an alarm bell in her mind. He saw it and softened his expression.

"Look," he said. "Be logical, Doctor. This is why I've bothered with you in the first place. If I walk in there, people who might have seen that picture in the paper will think it's me and create a scene even before I get to speak with the bartender. Naturally, she's going to wonder why I don't come in with you. This just helps alleviate those concerns," he said waving the bills. "Money is and always will be the great convincer."

Slowly, she took the bills from him.

"I don't want to frighten her," she said.

"After she's out here, just leave it all to me," he added. "I don't want to frighten her either. If I do, she won't be of any value to us, now will she? We're running out of time," he added, directing himself to her hesitation.

She looked at him, opened the door, and got out. He reached over to keep her from closing it and looked out at her.

"Remember, Doctor, there are innocent lives at stake, deaths we can prevent," he warned.

She nodded and turned to the rear door of the tavern. As she walked toward it, she debated. She could call Will Dennis. She could have policemen around this place in minutes, but what would that accomplish? Even Will said he would have little or no chance of convicting the man of anything more serious than impersonating a policeman, while, if this story were true, the real killer would be out there raging on, each death her responsibility.

On the other hand, she still had this instinctive feeling that Garret Stanley wasn't exactly all he claimed to be. This was the man who had attacked Curt, after all, and had incapacitated a policeman. How far would he go?

The conversations in the tavern were so loud and spirited that the music of the jukebox was nearly inaudible. Seconds after she had entered, however, many people stopped talking, looked her way, and then began again with even more energy and interest. Griffy, who recognized her first, left the two men he was talking with and approached her quickly.

"Dr. Barnard, right?"

"Yes."

"Well, what brings you here? I hope it wasn't someone complaining about our food," he added smiling.

"No," she said. "I need to talk to your bartender, Darlene."

"Oh. Well, sure," he said after a moment. "C'mon."

He escorted her to the bar where Darlene waited, curious, leaning back against the corner, her arms folded under her breasts.

"You know Dr. Barnard?" Griffy asked her.

She shook her head.

"No, but I've heard of her," Darlene replied, her eyes still on Terri.

"She wants to talk to you. Go on. I'll cover for you," he said and went around to serve the customers.

Terri looked at the two men sitting on her right, both watching and waiting. Darlene noticed her concern and moved through the opening.

"What do you want?" she asked immediately.

"Can we go out through the back?"

"Why?"

"I need you to speak with someone," Terri told her.

"Who? A cop?"

"Not exactly."

"What is this?" Darlene asked, obviously nervous and disturbed with the request.

"There's a man outside who is investigating not only what happened to Paula Gilbert, but others. He is not with the police, but he represents people who are so interested, I was told to give you this if you will speak with him," she added, turned so her body would block it and showed Darlene the bills. Darlene's eyes widened as she counted.

"Seven hundred dollars? Just to talk to him?"

Terri nodded.

"Why didn't he come in?"

"You'll understand when you see him," Terri said. She hated to add it, but she did, "Trust me."

Darlene glanced at the men trying to hear and to see what was happening and then shrugged.

"If you can't trust a doctor, who the hell can you trust?" Darlene asked, took the money quickly, and started for the rear of the tavern. Conversations stopped again and heads turned in their direction until they went in through the kitchen doors.

Dorothy looked up from the skillet as they began to pass through.

"What's going on?" she asked.

"I have to speak to someone. Griffy's covering the bar for me," she told her quickly.

Terri just nodded at her. As soon as she recognized her, Dorothy's face blossomed with surprise, but before she could say anything else, Terri and Darlene walked out.

"Over there," Terri nodded toward the car.

Garret Stanley kept his face turned away as they approached. Darlene's steps grew slower, more cautious. She glanced at Terri who didn't look all that comfortable herself.

"Who is this guy?" Darlene muttered.

Before Terri could provide any additional information, Garret opened the car door and stepped out. Darlene gasped the moment she set eyes on him.

And so did Terri.

He had her police escort's .38 in his hand and he was pointing at the both of them.

"Get in behind the wheel, Doc," he said. "You," he told Darlene, "get in the back."

"What is this? What are you doing with him? This is the man. I thought you were a doctor," she told Terri.

"She is," Garret said. "So am I. Move," he ordered.

"This wasn't what you told me you would do," Terri protested.

"Don't make me do something else I didn't tell you I would do," he replied and pulled the hammer back on the pistol, keeping it fixed on Darlene.

Terri looked back at the restaurant's rear door. There was no one around and it was too far to run back to it. With all the noise within, any shouts for help would not be heard. She nodded at Darlene.

"I'm sorry. You had better do what he says," Terri told her. Darlene looked at the gun. Garret Stanley held the rear door open for her and Darlene slipped into the back. He followed.

"What now?" Terri asked.

"Just drive away," he told her. "Slowly," he emphasized and turned to Darlene Stone.

EIGHTEEN

He sat in the motel owner's chair and stared at the front door. When he saw himself reflected in the window of the door, he saw he was pouting. Nothing that he had done over the past twenty-four hours had pleased him. This was a totally new and unexpected feeling. In his mind he was really born the day he had escaped, whenever that was. Time itself was so confusing a concept. It made even his recent history vague, especially now with all these memory lapses. How long had he been happy, successful, traveling like a smooth rocket through space? Was he ever this unhappy and was it that he simply could not remember it?

Sitting there and struggling to understand made him more irritable than ever and it frustrated him that he had no one in particular to blame for his depression and dissatisfaction. Other people at least had parents to blame. Who were his parents? Obscure faces floated through his mind, wispy, faces of smoke, holding shape for a moment or two and then dissipating and disappearing somewhere in the darkness that clouded his thinking. There were bits of music, occasional voices, clips of sentences, words, all of the sounds coming at him over a continually inter-rupted transmission from a station so deep down in his memory, he could barely hear anything.

Not knowing who he was and from where he had come never bothered him as intensely at it bothered him at this moment. Surely it had something to do with his new physical problems. Whatever. Even that malformed, ugly creature he had stomped out back there had a his-tory, had pictures and memories to cherish. Where did he leave his pictures, his memories?

Someone had stolen all that from him, he thought. Someone had done something terrible to him and he didn't even remember it being done. What was most frightening was he couldn't recall who had done it, and that meant he might very well confront this person and not know he was his mortal enemy.

Therefore, everyone must be thought to be his mortal enemy, he concluded. He would trust no one, not that he ever put much trust in anyone he could recall, but especially now he would invest not even an iota of faith in anyone's words. He decided he was out in the world like Cain or like Judas. Once anyone discovered who he was, they would despise him.

He hated being this analytical, this philosophical about himself, and especially this paranoid. It had been so easy, so enjoyable just taking things as they were, glid-ing along, tasting, touching, never having a single responsibility, and concerned only with his own pleasure and well-being. Who needed anything else, especially all this deep thought? The more intelligent you were, the more unhappy you are, he concluded. Pity the ant who suddenly realizes how small and vulnerable he is among the moving humans around him. Be oblivious to your own mortality and weakness and you will never be unhappy, he told himself.

The headlights of an approaching vehicle swept over the office walls and ripped him out of his musing. He was grateful for that and sat up quickly to watch as a slightly built, dark-haired man with glasses emerged from the car that had just pulled up in front of the motel office. When the door opened, he could see the woman in the passenger's seat. She didn't look very happy.

"Evening," the man said after entering. "I think we've gone off the beaten track, so to speak. How far is it to Kingston?"

"Kingston," he repeated. "That's a good eighty miles," he said, even though he wasn't sure. From his understanding of the area, it seemed reasonable, however. At least he would appear to know what he should know.

"Eighty? Wow." The man scratched the back of his head and then looked toward his car and his wife. "She's not going to be happy about that. We've been driving all day. You have any availability?"

He really wasn't in the mood for anyone, but he also realized he had to keep up the charade of being the motel owner so he wouldn't cause any undue interest and attention. He didn't have time to think about any of that. He had to work on where he was going, when, and how. He had to free his mind of everything else so the messages would come, as they always had before, the sense of direction, the new target, so to speak. He had to be receptive, and as long as he permitted all this static in his head, it wouldn't happen.

"Yeah, sure," he said quickly and got up. He scooped a set of keys off the rack. "Ten will be fine for you," he added handing the man the keys.

The man stood there looking at them and smiling dumbly.

What am I doing wrong? he wondered. What have I left out?

"Well, don't I have to sign in first?" the man asked.

"Sure, sign in," he said and turned the book toward him.

The man still stared at him, a confused smile on his face.

"How much is the room?" he asked.

"Thirty-eight fifty," he said. "All the rooms are thirty-eight fifty."

"Oh." He looked out at his wife again. "She gets annoyed when we don't stay at places that advertise on TV."

He started to take the key back. Maybe the man wanted to go. Good. Go, he thought. I have to have peace and quiet so I can hear the voices.

"But I'll tell her that we've gone far enough," the man suddenly decided and reached for the keys.

"Suit yourself," he told him and gave him the keys.

The man took them and then signed the book. He reached into his jacket to produce his wallet and slip out the credit card.

It put him in a small panic. He had to process that. Where was the credit card device?

The man watched as he searched.

"Everything all right?"

"Yeah, yeah, my brother puts things where I can't find them," he replied.

"Oh." The man smiled with relief as if he had a brother who was always doing something similar to him as well.

"Here it is," he announced and produced the device. He took the man's card and slapped it on. Then he wrote in the amount and gave the receipt to the man to sign, which he did quickly and handed it back.

After he ripped off the customer copy, he handed it to him.

"Oh, my card," the man said.

"What? Right, Mr. Samuels," he said reading off the card before he gave him that too.

"So I suppose there's a good place for us to have some dinner nearby?"

"Yeah, sure," he said.

"Any recommendations?"

"No, they're all about the same," he told him. "Just go east."

Charles Samuels stared at him with some surprise and then nodded and smiled. He started out and stopped.

"Any of those advertisements, pamphlets about the area, something that would describe the nearby restaurants?" Charles asked. "My wife is very particular about what she eats. Is the place clean? That sort of thing, you know."

He shifted his gaze and searched the lobby. There wasn't anything.

"No, I'm sorry."

"Maybe the phone book in the room then, or a newspaper. Thanks," Charles Samuels said and hurried out to the car. For a few moments, he sat there talking to his wife.

He could see Samuels raising and lowering his arms and shaking his head. Finally, he started his engine and drove slowly toward the units, pulling in at Unit 10. He could see the woman getting out slowly, reluctantly. In the dim light of the motel walkway, he could see she was wide in the hips and had her hair cut short, almost shorter than her husband's. She walked like someone pouting would walk, refusing to take anything out of the car. Charles Samuels opened their trunk and brought out two bags. She stood by the door, facing it like a woman on death row. Samuels fumbled with the key. She offered no assistance. Finally, he opened the door and they disappeared within.

He sat back, hoping he wouldn't have any hunger

tonight, or if he did, hoping he could find someone better than a woman like that from whom to draw what he needed. He was tired, and being tired this early in the evening was not something he was accustomed to experiencing. Rising with concern, he went into the bathroom and looked at his face. He didn't have as healthy a complexion, he decided. The fatigue he felt was showing itself in his eyes and the deepened lines in his face. This wasn't good. This wasn't good at all, he thought. He had just fed, just renewed his bodily needs. Why was he still tired?

He went back to the lobby and sat thinking again. It wasn't until he heard a noise, the sound of a car door opening and closing, that he opened them just in time to see Charles Samuels and his wife. Samuels had returned to the office, apparently to get a newspaper to read the advertisements for a restaurant and then drove away.

He closed his eyes again. He was so sleepy, and this was so unusual.

Maybe he would have to visit Unit 10 later, he reluctantly thought. He would wait for them to return. At least, he should be grateful it was all still coming to him, all still easy to acquire. Get rest. Get strong, he told himself and permitted himself to doze.

"Go on," Garret Stanley ordered Darlene Stone. He waved the pistol at her as well.

He had forced Terri to drive them toward Neversink and then pull into a side road that had once been the driveway for a moderate size tourist house, now deserted and left with a foreclosure poster on its front door. The poster was faded enough to suggest it had been closed down for some time. Windows were broken, shutters hung on a single hinge, grass and weeds grew wildly around the chipped and cracked cement front steps. The bannister was broken on the left side and had fallen to the ground.

"He said he was staying at a small tourist house and the old lady who ran it told him about the tavern," Darlene continued.

"Did he mention the Martins?" Terri interjected.

She shook her head.

"He didn't mention a name, just that."

"That's how he came to Kristin Martin," she muttered, "and the fire. . . ." She looked at Garret. "He probably set that. He must have harmed the old lady too and was just covering his tracks."

Darlene's eyes brightened even more with fear as she looked from Terri to Garret Stanley and then back to Terri, who could see the confusion in the woman's face. Was Terri a conspirator or what?

"You didn't have to pull a gun on her to get her to tell you all that, Dr. Stanley," she chastised.

Doctor? He was a doctor, too, Darlene thought. What was going on?

"You're talking too much," he told Terri.

Terri tried staring him down, but out of the corner of her eye, she saw that Darlene Stone was losing it fast.

"Just finish and let me take her back," she said.

He turned to Darlene.

"You spoke with this Paula Gilbert, didn't you? I mean afterward, when she was found in the parking lot."

She looked at Terri and Terri saw that her eyes were full of questions, the first one being, how did he know?

"Yes," she said nodding. "For just a few minutes."

"I want to hear every word she said. Talk!" he ordered.

"I told it all to the police."

"Tell it again," he said waving the pistol.

She gasped and continued.

"She said he hurt her while they made love. She said it felt like he was sucking out her blood. When he was finished with her, he left her naked in the rear and drove back to the restaurant. She said he was very happy, singing. She thought it was all just a nightmare because she was going in and out of consciousness. She remembered waking up when he was transferring her back to her own car. He told her she should go home now, that he was going home now."

"Going home now?"

"Yes."

"What did he say about that? What did he say about home?"

Darlene shook her head.

"That's all I remember she said."

"You're lying," he said after a moment. "Someone told you not to say anything else, anything about home, right?"

"No," she said shaking her head. "No one."

He sat back and thought a moment.

"Does that mean he's going back to where he was created?" Terri asked.

Garret looked at her sharply.

"I told you you were talking too much."

"Created?" Darlene couldn't help saying. "Who are you? Aren't we talking about you?" she asked after a surge of some courage.

Garret nodded at Terri.

"Satisfied now, Doctor?" He looked down and thought aloud. "He was definitely replenished. It's just not lasting as long. Arrogant. . . ."

"If he is as intelligent as you claim he is," Terri asked, "why doesn't he try to hide his victim? Why bring her back to her car? Why leave Kristin in her car?"

He looked up at her and then at Darlene.

"She just told you."

"She just told me? I don't understand."

"He wants to go home. Don't you see? Home? I'm his home. He's deliberately leaving a trail for me now. Maybe he doesn't even realize it himself. It's part of the great mystery here," he said, his eyes lighting with excitement. "Cellular affinity, I'd call it, a driving, almost primeval need to reunite. Maybe," he added smiling, "that's the soul the critics are so worried we would eliminate. Very complicated, but very fascinating, wouldn't you agree, Doctor?"

"No," she said. "I'm not fascinated. I'm more disgusted."

"That's disappointing, Doctor, tragically disappointing."

"What is this all about?" Darlene Stone demanded. Her confusion and fear had merged and become frustration and indignation.

Garret smiled at her. The coldness and calmness in the man's eyes splintered her wall of bravado. She wrapped her arms about herself protectively, looking like she wished she could shrink and disappear.

"What's it all about? Just everything—life, health, immortality, God, man, you name it. In the end I suppose it's about power. Everything eventually is," he said a little sadly.

His cell phone rang, shattering the deep silence that had followed his words.

"Excuse me," he said and took it out of his inside pocket. He snapped it open and said, "Yes?"

Terri looked at Darlene and gave her what she thought was her best look of assurance, urging her to remain calm. Darlene squirmed and bit down on her lower lip. Terri could see she was tottering on the verge of hysteria.

"When was this?" he asked whoever called. "Okay. Just give it to me. You nearly messed this up. I'll handle it from here," Garret said into his phone. He listened and then just closed the phone. "So," he said gesturing at the degenerating tourist house. "Another monument to a bygone era, eh?"

"Can I drive back to the tavern now?" Terri asked him. "We've kept her from work long enough, don't you think?"

"Not just yet. There's more to discuss."

"What? She's obviously told you everything she knows."

"Oh, people don't realize what they do and don't know," he said smiling. "Let's change the setting. Maybe that will stimulate the memory. Get out," he ordered. "Both of you."

"Why?" Terri demanded without moving.

"We never stop asking that. Do you realize that, Doctor?" Garret asked her. "When we're very little, we're always coming at our parents with why this, why that? Why, why, why? Some parents get to hate it. Some think it's cute for a while and then get tired of it and before we know it, we have to go elsewhere for the answers, but to the day we die, that is the primary question on our lips. Why?"

"I want to go back," Darlene said simply, so simply in fact it sounded like the most obvious thing to do.

"We all want to go back. Life is a journey home.

Maybe that was what he meant when he told that to Paula Gilbert, eh, Doctor?"

"Please," she said. "I've helped you. You're frightening Darlene, and you're frightening me, I might add."

"And what would we be without fear, Doctor? Fear protects us. It's our ability to foresee bad things happening to us that keeps us cautious, careful. Animals have it instinctively. We did, but we've lost the edge, I'm afraid as we evolved and became civilized." He stopped smiling. "Get out," he ordered again, but more sternly. "Now," he screamed at Darlene, pointing the gun at her as well.

She jumped, turned, and opened the door.

He got out on his side and turned to Terri, who hesitated, asking herself, what had she done?

Seeing she had little choice, she opened her door and stepped out of the car.

"What are you doing?" she asked him in the tone of voice to make him think about it.

"Let's go look at that old house. I'm interested in historical sites," he said.

"I told Dr. Templeman I was going with you. I told him who you were," she said, relying on her powers of convincing people to have hope where there was very little. Was she as good a bluffer as she thought she was?

"I doubt that, but even if you did, Doctor, you're with a mad schizophrenic. That's all anyone would think."

"Why are you doing this?" she asked, changing her

tone now to one of pleading. "It's only going to add to the mess, to the questions and to further investigations."

"The house," he said. He pointed the pistol at Darlene who gasped.

Terri put her arm around her.

"Walk to the house. Don't panic. Just do whatever I tell you to do."

Darlene couldn't speak. Don't panic? she thought. Easily said. Her throat was closed with panic. Her body felt numb, cold. It was as if she had already been killed and she was in the process of leaving it behind.

"Open the door," Garret ordered when they stepped on the porch. The floorboards creaked so loudly, Terri thought they might just crack beneath them.

She tried the door. Amazingly, despite the broken windows, the crumbling wood siding and shutters, the door was locked. She tried the handle and then turned to Garret.

"Out of the way," he ordered and kicked the door with the style and effectiveness of a karate expert. It splintered around the lock and swung open, revealing a dark, dank room that Terri thought must have once served as a lobby or living room area for the seasonal guests. With twilight falling quickly now, there was not very much illumination.

A body left in this place will probably not be discovered for some time, she thought. Darlene, trembling helplessly now, was also whimpering and gasping for breath. She could simply faint any moment, Terri thought.

"Well, isn't this cozy," Garret said. "Must have been a very nice place once. Move," he told Darlene who stopped and now looked incapable of taking another step. She didn't, so he poked her in the ribs with the barrel of the pistol. It had the effect of a gunshot. She took two steps forward with him still holding the pistol barrel against her, but then her eyes went back and she folded so quickly at his feet, it was as if all of her bones had turned to jelly.

Garret was moving forward aggressively at that moment. Caught by surprise, he tripped over her and struggled to maintain his balance. Terri spun and with desperation and a gathering of all her physical strength, pushed him while he was still off-balance, and he fell forward, losing the grip on his pistol. It flew a few feet ahead of him as he went to break his fall with his palms out.

Terri considered her options in an instant. She was obviously no match for the man in any physical struggle. Her only hope was to get away, but that meant leaving Darlene behind. The now-unconscious woman was sprawled awkwardly on her right side. Terri turned and shot forward, through the dark corridor, choosing not to go up the stairs, but instead continue toward the back, through what was once the kitchen. The dwindling daylight spilling through the broken windows gave her just enough illumination so as not to bump into things.

She heard Garret scrambling behind her, cursing and calling after her, warning her that she was making a big mistake. The rear door of the old house was locked, but it was a rusted tumbler. She pulled it open and jerked at the door, which resisted at first. She didn't know from what source she drew the surge of strength, but it was sufficient for her to get the old, heavy door opened enough so she could squeeze through. She pulled it shut behind her, hoping to cause Garret any delay she could.

Once outside, she stood on the back porch and considered the woods. There was a distance of at least five hundred yards to cross before she entered the forest. It was darker, but she knew she would never make it before he would be out and taking aim. Knowing she had to do something fast, she hurried down the four steps and then turned, now in a desperate panic herself.

Under the porch she saw a basement window that was completely blown out. She knelt and reached the window just as Garret opened the back door of the old building. As quietly as she could, she slipped through the window, falling and crawling her way down the old fieldstone foundation until she hit the cement floor. She swallowed her grunts and cries of pain and moved like some sort of rodent deeper into the darkness. There, she pressed herself against the wall and waited, watching the window and listening.

Garret came down the stairs slowly and stood there. He had to consider that she had run around the building, and his first thought was she was heading back to the car. She had left the keys in the ignition. Alarmed by that thought, he hurried to the corner and looked back toward the vehicle. Seeing she wasn't there, he relaxed, took a deep breath and then slowly made his way to the car to take the keys out of the ignition to prevent her from using the vehicle should she somehow get past him. That done he turned and headed back to the rear porch. He considered the woods but as he looked around, he saw the open window and smiled to himself.

Below, Terri realized she was still quite vulnerable. There was barely any light pouring through the open window, but she was growing accustomed to the thick shadows and was able to see some old piping. Grasping a length of pipe she could handle, she crawled closer to the window and waited.

Garret was now convinced she was down there. He approached the window slowly, a cold, confident smile on his face.

"Doctor," he called through it, "you're not behaving like an intelligent, educated person. Come on out and we'll talk and figure out a way to make everyone happy. I'm not interested in seeing anyone else hurt. You know that," he said.

She held her breath and pressed her back against the fieldstone wall. The jagged edges of some of those stones were painful, but she ignored that and remained as still and as poised with the pipe as she could be.

"Okay, Doctor, I'm coming in and when I see you, I'm not going to be very pleasant," he warned, waited another few seconds, and leaned into the window.

"You're a damn fool," he shouted, his rage rising. He couldn't see her, and he was unhappy about having to go in, but that was what he had to do.

He turned and lowered his legs slowly into the old basement. When he was almost completely in, he held onto the windowsill to gradually find his footing below. He turned his head to look down and that was when Terri swung the pipe and caught him squarely in the forehead. The blow snapped his head back sharply. He lost his grip on the sill and fell to the basement floor. His cellular phone dropped out of his pocket and bounced once, but he held the gun in his hand.

He groaned and she struck the gun hand, sending the weapon into the darkness where it bounced against the side wall. Garret moaned, fighting for consciousness. Terri threw the pipe down, scooped up his cellular phone, and leaped for the window, pulling herself up with all the strength she could muster. Below, Garret groaned again. Pure terror lifted Terri out the window. She fell to the ground under the porch, caught her breath, and scampered around and up the back steps.

Once inside the old tourist house, she ran through the kitchen, down the corridor to the lobby, where Darlene was sitting up, dazed.

"Quick!" Terri screamed at her. She reached down for her arm and helped Darlene to her feet.

"Whaaa . . ."

"Just run with me. Run!" she shouted and pulled her

along, through the front door, down the stairs, and toward the car. She lunged for the door on the driver's side and then stopped dead with disappointment when she saw the keys were not in the ignition.

Behind them, she could hear Garret bellow, his voice echoing in the old house.

"C'mon," she urged Darlene and pulled her toward the now dimly lit woods. Some early starlight and a quarter moon was enough to light up the way. They ran past the first set of birch and maple. Without leaves, the forest wasn't all that protective, but with darkness thickening, Terri was hopeful. She tugged and urged Darlene along until they were deeper and deeper into the woods, finding even more protection provided by a group of pine trees.

"I can't run anymore!" Darlene cried.

"You've got to keep moving. If we stop, he'll catch up. Move," she ordered.

Darlene gasped and followed. They went through the area of pine trees and then down an embankment where there was a stream of water bubbling over rocks. She saw a heavy overgrown area across the way and directed Darlene to it. Once there, she paused and indicated they should crouch so she could listen. Their heavy breathing almost made it impossible to hear anything.

Then, there was the sound of branches cracking. After a long moment, that sound stopped and then they heard the most primeval, horrendous scream of frustration.

Darlene gasped and whimpered.

"Oh Jesus," she said.

Terri didn't move a muscle.

"Quiet," she told her.

They waited. The sounds grew more distant until finally, they heard the distinct roar of a car engine.

Terri released a hot breath of relief.

"He's going," she told Darlene.

"Who is he?" she asked.

"A modern-day Frankenstein," Terri replied. "Let's get some help," she added and held up the cellular phone she had been grasping tightly during the whole flight. Before she could flip it open to punch out a 911 call, it rang.

For a moment it was as if she was holding a hand grenade that had just been triggered. It was truly like a small explosion. She nearly dropped the phone.

Then, she flipped it open and brought it to her ear slowly. She didn't say hello. She held it there.

"Garret?" she heard. "Doctor Stanley? Are you there?"

That voice.

She couldn't mistake it.

It was Will Dennis.

"I now know how he knew you had spoken to Paula Gilbert," she muttered as she closed the phone.

"I don't understand," Darlene said.

Terri shook her head and looked at the cell phone. She truly felt as if the legs had been cut out from under her and sat back stunned.

She looked at the phone.

It had been a hand grenade after all.

NINETEEN

Anxious and impatient, he decided to wait for the Samuelses in their room. Surprise was always his best friend in situations like this, he thought. There would be no need to manufacture some reason to be there. No reason to tax his brain. He found the master key for all the rooms and just sauntered down as if he was carrying out some mediocre, simple responsibility. When he entered the room, he saw they had left a lamp on next to the bed and a light on in the bathroom.

"Sure, what do you care about my electric expenses," he muttered. He liked playing a role, enjoyed slipping into identities, assuming someone else's life, even that ugly man decomposing in his living room. At least, he had a life of some sort.

When you're desperate for an identity, you take what you find, he told whatever part of him even suggested criticism. Survival takes precedent over everything and anything else. And what great difference did it make anyway? Very soon he would drop this identity and leave it behind like an old suit of clothes. In a sense he resembled a snake, shedding its skin. He didn't mind the analogy really. How clever it was to be able to take off your skin and replace it with a brand-new covering?

Curious about these people now, he passed the time by going through their bags. He held up Mrs. Samuels's undergarments, deciding she was quite conservative and obviously very wide in the hips. Charles Samuels had very uninteresting clothing, too. His suit and two sports jackets were bland, simple, and not very expensive.

He found some personal papers, business cards that told him Charles Samuels was a loan officer in a bank. There was a letter from some cousin in Kingston describing her new home and inviting the Samuelses to visit. The directions to the house were in the letter. He thought about it a moment and wondered if this was a sign. Should he be heading there? Nothing dramatic happened, no ringing in his head, but still, he thought he should give it consideration, so he folded it up and put it into his pants pocket.

It was time to plan. What would he do exactly when the Samuelses arrived? He had thought of something, he realized. Before he had ambled down here, he had made something of a plan. What was it? Damn this memory thing. He had to restore whatever it was in him that was bringing about these lapses. That was for sure.

He looked at the bed and saw the long, serrated bread knife he had brought along.

"Oh yeah," he said aloud. "The best way to say hello."

Remembering restored his confidence in himself. He

sat comfortably now and waited. They couldn't be much longer. People who didn't know an area wouldn't spend much time out there at night. They would find the restaurant they wanted, eat, and come right back. He checked his watch. It occurred to him that he wasn't sure exactly when they had left. Time was becoming very obscure again, liquefying and freezing into a piece of ice. He couldn't hold on to it at all. Had ten minutes passed or an hour? When did he walk in here? All these little confusions were mounting.

He felt a buzzing inside his head and soon he couldn't sit still. He rose and paced and went to the window to check the parking lot and then paced and began to talk to himself, reciting words, names, events in no special order or logic, babbling as if he was some sort of cauldron of memories, overflowing.

"I'm literally losing my mind!" he cried. "Damn you," he raged, waving his fist at the ceiling.

Who? He thought he heard called back.

Damn who?

He didn't know and it was stupid to behave like this anyway.

He paused and then seized a grip on himself and sat again. When he looked at his watch, he thought only a minute or so had gone by. How could that be?

His lips were drying.

His eyes burned.

His very skin felt as if it were writhing on his bones

and inside himself his organs were turning and twisting, tugging on his bones.

I am not a well man, he thought, and then he thought, I am not a man.

What am I?

On his wrist, time, like a persistent termite, continued to bore a hole in his wooden heart.

Finally, he heard the distinct sound of a car entering the motel lot. Excited, he rose quickly and peered through the curtains. It was the Samuelses all right. About time. He backed up and pressed his back against the wall so when they entered, they would not see him there until they had closed the door behind them.

He heard the key being inserted and braced himself. The door opened, but only part way.

"All right," he heard Charles Samuels say in an irritated voice, "I'll just get everything myself. Stay in the car."

Stay in the car? That wouldn't work, he thought.

The door opened farther. Charles entered, but didn't look in his direction. Instead, Samuels started for the open suitcase.

He pushed the door so it shut and Samuels turned around.

"What?" he asked as if he had said something to him. Samuel's face collapsed in fear. "What is this?"

"You left the lights on," he said. "You went out to eat and you left the lights on."

"Huh?"

"That's inconsiderate," he told him stepping closer. Samuels had yet to see the knife he was holding just behind his back. "And when people are inconsiderate of others, they should be punished," he continued.

Samuels looked at the closed door, considered his options, and started to back away.

He smiled, raised his left hand abruptly, which caught Samuels's attention, and then drove the knife into and just to the left of Samuels's sternum. With the accuracy of a heart surgeon, he sliced the pulmonary artery. Samuels gasped, raised his hands as if to surrender, and then coughed, brought his hands down surprisingly hard onto his shoulders, and held himself there for a moment, gazing into his face, his own eyes full of wonder as though he had a preliminary view of where he was now going before collapsing at his feet.

"Turn off the lights when you leave next time," he muttered down at Samuels.

All was quiet. He turned to the door and listened. Mrs. Samuels had not gotten out of the vehicle yet. He waited and suddenly, he heard the car horn. He went to the window and saw her leaning over to press it. She did it again and then, frustrated and angry, she opened the car door and came toward the unit.

Once again, he backed away from the door. When she opened it, she was in midsentence.

"What's taking you so damn long, Charles? We've got to get out of here before . . ."

She stared at her husband's folded body on the floor. It took the breath out of her and all she could do was gasp and bring her hands to the base of her throat.

Quietly, calmly, he closed the door behind her and she turned.

He smiled.

"Now if you don't put up a struggle, you might live," he said.

He knew there was no chance of that, but when someone was in a state of pure desperation, even empty promises bobbed about like lifesavers.

He raised the bloodied knife so she would see it.

"Go to the bed and start to take off your clothing," he ordered.

And then he said something that put even more terror into her, not that she thought that was possible.

"I'm hungry," he said.

She was unable to move, unable to speak, barely able to breathe.

"Move!" he shouted and suddenly she found the strength to do so.

It was toward the end when he felt regenerated that he suddenly realized the Samuelses had returned to leave. Charles was getting their suitcases and she was too afraid to get out of the car and help him pack up.

Why would they do that? Why would they come here, book and pay for a room for the night, and then leave? What frightened the woman?

He searched his memory, which was better now, sharper, and recalled they had stopped at the office to pick up a newspaper to find advertisements about restaurants.

The picture.

They had recognized him. What else had they done?

He had to move quickly, he thought. He had better leave as soon as he could.

Once she regained her composure, Terri picked up the phone and again began to punch out 911. All the while Darlene Stone stood like she was indeed made of stone, her eyes glazed over with exhaustion, fear, and confusion. Terri decided to describe them as being in a very bad car accident. She didn't even give her right name. Then she gave the police dispatcher as good an idea of where they were exactly located as she could before turning back to Darlene.

"C'mon," she said reaching for her hand, "we've got to make our way out to the highway."

"Why did you tell them you were Grace Robbins?" she asked.

"Grace was my roommate in undergraduate school," she said moving her forward as she spoke. "Her name just came to me."

"But why didn't you use your real name?"

"It's a complicated mess, Darlene. Right now, all I

want to do is get us home. I want to soak in a hot bath and not think about it all. You need a good day or two of complete rest. I'll call in a prescription for you, get you something to help you sleep and forget all this for a while."

"What about that horrible man?" she asked.

Terri thought for a while before responding. They trekked on through the bushes, past some more pine trees, toward a field that ran adjacent with the highway. She was familiar enough with this area to guide them.

"He has other, more compelling business to consider," she replied.

Terri really had no idea what Garret Stanley would do next and if he would decide he had to come after them again. As she walked along, she considered all the possible options, not the least being to contact someone at the FBI. She had doubts now that they were ever brought into this mess here. She recognized how difficult it was going to be to get anyone to believe her story, but at the same time, she thought it would be their best insurance. Perhaps, Garret would realize that if he left them alone, people would just not believe them and it would go away.

All of the potential scenarios loomed out there, but at the moment, she was far too exhausted to make any quick decisions. The advice she had given Darlene was probably the advice she should be giving herself, she thought. She laughed to herself just imagining being in

Hyman's office and beginning with a line like, "Hyman, here's the reason why these young women died of severe vitamin deficiencies." Envisioning the look on his face brought a smile to her own. Hyman Templeman, the medical iconoclast, confronted with the horrors of the new millennium: cloning humanity.

It occurred to her of course that she just couldn't go home, or go to Curt's home and go to sleep. Hyman, Curt himself at the hospital, her parents, her in-laws, everyone was going to want to know where she had been. She wasn't even sure what she looked like. She felt some deep aches and some sharp sticking pain in the area of her back. She touched her forehead where her skin felt raw and imagined some sort of scrape there as well. Of course, she couldn't let Curt see her this way, and she could not tell him everything yet. He was in no condition to be burdened with all that worry. It would just impede his recuperation.

Maybe the fabrication she gave the dispatcher was the best story to use at the moment . . . claim she had been in a minor traffic accident. At least that would give her some time to work out a solution, if there was any.

Almost twenty minutes later, they broke out of the woods and stepped onto the highway. It was close to perfect timing. A highway patrol car followed by an ambulance rounded the corner, lights blinking, sirens screaming. She held Darlene, who was wavering, her eyes closed. The patrolman spotted them and put on a blinker as he slowed his vehicle. When he pulled up and stepped out of his car, she recognized him to be the first highway officer who had been sent to her house. He recognized her as well.

"Dr. Barnard?"

"Yes," she said.

The ambulance attendants started toward them as well.

"What happened?"

"We got lost, into an accident, and then lost again," she said.

He stood back as the attendants approached, both of them recognizing her as well.

"Dr. Barnard?"

"Yes, please get her inside the ambulance. Let's get her blood pressure."

Darlene gave in to her exhaustion just at that moment and sank in Terri's arms. The two attendants moved quickly to put her on a stretcher and get her into the ambulance, while the patrolman and she stood back watching.

"How did you come to be out here? Who is that?" he asked her.

"Someone I was helping," she said, keeping it as cryptic as she could.

"What about the car? Where about is it?" he asked turning toward the woods.

"I don't care about the car right now," she said. "Thanks," she added and got into the ambulance as soon as Darlene was rolled inside.

One of the attendants turned to her.

"You have a bad gash on your forehead, Doctor. Might need stitches," he said examining it.

The patrolman stepped closer to the open door.

"I'll follow you to the hospital," he said. "We can send a tow truck later."

"Good," she called back. "Let's get going," she told the attendant and he closed the door.

Moments later they were on their way to the emergency room, and she wondered if the patrolman would report back to Will Dennis or a superior who would report to Dennis.

Wasn't it horrible to have to be afraid of the very people who were employed and supposedly dedicated to helping and protecting you?

She sat back and let the attendant begin to clean her wound, while the other one began to monitor Darlene, and she realized she had been as close to death as she had ever been in her life. It was a rescue that had the potential for geometric impact. Whenever or if ever she saved anyone else's life with her medical skills, she would think it would have not happened if she had not effected this escape.

Somehow, she thought, she would be an even better doctor because of all this.

Like some child hoping and searching for a rainbow, she closed her eyes and listened to the ambulance siren clearing their way toward home.

TWENTY

He closed the door of Unit 10 behind him, and rushed back to the office to gather up the money he had discovered in the motel owner's apartment. Before he had left Unit 10, he had taken all he could find on Charles Samuels as well. In his way of thinking, money was a sort of fuel, and every person he robbed was a fueling station. He favored cash over anything. He was fearful of using credit cards and leaving some sort of trail. Occasionally, he had taken some jewelry, but he had yet to pawn any of it. That, too, might leave tracks and he knew in his heart that his pursuer was a very sharp, capable, and effective predator, at least as able as he was. It was a frightening thought to envision himself hunting himself. That was a nightmare he recalled vividly. It was what gave him his all-knowing sixth sense.

But he was in a particular hurry now, fleeing with an intensity he had not experienced. Never before did he feel this degree of desperation. He hated it and didn't want to look at himself. He was ashamed of his fear. It made him weak, made him more like . . . them, his prey. If there was one thing that terrified him above anything else, it was the thought that he was someone else's prey. He was the hunted and not the hunter.

He was practically running now, running toward the motel office, blind to everything but the tasks at hand. Focused, intense, a projectile of raw determination, he charged through the door and into the apartment. He went right for the can of money he had left in front of the closet, filled his fist with the bills, and stuffed them into his pockets. Then he rose and walked slowly back to the living room, feeling more confident, feeling more in control of events. But when he stepped into the room, he paused. In his haste, he had run right past the motel owner. For a moment he was confused. The dead motel owner wasn't against the wall where he had left him. The man was in his easy chair, his head back, his eyes open, facing the television set that was on, the volume low.

Did I leave him that way? he wondered. Did I turn on the set? Was I having some fun?

"It's better this way," he heard himself say. "This way it looks more like he had a heart attack while watching television. I'll make sure of that."

Did he think aloud?

He turned very slowly and looked at himself and saw Garret Stanley.

"Boy, have you made a mess of things," he heard himself say. "You have no idea what I have gone through covering all this up. Some important people had to use big muscle."

He looked at the dead motel owner and then turned back to Garret.

"What else have you done here? What else do I have to clean up? Well?" Garret followed after a moment. "Are there any other bodies in the vicinity? Hello! Those two cars parked in front of the motel units?"

He nodded.

"Great." Garret stepped closer, moving more into the illumination. There was a nasty looking bruise on his forehead. He raised his hand to his own forehead and felt for it. "No, this is particularly my own trauma. Thank you for caring. Seems a local physician, a Dr. Terri Barnard, was a bit more resourceful than I imagined she would be. Did you know she had the pleasure of confronting two of your pieces of work, and eventually, might have made a lot of trouble for us? You don't read newspapers? You didn't see our face on the front page?"

He nodded.

"Oh, you did. Great. Well, why are you still here then?"

"I'm leaving," he said.

"Yes, you're leaving. We're leaving. You can't continue like this. You understand that, don't you? Well? Don't you?"

He nodded.

"Good. We'll get you back and help you."

There was something in Garret's face he recognized. People lie to themselves, but they know they're lying to themselves. They can't look into the mirror and not know the truth. They can put on a facade to hide the truth from others, but there is no mask thick enough or good enough to hide the truth from yourself.

He saw the deception in Garret's eyes. He saw the looming betrayal.

"You can't lie to me," he told Garret.

Garret's eyes widened.

"I'm your mirror and you're mine."

He saw that Garret understood. He saw the look of fear now. He reached for the pistol in pocket and brought it out, but just as he was doing so, he lunged at himself and grasped his wrist. They struggled and turned, a strangely beautiful dance of death, mirror images, each anticipating the other's steps, looking into the duplicated eyes, the duplicated twisted lips of effort, their arms equal in strength. The spinning grew faster, a little more awkward.

Garret's head trauma sang and shortened his ability to keep his balance.

Then, he did a surprising thing to Garret. Maybe he had to duplicate that head trauma. He brought his head back and snapped it forward so his forehead would strike Garret just at the bridge of his nose. The nose cracked and the pain was electric, shooting up in a dozen directions, tearing through Garret's eyes, into his brain where it exploded like a big lightbulb.

Darkness came rushing in. The grip Garret had on

his hands loosened. His legs began to retract as if they were receding into his hips, the calves into the thighs, the thighs into his lower torso until they were completely gone and he was dangling in the air.

It felt like water rushing over him, a great wave washing him farther and farther down until he was too deep to ever come back up.

Garret died in little ways first, first losing all sensitivity in the tips of his fingers and toes, the tip of his nose, his lips, his ears, every extremity falling away, crumbling. It was truly as if his skin was peeling off. There was bone showing everywhere.

There was no sound possible, just the tremendous urge to make one.

How remarkable, Garret thought, is death.

What a fool I have been to avoid it.

Garret's body folded at his feet. He stood looking over him for a long moment. First, he felt relief. The organism felt relief. It had survived, but that was followed by a tremendous sense of sadness, of sorrow and desolation. He was literally mourning himself.

He dropped his head back and squeezed his eyes closed and then he howled like a wild animal that had lost its loving offspring. He was, after all, now truly alone, not connected to anything, floating out there. Prey needed its predators. He had no purpose. From what would he flee? After all, that was all he really existed to do: flee. Refuel, refurbish, and then flee.

He howled again and then he lowered himself to his knees and looked at Garret. What was more terrifying than looking at yourself in death? This was a nightmare come to life. He shook his shoulders and his head bobbed and swung about, those dead eyes like two glass marbles threatening to fall out of his skull.

Then he embraced him and held him; held himself and rocked back and forth for a while.

Afterward, maybe out of a need to deny what was true, he changed clothing, even down to underwear. He put on his watch, took his wallet and identification, slipped, as it were, into him, the way he had slipped into so many other identities. It gave him some consolation, some relief. He rose with a renewed energy, especially when he looked at him in his clothing.

The weaker part of me is dead, he thought. That's all. I go on. A sacrifice was made, nothing more.

"Thank you," he told the new corpse and turned to go.

Before he reached the lobby, he heard the car drive up and saw a tall man get out of a black automobile. There were two men alongside him, both looking rather aggressive, military, even though they were in suits. He stepped back as they came to the door.

"Dr. Stanley, are you all right?" the tall man asked as he entered.

"Yes," he said.

"What's happening?"

"It's over," he said. It just came to him to say that quickly.

"Oh good. What went on here?"

"I'm afraid a few more victims. You'll find them in the two units: a woman and her mother, and a couple. Both of the women are . . . depleted," he said.

The tall man nodded and turned to the two men.

"I suppose you're going to want to go check it out," he said.

"Right," the taller of the two said and turned to his partner. "I'll do that. You stay with Mr. Dennis and assist him and Doctor Stanley here."

Dennis turned back to him. "Where's . . . ?"

"He's back there with the motel owner," he said quickly.

"Let's take a look," Dennis said and he and the other man followed him into the living room. "Christ, he looks exactly like you. Just as you described. Jesus," he added turning to him, "you both have a bruise on your foreheads, too. That's eerie. How's that?"

"We struggled. He knew why I had come. I didn't have a chance to shoot him. I hit him with the handle of the pistol. Just a coincidence," he added.

"Nevertheless, it's eerie. Anyway," he added while the other man checked out the motel manager, "we'll have a bit of a problem with that doctor, Dr. Barnard. I still don't understand what you were trying to do there, taking her and that bartender out to the old Feinberg property. I had her under control, had her believing I had taken her into my confidence. I don't know why you didn't trust what I told you from my interviews. Now that she has escaped . . ."

"Who's going to believe her after you speak to the press?" he asked Dennis.

"Well, I'll have a bit of a time with her. She did attend to two of his victims, remember? She is no fool, as you now know, and if she wants, she can contradict intelligently. I'll need a little more help," he added with a wry smile. "To pay for a complete coverup. I'm sure your people will understand the added costs."

He looked at the other man who looked at him and nodded.

"Whatever it takes," he said. "Just do it. This is your territory."

Dennis smiled.

"Good." He turned to the other man who stepped forward and looked at Garret Stanley's body.

"What do you want done with him?"

"Done? Oh. Send him back to the research center, of course."

"We'll see to it," Will Dennis said nodding.

"Good."

Mike returned.

"A mess," he said. "Ugly. Major cleanup, Doctor."

"Just do it," he said.

"At least it ends here," Will Dennis said nodding at Garret Stanley's body.

"Yes," he said. "It ends here."

"Let's get on the phone," Mike told his partner and they went out to the office.

"I guess my having that police sketch put in the paper wasn't a mistake after all, was it, Doctor?" Will asked, smiling with an annoying arrogance. "I guess we're not all country bumpkins after all."

"Apparently not."

"If I had done it earlier, using Dr. Barnard's description, all of this might have been avoided."

"Hindsight is always twenty-twenty," he said.

Dennis nodded.

"Well, I hope this is all going to be worth it someday, Dr. Stanley."

He smiled.

"Oh, it will be. I'm sure. In fact, it's already worth it in so many ways. I'd better get going. I have lots to do."

"I bet. Don't forget to put a good word in for me with those people in high places we discussed. I guess I'll have enough money now to launch a senatorial campaign and you'll be able to count on my vote when you need it."

"Absolutely," he said. "We both want the same things."

"Oh?" Will Dennis smiled. "What's that?"

"More. Always," he said as he started out. "You and I. We'll always want more."

He nodded at him and walked out of the motel.

The moment he did so, he felt like a man who had just been freed from a long prison sentence. Never had he experienced such a surge of elation. I'm gigantic, he thought. He did all he could to contain himself and not scream it at the night sky. I really will go on forever.

He watched the agents in the office behind him talking on the telephone, one on the land phone, one on a cellular, both working diligently to clean up the mess he had left behind. The whole world was working for him. At least for now, he thought as he made his way toward the vehicle he knew belonged to him, to Dr. Garret Stanley.

Finally, he didn't have to share his identity with any other living thing.

It was as if he had thrown off a heavy weight, taken off a shackle.

He could breathe easier.

At least for now, he thought again.

He didn't like the sound of that.

There was some threat still looming. It was like a pebble in a shoe. He could feel it and he knew he had to get rid of it.

What was it?

He drove off, his forehead a bit bruised, but folded in

deep thought as he struggled to determine the answer. It came, right from Will Dennis's lips.

All he knew at the moment was it was out there, waiting for him.

And once again, he could be the predator.

TWENTY-ONE

Terri had her head down on her folded arms. She was at Curt's bedside. He had been sleeping when she entered the room. An hour earlier, she had been with Darlene Stone in the emergency room. Except for emotional trauma and exhaustion, the woman was well enough to go home. Terri arranged for her to have some sedation and told her to just go home and rest. She would talk to her in the morning.

"Don't we have to speak to the police?" she asked.

"I'll take care of all that, Darlene. Just rest," Terri told her.

Darlene's mother and her mother's live-in boyfriend came to pick her up.

Terri did need a half dozen stitches. The bandage made the wound look much more serious than it was. Exhausted herself, she somehow garnered enough energy to go up to see Curt. First, she would assure him she was fine and then she would tell him the story, she thought. Finding him asleep, she made the mistake of lowering her head and closing her eyes.

A gentle nudge on her shoulder awoke her. For a long

moment, she forgot where she was. Then it all came rushing back. She turned and looked up at Will Dennis. Instantly, her heart began to pound.

"Let's go down the hall and talk," he said. "There's an empty room two doors down."

She hesitated and gazed at Curt, who was still asleep.

"I promise. I'll tell you everything now," Dennis said. "Nothing more is going to happen to anyone. It's all right," he added.

She rose slowly.

"It's all right? Funny way to describe the events of the day," she told him.

He turned and walked to the door. The highway patrolman who had been with the ambulance was standing in the hallway speaking softly with another highway patrolman. The two stopped to look her way.

"I found your vehicle, Doctor," the patrolman said. "It was in the parking lot here. The keys are in the ignition."

"Yes, well, it won't start," she said looking at Dennis.

"Take care of it, will you, Paul?" Will Dennis told the patrolman. He nodded and left with his partner. "Right over here," Dennis said leading her to the empty room.

She entered behind him and he pulled the one chair out for her to sit. She did so and looked up at him.

"Let me begin by telling you he's dead," he said.

"Who? Dr. Stanley or his creation?"

"His creation. That's the more important matter."

"That's a matter of debate. In my opinion Dr. Frank-enstein was as bad as the monster he created. Do you know what he intended to do to us, Darlene Stone and myself? Do you know why he took us down that dirt road to that deserted tourist house?"

"I've passed all that on to his superiors," Will Dennis said.

"His superiors?" She laughed. "That's like telling Hitler what Goebbels did."

"Whatever. It's out of my hands now and I'm not terribly upset about that."

She narrowed her eyes and sat up firmly.

"Why should I believe anything you say, Will? You lied to me about all this, and if I didn't happen to have Garret Stanley's cell phone, I doubt I would have known."

"Probably not," he candidly admitted.

She brought her eyebrows together.

"What was your involvement here?"

"I'm sorry. I told you as much as I thought you could know without being in any danger yourself. I didn't know what was going on until late in the situation myself, Terri," he said. "After Kristin Martin died and was diagnosed, I was contacted by people pretty high up the ladder. They told me basically to cooperate with Dr. Stanley, that he was the lead man in this pursuit of this unusual perpetrator. I wasn't given great detail, just that someone very dangerous was on the loose and if the whole story got out, it would create even more havoc in our small community than we already had. I was on a need-to-know basis and prohibited from telling anyone else what I had been told.

"When you called me about Paula Gilbert that night, I was in a real panic myself and that was when Dr. Stanley was forced to meet directly with me. I told him you didn't know all that much more than I did, but he convinced me he could ask you and any witness or any person in contact with the perpetrator questions that would give him essential information."

"Why didn't you or someone from your office accompany the madman?" Terri asked.

"I was hoping not to have to reveal to anyone, even you, what I was told, what I knew, and it was obvious no one else on the outside would be permitted to know anything, be part of any of this. It's very tightly contained.

"And," he added, looking penitent, "I had no idea how far Garret Stanley would go. He became somewhat of a desperate man after Paula Gilbert's death. I should have realized that. I'm sorry.

"The bottom line is he has taken care of the situation. It's over."

"Is it? He'll continue his work, won't he?"

"That's beyond us, Terri. Believe me, that's beyond our control and if either you or I went public with this, nothing would change except we would both be destroyed professionally. There are forces at work here, very powerful forces. I'm here to apologize to you for what you've been through and to assure you it's over for us. We'll have no more victims in our community. You should go back to your practice. I'll find a way to compensate Darlene Stone, get her a better job, perhaps. In time she'll put it behind her, too."

"What about the Thorndykes, the Martin relatives, the Gilberts, and who knows how many others?" Terri asked him.

"It's not in our power to do anything for them, Terri. If I could, I would. Believe me."

"People are still going to want to know how these women died of gross vitamin deficiencies, Will. You can't cover up what has already been revealed. You can't unring a bell."

He shrugged.

"It will be a mystery and as long as it is over, it will be one of those mysteries that drift off in time and is eventually forgotten."

"And you're satisfied with that?"

"I have no choice," he said. "And neither do you. If you go public with anything, I won't support you. What are you going to say, Terri, that a secret research organization created a vitamin vampire? Just imagine what you would do to your own and Hyman's reputations. Who would want to go to either of you for medical concerns? They have ways of coloring you in the media. You'll come off being some sort of a kook, like someone who believes extraterrestrials kidnapped her to study her body and then let her free.

"No," he said shaking his head. "Let it go. Take Curt home. Help him recuperate. Get married and have a wonderful life."

"Is that what you're going to do, Will? Have a wonderful life?"

"I'm going to try," he said smiling.

"You should reread the *Tragedy of Dr. Faustus,*" she said, "unless you never read it. Then read it. You've made a similar deal with the devil, Will. There is no wonderful life after that."

He stopped smiling.

"I've given you my best advice. Do what you think you should," he said. He nodded, turned, and left her sitting there staring after him.

As long as there are political animals like that left in charge of the public welfare, we'll never be safe, she concluded, but she also concluded that he was right: there was little she could do about it now.

She rose slowly. Her head was throbbing and not just from the wound. One thing was for sure, she thought. She and Curt both needed time off.

He was awake when she returned to his room.

"What happened to you?" he asked as soon as he saw the bandage on her head.

"I'm going to tell you," she said, "but you won't believe me."

She sat and took his hand into hers.

"I'm all ears," he said sitting up.

"Once upon a time," she began, "mankind decided it had to improve on God's work."

He didn't drive that far. Refurbished and re-energized, he was now like an overly charged battery. All the immediate events played back as vividly as they had when they occurred. He relived every action and again heard every word spoken. It overwhelmed him and he had to pull off the road. It was too difficult to keep driving.

He found another motel, much more upscale, and took a room. There was a restaurant attached, one of the chain restaurants he had seen during his travels. He went right to it and ate like someone who had been on a deserted island for weeks. The waitress, a flaming redhead with an ample bosom but hips that reminded him of Mrs. Samuels, was amused by his appetite.

"How do you stay so slim eating like that?" she asked him.

"Exercise. I'm a jogger. I'm always in motion," he added, giving her his best smile and turning his shoulders.

She laughed and went off. He followed the sway of her hips, and thought how wonderful it was to still be alive and in the game, still be meeting challenges, having thirsts and hungers and wanting pleasure.

What a work of art am I, the quintessential man, the paragon of all things, the perfection of life and the ultimate goal of evolution.

When he was finished eating, he returned to his room and lay on the bed, gazing dumbly at television. Pictures and words to stave off loneliness, he thought. How pathetic it must be for some, those inferior. It was as though they were truly in God's Waiting Room, and instead of thumbing through magazines, they were watching television. A door would open and they would be beckoned.

But not him. God didn't know he existed. He came from another place.

As more time passed, it occurred to him that he was waiting to be beckoned. But not by Death. He was waiting for some signal, some urge. He felt good, strong, vibrant, but he had no sense of direction, no urging, no mysterious calling. Based upon past experience, he concluded that if it didn't come soon, he wasn't meant to go anywhere else.

Perhaps that was also part of this nagging and annoying feeling that returned. Something yet remained that threatened his very existence. Of course, he understood that once they realized that the body he left behind was not his, some sort of pursuit would begin again. He had renewed confidence concerning that hunt. The predator was no longer as capable. He was in far less danger.

But something else threatened him. As the immediate

past replayed itself again, he centered in on words and narrowed it down to what that tall man had told him. It was about this doctor. He was going to have a bit of time with her. He needed more help.

He had no confidence in the tall man. He certainly didn't want to leave his fate in that man's hands. Maybe that was why he had no calling, maybe that was why he had to stay.

"I have unfinished work here," he thought. "In fact," he decided, "I actually have to go back."

That was something he had never done yet—retrace his steps, return to anything. It was always a forward motion, always new discoveries. Going back made him nervous, but it had to be done. What he had to do of course was be sure he was in tip-top shape for all this. He had to pay more attention to himself. At the first sign of any weakness, memory lapse, whatever, he had to go out and refuel.

He closed his eyes. A little rest is good, he thought, and drifted into a deep sleep much faster than he had anticipated. He had a strange dream, not a nightmare as such at the start, but troubling enough to make him uncomfortable. He moaned and turned on the bed. In his dream he saw himself liquefy and flow along until he poured into a river and was carried into a great pool in which there were others like him, streams of people, faces, bodies meandering about, locked in by the shoreline and a dam at the very south end of it all. As he drew closer to that, he saw a very tiny opening through which some flowed before the opening was closed down again.

It was when it opened once more and it was his turn to go that the dream turned into a nightmare. He started out and then fell forever until he hit a bed of sand into which he gradually seeped and disappeared. This was his grave.

He woke with a start, pounding on the bed to keep himself from sinking. He was screaming, too. Finally, he realized it and stopped. His face was coated with sweat. He looked around and realized he had slept through the day. When he sat up, he didn't like the dizzy feeling. It took a moment to settle. Then he went into the shower. As he was drying himself, he gazed into the mirror.

There was something different. What was it? He drew closer to the mirror and studied himself. Those were very distinct gray hairs, he realized. And there were lines around his eyes he had never seen before.

He pulled back from the mirror as he would had he looked through a window at his own death.

I'm getting old, he thought. That process to mature me—it's running amok. I'm like a vehicle that's lost its brakes and is going down a steep hill. I need to slow it up. I need whatever fights aging.

With a new sense of desperation, he dressed and went out into the night. He got into his vehicle and drove. The direction didn't matter. Movement mattered.

Concentrate, he told himself. It will come to you. What you have to do will come to you. You don't just need to feed off a healthy woman. You need something more. You need something of youth. You need. . . .

He slowed down.

He had pulled into a mall parking lot and three of them were walking toward the movie theater complex. They were laughing and their voices were so full of vibrancy. Three teenage girls. Young girls with young thyroids, their skin soft and healthy, their bones strong, all the juices within them fresh.

Go younger, he told himself.

Simply go younger and you will be all right.

You can still go on forever, even if it means going younger and younger and younger.

He parked his car and he waited. Eventually, they would come out and he would follow them and he would find an opportunity.

Afterward, when he was rejuvenated, he would turn his attention to that bigger problem, that threat he had left behind. Just be patient, he thought. Just be patient and calculating and you won't fail.

After all, now you had to carry on for more than just yourself. You had to do it for him so that he wouldn't be dead and gone, so that he would never die.

That was about all the conscience he possessed and all the remorse he could mine in himself. But it was enough. It gave him more purpose, and when he thought about it, he concluded what was any life if it didn't have reason for its existence?

His reason happened to be existence itself.

Like an echo trapped and bouncing back and forth forever, he would go on and on.

What difference did it make who heard him?

He heard himself and that was all that mattered.

"It'll be like a test run for our honeymoon," Terri told Curt when he showed some resistance. "I need the week off and so do you. I don't like the idea of your going back gradually. That prescription was given to you by a doctor without courage. You frightened him. Doctors are afraid of lawyers," she continued and Curt finally threw up his hands in surrender and laughed.

"Okay, okay. It's Hyman's cabin. We'll live like wild mountain people."

"Yes, wild in nature with Hyman's big-screen television set, the electric stove, central heating, and downy pillows on the beds, not to mention the full bar and the pool table."

"I do like to fish," Curt said.

"Hyman has the boat for us to use, but I hate putting worms on the hook."

He laughed.

"You can sew up people but you can't put a worm on a hook?"

"I am trained to end pain and suffering, not initiate it," she replied.

"Okay, forget fishing. We'll read, take walks, make love, eat, make love, read, make love."

"I get the idea," she said and kissed him. He touched her bandage.

"I still think we should go after that guy. Will Dennis doesn't scare me."

"He doesn't scare me either, but unfortunately, he makes sense," she said. "Let it go, Curt. Let it go."

Reluctantly, he nodded and backed away.

"All right, let's start packing."

"I'll make a list of what we need," she said, suddenly filled with an excitement that revived her. She truly felt like a young girl again and it was wonderful. Perhaps after a week of R and R, she would be restored and be able to put all that had happened behind her.

The ride up to the cabin was easy. They stopped at a shopping market and bought way more than they needed. She was sure of that. Casting off responsibilities, just letting go of their busy, full everyday lives filled them both with a grand sense of abandon. They could be as silly as they wanted, look as foolish as they wanted.

Hyman's cabin was really more of a lake house. There were two bedrooms, a den, a nice size living room with a fieldstone fireplace, a dining room, a relatively modern kitchen, three bathrooms, a back porch that faced the lake, and about an acre of surrounding trees. He had his own dock and a small boat with a 15-horsepower out-board. There was a shed behind the house as well.

The house itself had a cedar facing and a crawlspace. Television reception came from a satellite dish, and the set was in the den. In front of the fireplace Hyman had a large, thick, and fluffy white shag rug. The remaining flooring was all wood and some stone.

"Not too shabby," Curt said after inspecting most of it. "How long has he had this?"

"Ten years or so, I think. It's a nice escape for him because he's close enough if there are any real emergencies, but far enough out of it here to feel isolated and undisturbed. He assures me we'll enjoy the sunsets and the sound of the owls."

"Owls? I guess at a certain age, owls become a romantic bird," Curt said laughing.

They set about putting away the things they had bought, and then they went exploring, following the paths to the lake and through the woods. In the evening, they worked on dinner together.

"I wonder how often we'll do this after we're married," Curt said.

"After you taste my meatloaf, you might hope not often," Terri told him, but his point was made.

How do two very busy people with full professional lives hold on to a marriage? Their work will make most compromise impossible, she thought, but she also thought hers would obviously be the more demanding job. Curt could turn off his pager. She would forever be hooked into a service that would reach her at any hour, at any time, unless she was away on a vacation.

And what would happen when they had children?

This was a marriage that would demand so much more. Were they up to it?

It was as if he could hear her thoughts as they stood side by side in Hyman's lake house kitchen. Suddenly, Curt took her hand and stopped her. He turned her to him and looked at her with that steely-eyed focus that unraveled people on the witness stand in courtrooms.

"Terri, I'm going to love your meatloaf, and you're going to make it whenever you can, and we're going to find every possible way, every little opportunity, every bonus minute to spend more of our lives together. We won't sacrifice our clients and patients, but we won't always put them at the top of the list. Just don't expect me not to object whenever I can," he added.

"Objection sustained," she said and they kissed.

As simple as the meal was, it turned out to be one of the best they had together. They drank too much wine. They laughed a lot and kissed a lot and held each other impulsively all night, and when they made love, it was slow and graceful and full of promises.

Afterward, lying side by side and seeing the moon over the lake through the bedroom window, Terri talked about Garret Stanley.

"I've seen many arrogant, confident Godlike doctors

in medical school and when I interned, Curt. Some looked carved out of an iceberg. They looked right through personalities, identities, families and saw blood clots or tumors, diseased livers, infected gall bladders, and they attacked them with great art and knowledge, with determination I envied at times, but when they were done and they saw that patient for the final time, I often felt they just visited a complete stranger. I vowed that wasn't going to be me."

"It won't be," he said.

"After being with Garret Stanley even a short time and seeing how obsessed he was with his work, regardless of its impact on humanity, and then seeing how much power was behind him, I fell into a deep depression. It was truly being told what I think, what I do, won't matter."

"That's not true, Terri. You're going to influence the lives of hundreds of people and they will in turn influence a hundred more. It will matter."

"I want to believe that, Curt. Then I stop and wonder what new monster will be out there tomorrow, a product of greed and the hunger for power."

"Whatever it is, we'll stop it," he said.

"As long as you're there to hold me," she told him, "I'll believe it."

"Then you'll always believe it," he said. "For I'll always be there to hold you."

She fell asleep in his arms, truly feeling secure and safe.

She woke before he did and let him sleep. While he did, she put on her running shoes and sweat suit and went out for a jog. There was a beautiful mist over the water. With the sun on it, it looked like an abstract painting. Birds were flitting about excited at her presence. She saw a pair of beavers scurrying at the edge of the water. The air was cool, fresh, and reviving. Instead of growing tired with every passing thousand yards, she seemed to grow stronger. She had no idea if the path along the water went all around the lake, but midway, she realized it probably did and she continued.

Finally, she had to stop to walk and catch her breath. She was still a good quarter of the lake away from the cabin and now berated herself for going too far. Curt was surely up by now and wondering where she was. He would worry.

It put more speed into her steps and she started to jog again. The path thinned out in places and was barely visible. Some wild bushes became hazardous, their branches pulling at her sweat suit. She had to go slower. At last, the cabin came into view. She sprinted the last hundred or so yards and then stopped at the stairway in front, holding the railing and catching her breath.

The door opened and Curt stood there gaping out at her, a mixture of confusion and annoyance on his face.

"Where the hell were you?"

"I didn't realize how long it would take to run around the whole lake," she said. "Sorry."

"Why didn't you leave a note, Terri?"

"I really didn't expect to be out this long. Sorry," she said. She straightened up. He wasn't smiling. "What?"

"You had a phone call."

"This early? What?"

"It was Hyman."

She held her breath.

"What did he say, Curt? Is he sick or something?"

"No. He wanted you to know there has been another bizarre death."

"What?"

"A teenage girl. He said to tell you it looked like another case of Frank scurvy," he added.

The fatigue she had enjoyed suddenly turned into pure exhaustion. Her legs ached and weakened. She stared up at him and shook her head.

"But . . . Will Dennis said it was over. He said he was dead. He said. . . ."

"I've got the coffee made," Curt said sharply, turned, and went inside.

She stood there on the steps.

Behind her, a crow, annoyed by something, screamed so loudly it carried across the lake and woke whatever was left sleeping.

TWENTY-TWO

He didn't sleep all night. This feeding left him far too wired. He had seen young people juiced up on Ecstasy and other recreational drugs when he was in dance clubs, and he thought he resembled them. He wanted to play music loudly in the car. He moved to the beat, pounded the steering wheel, sang along whenever a song was familiar to him, and drove much faster than he usually did.

There was something extra in his feed this time, he concluded, something he needed all along. Whatever it was, it had a great deal to do with his energy level. It made everything else work more efficiently within him. He was truly running on all cylinders, and, he thought, for the first time ever. Even when he was home, there, wherever, and they were taking care of him, he didn't feel this good. So much for what they knew.

Young teenage girls, he concluded, they're the ticket, girls who were just a few feet past puberty, like fresh eggs. Time, that wicked thief, had less opportunity to steal their radiance, make it duller, coat it in minutes and seconds and hours, thicken it over with days and weeks and months until they were so old, you had to scrape away to find the glitter.

Now he would go to a different supermarket in which there was nothing older than sixteen. He would hang around schools. He would stalk the Brownies and the Girl Scouts, or he would simply wander through malls. They gathered there like birds on telephone wires, chattering, giggling, parading, and flirting, trying out their wings.

Maybe he would never need to sleep now. Sleep was really to refresh oneself, to rest tired limbs, to restore and rebuild dying cells. He did that instantly so why sleep? He would truly be a shark, always on the hunt. What an advantage he would have? They had to sleep. They grew exhausted. They were more like vampires than he was, crawling back into their temporary coffins every night. He was the mythical bird that never lighted, pausing only to consume its nourishment.

He actually felt as if he had grown inches, widened, thickened. He was truly bigger than life. Still, he recognized that he had to be cautious. They would be coming after him again, more intently, more determined. He was no fool. If anything, his mental capacities were as heightened as his muscles. Too little time had passed. That picture in the paper was still vivid in the minds of some people, he concluded.

Memories of the motel owner returned and he nodded at an idea. As soon as he came upon a mall, he pulled in and went to the large drug store. He bought black hair coloring and then he returned to his motel room and washed it in. He decided that although it still looked artificial, he had done a better job than the motel owner. It was passable. At least people wouldn't spot him from a distance, he thought. He even colored his eyebrows.

There weren't really all that many people who could recognize his face with certainty—our face, he thought. When he gazed into the mirror, he did see himself twice. He saw a duplicate of himself just under the skin as if he wore a mask. He'll always be with me, he concluded. As long as I live, he lives. Yes.

Now it was time to protect him, to protect us, he decided. When you pursue a shark, don't lose sight of him, he warned the predators. If you do, you will soon find yourself pursued. Predator will become prey.

I'm standing behind you, he thought and sang, I'm standing behind you, on your dying day.

It made him laugh so hard that he had tears in his eyes. Suddenly, he became serious and went to the telephone. He found the telephone book in the drawer beneath it and looked for the number. Then he punched it out and waited.

"I'd like an appointment with Dr. Barnard today," he said as soon as he heard the office identified.

"Oh, I'm sorry. Dr. Barnard is on vacation this week."

"Vacation?"

"Yes. I do have an opening with Dr. Templeman at four-thirty, if you would like."

"No, I want to see Dr. Barnard. Where is she? When will she be back?"

"About a week. I'm sorry. The best I can do for you is schedule you for a week from this coming Wednesday. Would you like a morning or afternoon appointment?"

He just hung up.

And sat there, fuming with frustration. One of the consequences of being at so heightened a level of activity was the difficulty of slowing it down, stop going in one direction and take another, pausing. The urge to keep moving burned like a hot coal in his stomach. He raged, threw the phone across the room after tearing the wire from the wall, and then kicked over the chair.

Nothing stops me, he thought. Nothing stops me. He walked to the front windows and looked out. The day was grayer than he had realized. It might rain here. There was light traffic, about seven other cars in the motel lot, but no one walking about, no real activity around him. How dull it all suddenly looked. Why stay after all? He could get into his car and drive off, forget about it all, just go on. Maybe he should.

No, he heard and turned.

He was standing there shaking his head.

What?

We can't just go on. They'll come after us, armed to the teeth with information, pictures, witnesses. They'll hunt us down and they'll stomp on us.

He saw that his hair wasn't dyed.

"Your hair isn't dyed, too," he said.

He smiled back at him.

"Doesn't have to be. I'm inside you most of the time, remember? Thanks to you, that is."

"Oh. Right. Well, what do we do?"

"You'll know what to do. Just go on," he said nodding at the door.

"Right. I do know what to do."

He opened the door. The rush of cool air washed over him and despite the clouds, the light made him squint. He pulled up his shoulders. He could feel him slipping back inside him, strengthening, supporting. He was confident again and started for the car.

Yes, he thought as he opened the car door. I know what to do.

I know exactly what to do.

Curt sat beside her when she made the call. It took quite a while to track Will Dennis down, and at one point his secretary tried to talk her into calling later.

"No, I must speak with him now. You have to get to him," she said firmly.

"Well, I'm trying. He hasn't responded to the page yet. You want to continue holding?"

"Absolutely," Terri said. "We'll hold until hell freezes over."

She heard the secretary blow air through her lips and then the elevator music began again, periodically interrupted by messages and information from the district attorney's office, the county clerk's office, and the tax assessor's office.

"He's busy composing what new lies he's going to tell you," Curt said.

"My next call will be to the newspapers and radio and television stations," she threatened.

It was nearly fifteen minutes before the secretary came back on to say, "Please hold for Mr. Dennis."

Terri sat up.

"Before you start, let me tell you I've been on the phone all this time with Dr. Stanley's people," Will Dennis began.

"And?"

There was a truly pregnant pause.

"Apparently, we sent Dr. Stanley back in a body bag and not, what shall I call him, It?"

"What? How could that be?"

"You know he's a perfect duplication. If I had any doubt, which I didn't at the time, you would have ended it when you described how you had struck him in the forehead. Both of them had head bruises, and practically in the same place. He wore Stanley's clothing. He responded to everything the way I expected Doctor Stanley to respond. There just wasn't any way to tell," he claimed, his voice now high-pitched.

"What do you intend to do?" she asked.

"I'm working on it with the higher-ups," he said. "They're bringing in everyone they can. There hasn't been a manhunt like this since we went after bin Laden."

Curt, who was sharing the earpiece, pulled back and shook his head.

"Tell him, they have to have a press conference and let the public know it all," she told Will Dennis.

"It's not my decision, Doc. I've made that suggestion myself. It's out of my hands."

"It's not out of mine," she said.

"Nothing's changed in that regard, Terri. You do that and they'll paint you into a corner. They . . ."

"They've lost control now, Will. If you care at all about the people who elected you, and the people who are vulnerable to this, you'll take a leadership position. I'll stand beside you," she said. "We'll do it together."

He was silent a moment.

"Will?"

"Let me think about that, Terri. You might be right," he admitted. "I'll call you later today. I want to hear what they've got to say, what they're doing. Okay? I'll call you this afternoon."

"I'm not back home. I'm at Hyman's cabin in Willowemac. I'm supposedly taking a much-needed rest with Curt."

"Understood," he said. "I know the place. It's peaceful. I envy you."

"Yeah? Well, I'm not feeling very restful at the moment, Will."

Curt smiled.

"Squeeze the bastard," he cheered.

"If this goes on, Will, you will be the one blamed."

"Is that a threat?"

"Just a clearly thought-out realization, Will. You have the information and you're sitting on it and another person is dead, and a teenager to boot."

He was quiet.

Curt's smile widened as he nodded and whispered, "Yeah, right on."

"I'll call you later," Will said. The line went dead. She held the receiver a moment and then slowly cradled it.

"Maybe, I should go back to the office," she said.

"To do what? You're only an hour away, baby. Seconds away from reaching the media. Will Dennis knows that in spades now. We might as well go fishing. You've done what you can and very well, too," he added.

"I guess you're right," she said after a moment's thinking.

"Sure I'm right. It's like any negotiation. You deliver your best assault and then you let the other side stew. A watched pot never boils," he added.

She smiled.

"Who told you that one?"

"My grandmother always used it, and Dad never forgot it. He loved to move on to another case and leave the first one hanging there."

"Yes, well I don't know if this one is hanging or seeping," she said.

He leaned over to kiss her.

"You'll know soon enough," he said. "C'mon, I'll put the worms on the hooks."

She laughed and followed him out. He had their fishing poles set against the railing and a basket between them.

"What's in there? And don't tell me worms," she said quickly.

"No, some wine, some cheese, a loaf of that French bread. A loaf of bread, a jug of wine, and thou beneath me in the wilderness. Ah love," he moaned and she poked him.

"Curt Levitt, since when did you become the romantic?"

"It was that smack on my head," he told her.

"In that case I'll bop you every night."

"Big talker," he teased, kissed her on the cheek and started for the boat. She watched him a moment and then followed. Despite it all she couldn't help feeling guilty about enjoying anything. She should be doing more, she thought, only she had no idea what it was she could do now.

Pick on the unsuspecting fish, she thought and hurried to catch up to Curt.

• • • •

He sat in his vehicle and watched the front entrance of the county building. At one point he saw the two men who had accompanied Will Dennis to the motel and handled the cleanup. They went into the building and a little over an hour later, they emerged, but without Will Dennis.

He wasn't patient, but he looked patient sitting there in the car, calm. No one going by paid the slightest attention to him, he thought, actually, to us. He actually felt invisible. Finally, Will Dennis came out of the building. He was accompanied by two sheriff's patrolmen. They stopped at the bottom of the steps and spoke for a while. Then the patrolmen went to their vehicle and Will Dennis walked around and into the parking lot where his county vehicle was parked. He got into it and drove out.

Following at a safe distance behind, he could see Will using his car phone. He drove a good fifteen minutes before pulling into a self-service gas station about five miles or so past what was once the Monticello Trotters Race Track. Restaurants and gas stations, as well as motels had sprouted around it, but it all looked in hibernation now. There was nowhere near the bustling activity that characterized the area in its heyday.

Ghosts, he thought to himself. This place is haunted by its past. Memories lingered in old road signs that made promises no longer kept, hawking this bungalow colony or that small hotel, tempting visitors with now faded pictures of beautiful lakes and emerald-green golf courses. We've got to do our business and move on, he thought. There was an inherent danger to camping out in cemeteries. The dead might enjoy your company.

He pulled up behind Will Dennis, who was again on his cellular, talking while he filled his gas tank. Dennis had his back to him. He got out slowly, fingering the pistol he had used back in the motel owner's apartment. There was only one other gas customer, and he was finished, closing his tank and getting into his car. He watched him drive away. Will Dennis still had his back to him, still talked on the phone.

"Okay then," he said, "I'll be there in an hour."

He flipped his phone closed and turned to reach for the gas hose, which had stopped its flow. For a moment, probably because of the black hair, he didn't recognize him. He even flashed a smile and said, "Just about done."

"Leave it," he told him.

"Pardon me?" Will said. He stared and then rose slowly as his eyes began to reflect recognition.

He pulled out the pistol.

"Leave it," he repeated. "Just walk to my car."

Will Dennis looked about frantically.

"Move," he ordered firmly.

"Look, there are people who can help you. They're here now, and I was just going to meet with them, actually. Why don't you follow me in your car and . . ."

He pulled the hammer back on the pistol.

"Walk to my car or die here," he said.

Will nodded and started toward his car. He backed up to let him pass. The driver's door was still open.

"Get in behind the wheel," he commanded as he opened the rear door. "Go on."

"What do you want?" Will asked.

He smiled.

"I told you that before. I want more. Now get in and close the door."

Will did and he got in behind him and held the pistol close to the back of his head.

"Imagine," he said, "your brains splattered on that windshield. What a mess of thoughts and memories, huh?"

"I can help you," Will said. "Really. I'm on the phone with everyone involved. We have a solution."

"Oh, I know there is a solution. I know you can help me." He stopped smiling and added, "I want you to take me to her. Go on."

"Take you to whom?"

"The doctor, Dr. Barnard, the one who could make trouble for us. Go on."

"But . . ."

"Drive or decorate the windshield," he said putting the barrel of the gun against the back of his head.

Will dropped the shift into drive and pulled around his own car, looking at it longingly, as longingly as a man who was being swept past his last hope for rescue at sea.

"There's no need for this," Will said. "You're a very valuable person. They want to take you back, to help you, to make sure you're healthy and everything you need is provided."

"I know what I need and I know how to get it," he said.

Will thought.

"I don't know where she is," he said.

"Then make a call and find out. You can find out anything you need to find out, and believe me," he added poking him sharply just where his neck and head joined, "you need to find this out."

"She's at work for sure," Will said.

"See. You're screwing up already. I know she's on vacation."

"Well, then she's gone. She's out of the area."

"She's only away for a few days. She can't be far. If she is gone, you are gone," he said. "Either you will die or she will die today. Who will it be?" he asked.

"Why do you have to kill her, or me for that matter?"

"We've got to protect ourselves."

"We?"

"Yes, we," he said.

"Look, if you're including me in this, I want to assure you . . ."

"We're not," he said.

Will gazed into the rearview mirror and saw him, his eyes fixed on the back of his head. He's mad, he thought. Whatever he is, he's insane.

"This won't help you," he said. "They won't take you back if you do something like this. I'm the chief law enforcement officer in the county!"

"That doesn't matter to us. We don't want to go back now. We want to go forward. Are we going to her or what?" He leaned closer.

"Okay, okay, we're going to her," Will said.

"We knew you would make that choice," he said smiling. "We know you as well as you know yourself."

Will Dennis shuddered with a chill that brought him back to his childhood days when he first confronted something horrifying in a movie. He had gone with his older brother and his older brother's friends. His older brother wasn't supposed to take him, but he had to watch him that day and he wasn't about to be stuck in some G-rated film. He confronted his first vampire on the screen and cringed at the sight of blood dripping from those long, sharp teeth.

The creature seating behind him, for that was the only way he could think of him, a creature, revived those images. Would he lean forward any moment and sink his teeth into his neck, drawing out some precious nutrient and leaving him in mortal agony? Will Dennis thought his position had brought him face to face with some pretty cruel and violent people, but he always had the sense that he and the force behind him had the upper hand. They were there to punish, and punish they would. This was different. No court, no laws, no objections and motions to strike mattered. He was as helpless as the women who had fallen victim.

"You understand, I hope, that I was cooperating with your people. I've kept your existence secret, just like they wanted, and like I'm sure you want, right?"

"What did they promise you?" he asked.

"Me? I just do what I have to do to help. It's all for the better, isn't it? I mean as I understand it, you will be the answer to all diseases and illness, to aging itself. You're quite a wonderful thing."

Will saw him turn his eyebrows in. He had him thinking.

"You're absolutely right about this," Will continued, excited by the apparent breakthrough. "You've got to stop this Dr. Barnard. She doesn't have the same view of things. She's threatening to make trouble. She threatened me on the phone just an hour or so ago, in fact."

"Oh?"

"She said she was going to go public and expose you. She was going to put the blame on me. Actually, when you came up to me at the gas station just now, I was talking with your people, deciding how we would handle her."

"Well, now you know how we'll handle her."

"Yeah, right. That's good. She's at this cabin that

belongs to the old doctor she works with, Templeman. It's on the lake, in the woods. We're about forty minutes away. I know exactly where it is. I've fished on that lake, hunted around it, too. I grew up here, you know."

"That's nice," he said.

Will actually felt himself relax.

"Now she's not alone. I'm giving you important information here. She's with her fiancé, this lawyer, Curt Levitt. He's the one who you, I mean, who Dr. Stanley, confronted. You've got to be careful."

"Oh, I'm careful," he said. "Drive on and keep talking. It's better than the radio."

Will saw him smiling. Was he really satisfied or was he toying with him. Keep talking? Yes, that was the way to handle people like him.

I'll slip out of this, he thought. Somehow, I'll survive.

He drove on and he kept talking.

Although the day began quite overcast, the cloud cover thinned and weakened until direct sunlight wove through the gauzy layers and brightened the water on the lake. In the distance it looked like ice to Terri. The wind had died down and the boat barely rocked now. She was lying back in Curt's arms. They had just eaten their cheese and bread and had nearly finished the bottle of Merlot. She felt cozy and warm as she leaned back.

He leaned forward to kiss her on the forehead and move off some strands of her hair. She opened her eyes and looked up at him.

"Happy?" he asked.

"Content. Glad I followed your orders for a change, Doctor," she told him and he laughed.

"Why is it," he asked, "that I get the feeling this is really a unique occasion?"

"Don't worry. I'll settle down to just a mere twenty hours a day," she replied, and they both laughed softly. She closed her eyes again and he took a deep breath.

"I think I must have dug up sour worms or something. We haven't had a bite."

"Oh. I saw the bob thing bobbing."

"You did?"

He sat up quickly, moving her off him to seize the pole. When he wound in the line, he saw the hook was clean.

"Oh, that's great," he said. "We've provided a picnic for the fish, too."

She laughed harder, her voice carrying over the water.

"If we don't catch anything significant, don't tell my father," he warned. "He's never gone fishing without success."

"Stop competing with him. You're your own man, Curt."

"Aye, aye, Dr. Freud."

She smiled and shook her head. Then she turned serious.

"Do you suppose there is some kind of psychological drive to recreate ourselves in our children?"

"Are you kidding? If I heard him say, 'when I was your age . . .' once, I heard it a hundred thousand times."

"Maybe that's part of this unrelenting drive to clone ourselves," she offered.

"I'm sure it is. I'm sure it has a lot to do with ego. I'm so good. There should be more of me. Of course, there would have to be more of you or I'd be in competition with myself," he said. He laughed, but she didn't. "What?"

"That's what he's all about, I think, competition. In the end he wants to be better than his original self."

"He's already better. He's survived."

"Yes," she said. She looked worried.

"Terri?"

"Let's go back, Curt. I want to go back," she said with that final and firm tone he recognized.

"Why?"

"As far as I know there are only two people, three now counting you, who know the truth, Curt. The other person is Will Dennis, and we've handled him wrong, I think. This isn't a matter of negotiations. You don't negotiate with cancer or pneumonia. You eliminate it.

"Or," she added pulling in her fishing pole, "it eliminates you."

"Right," he said, somewhat annoyed. "I knew this vacation idea was a dream."

"It's not that," she began, but he pulled the cord and got the little engine going, revving it up as high as he could to drown her out. She fell back against her seat as he turned the small boat and headed for the dock. She saw him squinting.

"What?" she asked, sitting up and turning.

"Someone's on the dock waving at us. It looks like . . . our boy, Will Dennis," he said.

Her heart stopped and started with a thick, resonant pounding she could feel in her temples.

"Is he alone?"

"Far as I can tell he is," Curt said.

They drew closer.

"I guess you got to him," he added.

Will Dennis stood back as they brought the boat in, Curt cutting the engine and stepping up.

"Will," he said, nodding.

"I thought it would be better to come out here to speak with you, Doc," he told Terri as Curt helped her out of the boat.

"Something new happen?"

"Yes. We got him," he said.

"You got him?"

"How did that happen so fast?" Curt asked. He reached for the poles and the marine bag.

Will shook his head and smiled.

"These guys are good. I'll never resist calling in the Feds. Petty jealousies in law enforcement help only the perps."

"That's very big of you, Will," Curt said.

"Yeah, well, you grow with your problems, Curt." He looked toward the house. "Great place. How about we have some coffee and talk?"

"Okay," Terri said. She looked at Curt who nodded and the three of them started for the house. "Well, I can't deny this is a big load off my mind," she continued.

It was Curt who first heard the footsteps behind them and turned. Terri had her arms folded and her head down. She kept walking beside Will Dennis.

"Terri," Curt called.

She paused and turned.

Dr. Garret's duplicate was standing there, holding a pistol pointed directly at Curt. She looked up at Will.

"There was nothing I could do," he whined, his arms out. "He had me in his gunsights the whole time I was on the dock. He jumped me at a gas station about an hour ago and made me take him out here."

"Made you?" Curt asked.

"At gunpoint," Will added.

"What do you want?" Curt asked, stepping forward aggressively, ignoring the gun.

"Curt!" Terri warned.

Now that she was actually confronting him, she could of course see how perfect was the mirror image of Dr.

Garret Stanley, only she noticed some swelling in his cheeks, a reddening of his complexion, and a clear symptom of a thyroid problem—bulging in his eyes. He was breathing hard, too.

"What do we want, Mr. Dennis?" he asked Will, smiling. "Well? He wants to know. Tell him."

"He wants more," Will said obediently.

"More? More of what?" Curt asked.

"More of everything, just like everyone else. Let's all walk slowly to the house. Mr. Dennis had a good idea. We'll have some coffee and talk."

Curt hesitated on the balls of his feet, poised to charge.

"Curt, please," Terri cried. It wasn't only the sight of the pistol that frightened her now. The man was having some sort of physical reaction and from her perspective, it made him look even more maddening.

Curt looked at her and then joined her, glaring up at Will Dennis.

"This is your responsibility," he told him. Will said nothing.

Curt grasped one of the fishing poles tightly. Terri could see it in his face—he was thinking of spinning and striking him.

"Don't," she whispered.

"Don't be plotting anything," he said seeing them talk. "Stay together," he ordered when they reached the door. "Slowly, go ever so slowly. I'm right behind you."

Terri opened the door and they all entered. She looked back at him and saw he was sweating profusely now. His gun hand trembled a bit.

"Mr. Dennis," he said pointing to the rocker. "Why don't you take the center seat. You're used to being the center of things, aren't you? Go on," he snapped.

Will looked at Terri and Curt and then walked to the chair and sat.

"Comfy?" he asked him.

"Listen," Will began, but stopped and stared.

He had his hand up for silence and then tilted his head as if he was listening to something. He smiled and nodded. Then, he stepped forward and shot Will Dennis dead center in the heart.

In the house the .38 sounded like a cannon. Will Dennis's chest seemed to explode, the blood spurting down his white shirt. The impact made him rock in the chair. His look of surprise froze on his face and his head fell forward and the rocking stopped.

Terri screamed.

He turned to her and Curt, who were frozen in place, Terri clutching Curt's hand.

"My God," she managed.

"We had no need of him now," he said, nodding at the dead Will Dennis. "All he would do is wiggle and squirm, lie, and make every effort to save his pathetic life. It's his nature. He lacks the pure honesty of someone like me who never denies his true purpose.

"You two should feel honored," he continued, "I'm truly the New Man, the future of the species. All we've been up to now is God's little experiment, not yet perfected. Oh, well, at least He has given us the ability to finish His work, eh?"

He wiped his forehead with the back of his left hand and saw the layer of sweat. He glanced at himself in the mirror hanging on the wall and turned to Terri.

"What do you think, Doc?"

"You don't look well," she said.

"I know." He smiled. "But I know what I need to make myself well, better than well," he said. "You're not as young as I like them these days, but I know you can give it to me."

TWENTY-THREE

"I can help you more easily," she said. "You look like you're suffering a vitamin B_1 deficiency and acquiring beriberi. I have B-complex serum in my medical bag. A simple shot . . ."

He shook his head.

"No, that's not enough. Even with a continuous IV feed, they kept me in a nearly semiconscious state compared to how I can be," he said. "They were never very interested in my being a fully active individual. Everything has become more complicated. There's only one way to reach the level we need now. I have two mouths to feed, so to speak. You see," he said to Curt who moved protectively toward Terri, "that's what we really meant by more. We need more."

The look in Curt's face told Terri he was going to do something dramatic and drastic any moment. Surely he would die, she thought. There was no way to reason with this person. Something Doctor Stanley had told her about people who believed clones lacked souls returned. There was no remorse, no sense of morality in this laboratory offspring. Whatever Doctor Stanley had created, he hadn't foreseen a certain mad coldness.

Only one thing came to mind as a solution. She ripped the marine bag from Curt's hands and opened it to pull out the serrated fisherman's knife.

He laughed when she held it up for him to see.

"What do you think you're going to do with that?" he asked. "You can't stop me with that."

"I'm going to keep you from getting what you need, then," she said and brought the blade to her neck where she would cut quickly into her carotid artery. Death would be quick. "You know the human body," she said. "You know what happens once I do this."

"You won't," he said.

"Why not? You're going to kill me anyway, aren't you? That's what will happen. The only difference is, from how you are degenerating, I can be assured you will die too."

He shook his head and looked at Curt with a certain new desperate interest in his eyes.

"You won't do that, but just in case, Curt will precede me to the Afterlife."

"Or I'll go for you now and you'll shoot me," Curt threatened, not sure where Terri was heading with all this. He took a step forward.

Finally, the look of confidence left his face. He was getting redder, breaking out in what looked like hives.

He pulled at his neck collar, the sweat now dripping off his cheeks. He glanced at the dead Will Dennis and then back at them.

"Let Curt go," she said, "and I'll drop the knife. Once he's out that door and in our vehicle, I'll give you the knife."

"No," Curt said.

"Do it," she ordered, pressing the knife against her skin enough to cause some bleeding.

"Terri!" Curt cried. He didn't know what to do first, get that knife out of her hand or lunge for the killer.

"Maybe we'll just kill him first," he said, seeing their devotion to each other. "If you don't do what I tell you to do, I'll shoot him right now."

"Do that and I'll definitely have no reason to live," she said with such firmness, the smile left his face again. "You had better decide really soon," she added. "Time is not on your side. You're hyperventilating. You'll probably go into cardiac arrest any moment and I won't be giving you any CPR. That's for sure."

He tilted his head as if he were listening to another voice again.

"Okay," he said smiling and nodding slowly. "You," he told Curt, "get out. Drive away."

"I won't do it," Curt said, more to Terri than to him.

"You've got to, Curt. He'll kill us both for sure."

He studied her a moment. This wasn't just a sacrifice. She had some plan in mind. He had to trust her. Her eyes were pleading for it. He debated with himself. If he left and she failed, he would feel terrible, but if he stayed, what would he accomplish? Only their certain deaths.

"Okay," he said. He looked at the clone. "If she does die," he said, "I'll be coming for you."

"Or we'll be coming for you," he countered, the smile still there.

Curt glanced at Terri again. She nodded and mouthed, "I love you."

He turned and walked to the door. There, he hesitated, looked back, and then walked out.

"When he starts the engine," she said quickly.

They stood facing each other and waited. The automobile was started. She lowered her hand and he rushed at her, seizing her wrist and twisting it until she released the knife. He held onto her and looked into her face. She thought his eyes were two balls of ice.

"To the bedroom," he said. "Lead the way."

He released her wrist and she walked ahead of him. When they reached the bedroom, he closed the door behind them and locked it.

"Now," he said, "you will truly fulfill your oath and benefit your patient. You diagnosed us. Now, let's cure us."

"This isn't going to help you," she said. "It will be only temporary. Look at what's been happening to you. You need to replenish your nutrients more and more frequently. It's only a matter of time before it doesn't work at all and you'll die a horrible death. Go back to the laboratory."

Stall him, she thought. His onslaught of wet beriberi was coming faster and faster. The symptoms were clicking off in her mind. The vein pulse in his neck was rising. He was having more trouble breathing. The resistance between the arteries and veins dropped further and further, his blood flowing round his body more rapidly. His heart was struggling to maintain this higher output.

"I can give you this shot to tide you over and then you can . . ."

"Get undressed," he screamed. "Now!"

She backed away. He won't shoot me, she thought. He knows that would mean his own death as well. She shook her head.

"You're not living up to the deal. You're cheating."

"If you listen to me . . . ."

He roared with rage and somehow gathered the strength to literally leap at her, his feet leaving the ground, his hands landing on her neck. He threw her down on the bed with such force that he nearly knocked the breath out of her. Why wasn't he weaker?

She struggled, trying to keep his hands from tearing at her clothing and then, he brought his mouth to hers and pressed down with such determination and desperation, she was caught with surprise. She felt her own eyes bulging as if he was blowing air into her skull and pushing them out of their sockets. Then his tongue latched to hers and struggle as she would, she could not free it. She began to gag. Her arms weakened. He pushed them to the side as if they were broken and began to undo her jeans.

She jerked her torso in a vain effort to toss him off. His hands were on her naked buttocks. She felt her eyes going back in her head. This wasn't a rape as much as a ravishing, she thought. She was blacking out. Her final act of resistance was an attempt to clench her teeth. He put his finger into her mouth, beside his own tongue, and easily forced it open.

Moments later, she went unconscious.

Meanwhile, Curt drove as far as he thought would convince that creature he was fleeing for his life. He pulled over just after the end of the driveway and doubled back to the lake house. He knew he wasn't nearly a 100 percent recuperated yet from his minor concussion. This tension and terror, the effort to get back quickly, already had taken quite a toll on his physical stamina. He was breathing hard and his head was pounding.

He realized it would make no sense to just go bursting through the front door. He couldn't directly confront a man with a gun, especially a man who had no hesitation about using it. He went around the side of the house instead, and, staying close to the building, looked through the window into the living room. He saw Will Dennis's body, collapsed in the chair, but no one else. Then he moved around the corner of the house and came along the back to the window of the bedroom he and Terri were using. Slowly, he brought himself up to look in. At first he didn't see anything. Then he saw her, her clothes torn off her body, her arm dangling over the edge of the bed. Her hand moved with some weak effort to reach something.

The slam of the front door froze him. He listened until he heard the sound of Will Dennis's car engine being started. After a moment he went around the other side of the building and came out front just as the car started away. Without any pause, he rushed the entrance of the house and charged through the living room. When he entered the bedroom, he found Terri had fallen to the floor.

"Terri!" he screamed and rushed to her. He held her in his arms.

She was gasping, her eyes bulging, her skin looking like a fire had been started inside her and was climbing up toward her brain. She gagged, grunted, and swung her head to the right. He followed her gaze and saw her doctor's bag. Quickly he lowered her to the floor and seized the bag, opening it.

"What?" he cried.

She closed her eyes with the effort to speak.

"B," she said and he scoured the bag, pulling out medicine bottles until he saw the one labeled B-complex. He unwrapped a syringe and inserted the needle. As he filled it, he looked at her and she nodded. He kept filling it until there was no more room and then he injected it into her arm.

She closed her eyes and for a long moment, he thought it was too late. She did indeed appear to have stopped breathing. His mind raced and he began CPR. A good two minutes into it, she coughed, opened, and closed her eyes, and then took a deep breath and managed a small smile.

"Not bad for an attorney," she said in a loud whisper.

He couldn't help it.

He started to cry, the tears flowing freely as he reached down to embrace her and hold her closely like someone who would never let go.

When he saw their car parked at the end of the driveway, he went into another rage. The bastard hadn't run for his life after all. He had gone back. He pulled alongside the car and thought. This was an opportunity to make it a clean sweep, not an opportunity to pass up.

He looked in the rearview mirror and saw his second self sitting there.

"We don't want to give them any head start to come after us, do we?"

"No," he replied.

He turned off the car engine and got out. Clutching his pistol, he began to stride back to the house.

Inside, Curt lifted Terri and placed her gently on the

bed, covering her with the blanket. He caressed her face and kissed her cheek.

"Some water," she said, "cold water."

"Right. Then I'd better get on the phone."

She nodded and he went out to the kitchen. He had just filled the glass and turned when he heard the footsteps behind him and looked into that maddening face, only now it was vibrant and healthy.

He shook his head.

"You surprised me," he said. "You never left. Love is really weakness because it keeps the individual from doing the things that will protect it. If there was ever a lesson to be learned about survival . . ."

"What are you surviving for?" Curt asked him.

"Pleasure," he replied. "Now what I will do here after I kill you is make it look like you shot Will Dennis. That will confuse them for quite a while. You might have slowed me down if you had kept going and reported all this. Thanks for being a fool," he said and raised his pistol.

Before he could fire it, however, Terri, who had come up behind him quietly, the fishing knife in her hand, drove it down with medical expertise, cutting deeply through the medulla and severing that part known as the pyramid.

His eyes went up with surprise, and he managed to begin a turn. When he saw her, the shock was as much responsible for his total collapse as the loss of his motor functions. The gun bounced on the floor.

Terri hovered over him, breathing hard, struggling to keep herself from falling. Curt charged forward and grabbed her. They both looked down at him, watching him die. His eyes were open. The light in them dwindled into tiny sparks that faded.

"The only thing that frightens me now," Terri hoarsely whispered, "is that somewhere back there, there might be another."

The ambulance took both bodies away after the medical examiner was done. Curt sat out on the porch, dictating events as he recalled them. There were six sheriff's deputies, the sheriff himself, two county detectives, and a state BCI investigator, a real one, all gathered as his audience. Terri, exhausted still, remained sleeping in the bedroom. The skeptical and incredulous looks on the faces of the law enforcement officers amplified with every reference to the science Curt made. He did the best he could, but he could see he wasn't being very convincing.

Then they came.

Two FBI investigators.

They pulled the sheriff and the BCI detective aside, and when they were finished, the sheriff told his officers to get back to their regular tours and forget what Curt had said.

"I'll deal with the press," he insisted. The BCI man

looked happy to have any responsibility at all lifted from his shoulders.

That's the way it's going to be, Curt thought. No one wants to deal with this.

And that's why, he thought as well, it will continue.

He went back inside to check on Terri.

Despite her condition, which was mainly severe fatigue from the trauma of experiencing the first stages of beriberi and all that followed, she insisted he take her home.

"To our house," she said.

He loaded the car and literally carried her to it. She closed her eyes and lay back when he lowered the front seat as far as it would recline, and then they left the cabin and started for his home.

Curt called Hyman Templeman and he came over to examine Terri. Afterward, while she rested, he and Curt had tumblers of single malt scotches and sat in the living room. He listened to Curt's retelling of the chilling events.

"I saved her life and she saved mine," he concluded.

"Not a bad way to start a marriage," Hyman quipped, and Curt smiled.

They both looked up when Terri entered, wearing her robe and slippers.

"Just like men. You go to the booze to comfort yourselves," she said. "And don't offer me any," she added.

"A mere cc of that will knock you for a loop in the condition you're in," Hyman said.

"What's so bad about that?" she countered.

Curt looked at Hyman and he shrugged.

He rose, poured her a short shot on the rocks, added some water, and gave it to her. She sat, sipped a little, and then looked at Hyman.

"You know," she said, "a part of me was fascinated with all this when I heard what had been done. There is such promise in the future, especially the work with stem cells."

He nodded.

"Unfortunately," he said, "it's like every other major discovery from the wheel forward. The bad almost outweighs the good . . . gunpowder, rockets, nuclear energy. . . . I guess there was good reason to prohibit Adam and Eve from biting into the fruit of the Tree of Knowledge."

"Maybe, but it's too late now," Curt said.

They looked at him.

"Mankind will spend the rest of its history trying to get back into Paradise," he added.

Hyman smiled.

"Well," he said rising, "I'll leave it up to you two to continue the effort."

He gazed around and nodded and then smiled at them.

"From the looks of it, you have a little bit of paradise

to share already. You're still on vacation, young lady," he said sternly to Terri, "so don't even entertain the notion of returning to work."

She laughed.

He kissed her on the cheek, and then Curt walked him to the door and thanked him for coming over.

For a long moment he stood there, watching him drive off. Terri was suddenly at his side, holding his arm and resting her head against his shoulder.

"I remember Gramps coming in from the field. I could see he was tired, but it was a satisfactory exhaustion. He looked like he had accomplished something. Then he would see me standing here and his face would brighten with laughter and joy and the fatigue would fly off his face. I wasn't that small then, but I would run down to him and he would lift me with such ease, I thought he was the strongest man in the world and always would be.

"Grandma would yell at him for carrying a boy my size back to the house, especially after a day's hard labor, and he would shake his head and say, 'He's not heavy. He's just a thought, a dream, the future.'

"It's nice to be thought of as the future, don't you think, Doc?"

"Yes," she said. She lifted her face to kiss him. "No matter what, that's good. And they with all their science and experimentation will never take it away from us if we just hold on to our humanity."

"Funny thing for a doctor to say."

"Maybe I'm more like Hyman than I care to admit."

"That's not so bad.

"No, I guess it isn't," she said.

They kissed and turned to go back inside.

He paused and she looked off into the distance with him. She saw his eyes narrow and for a moment become the eyes of a young boy again. She could hear the words he wanted to speak.

It was on her lips to say it, too.

I see him.

I see him coming home, the future in his arms.

POCKET STAR BOOKS
proudly presents

The Hunted

Andrew Neiderman

Available in paperback Summer 2005
from Pocket Star Books

Turn the page for a preview of
The Hunted . . .

off and stopped him on his test that he didn't take the tom

PROLOGUE

Al Jones put his head down, folded his arms over his nose and charged right through the bushes. Normally, he would have circumvented this vegetation, but he had no time. Tiny branches found openings in the defensive wall he tried to create with his arms. It was truly as if the woods itself had turned against him. These branches scratched, tore and poked at his chin, cheeks and forehead. Thorns from blackberry bushes easily punctured his uncovered and unprotected thighs, but he didn't hesitate. There was no time to worry about any of the wounds. He had to go forward.

Naked, he was freezing. Fall was more like winter in the upstate New York Catskills this year. There were a few inches of frost in the ground and they had already had their first snow in mid-October. It had been weeks since the trees lost their leaves. That gray brush of Mother Nature had been wiped across the forest. Except for the Pine, there was no green, and with the foliage gone, no orange, red or yellow, but just the dismal charcoal frown everywhere he or anyone else gazed outside the small hamlet of Centerville, one of the oldest communities in Sullivan County.

Vaguely Al realized the cuts he was suffering were becoming serious because of how deeply they were going and how fast they were accumulating. Blood streaked down his forehead. It got into his eyes and made him blink. There was a constant buzz in his head. About a hundred or so yards back, he had caught himself on a low hanging maple tree branch. It had nearly taken his head off and dropped him on his rear, but he didn't take the time to evaluate any head injuries even though he had felt the sharp sting across his scalp and was dizzy for more than just a moment.

He had barely waited for his blurred vision to clear before he charged ahead again. Just like now, there wasn't even a second's pause available. Stopping to catch his breath had become a luxury. One step followed another, his bare feet pounding down and the soles of them getting punctured repeatedly by sharp small stones and broken twigs. He could see the little blood trail he was leaving behind.

Besides all that, his knees were complaining vociferously and his lungs were threatening to explode. However, he was afraid to think too long about any of it. If he did, his entire body might mutiny and just stop performing. Utter abject terror had already gripped him and was moving quickly up his legs, around his waist, squeezing toward his heart. It was one thing to be threatened with death, but another to be tormented, to be forced to strip and then be told to run for your life.

"Go on. Run like a frightened deer," he had said. "Run like you made him run, like he's still running."

"Who?" he wanted to ask, but he could see from the look in his eyes that there was not going to be any discussion, just a struggle to live.

Now, because of the great fear building in his chest, everything Al did and everything that happened around him reached his consciousness after a good ten seconds delay. It was as though he was already out of his body. He was so far from what it did and what happened to it that like an echo, everything reached him well after the fact. This intensified his terror. Death was already racing side by side with him and working its way into him. He flayed about like a madman who could actually see the Phantom dark spirit and was trying to drive it away. One watching might think he was being attacked by angry bees.

The overcast afternoon sky seemed to be descending, crashing down upon him. It was as if the whole world was closing in, cutting off his every avenue of escape. When he was a young boy, he thought of the forests here as endless. As he grew up, the world shrunk around him. And now, now he felt he might just run off the edge of the earth. He was that close to the end.

Finally, unable to take another step, he paused and leaned against an old maple tree. The bark smelled fresh, good, giving memory to a stack of pancakes. He rested there, breathing hard, listening to the thumping his own pounding heart made as it reverberated through every bone in his body. Then he took a breath and turned to tune into the sounds behind him, hoping to hear nothing.

But the chorus of his own impending doom was there, distinct, firm. He could hear the branches cracking and the bushes being pushed aside. There was no question that he was still coming. Carrying out the commands of Death and completely under its firm control, his pursuer was determined, definite, undeterred.

Al looked up. Birds sprang out of trees, their wings flapping frantically. Field mice, squirrels, and rabbits passed each other in flight. Something very ominous was upon them. Raw instinct sounded alarms in every living thing and he heard them clearly. In fact, in a strange way his senses were heightened now. Al could almost hear his pursuer's heavy breathing along with his own.

"Why?" he screamed, throwing his voice behind him without pausing to turn. "Why the hell are you doing this? Why now? Why me?"

There was no response except for the sounds of his pursuer's footsteps, relentlessly drawing closer.

Al Jones moaned to himself and pushed off from the tree. He thought a moment and then went down the slope to his right. He knew there was a brook that ran off Silver Lake. Maybe he could get far enough ahead to lose him in the water. Few men he knew could track someone through the water. The current would carry away his blood trail. He could escape.

His new direction took him up a small hill. On the way down, he caught his toe in some exposed birch tree roots and lost his footing. He tumbled, hitting the ground hard with his right shoulder. The blow nearly knocked the wind out of him and it took all his strength to get himself back on his feet. His ankle felt strained, but the pain was endurable, had to be tolerated, even though it did cause him to limp and slowed his flight.

He hit the water, welcoming the icy splash on his face. And then he jogged down the brook, taking as good care as he could not to stumble on the small, slippery polished rocks. When he rounded the turn, he paused and then ran toward the field of dry grass off to his left.

There, he paused again, lowering himself to his knees, and waited. The silence restored his confidence and his hope. It resurrected his courage and along with it his embarrassment. He was, after all, naked.

"You're going to pay for this, you bastard, you sick bastard," he muttered and rocked himself. He looked down right when something moved and caught his eye. It was a buck and with quite a good rack, maybe a ten-pointer!

Damn, he thought. You would have been mine for sure.

He rubbed his ankle and then he rubbed his chin and his cheeks where the branches had scratched him. He felt the bump on his forehead. It was like a small apple embedded under his skin. Rage tightened his jaw and he pressed his hands on his face as if to hold it together. The stubble of his two-day beard didn't bother his callused palms. He had been working for Cornfield Gas for nearly thirty-five years, delivering and installing tanks. It had given him heavy shoulders and put ropes of muscle in his back, but he was nearly sixty now, soft in the stomach and with nowhere near the wind endurance he used to have.

Old man Cornfield had been a hard man to work for, frugal, demanding, but his son Charlie was softer, more easygoing, lackadaisical about the business he had inherited. Everything came easy to him and he was easier to intimidate. Since he had taken over the business, he had permitted Al to use the company truck to go back and forth from work, and didn't keep track of the miles Al put on it. Al could get away with using it for something personal occasionally, as he had done this morning when he left the house early to hunt deer before the season actually had begun. It was illegal, but he had his reasons.

First, he couldn't afford to take off work on the day it started, and second, he wasn't going to be in this forest when all those idiots from the city, men who rarely held a rifle all year, much less all their lives, came up here equipped with radar scopes and all sorts of electronic paraphernalia and invaded the Catskills' big-game season. If they didn't get the best kills, they drove them so far and so deep, a hunter like himself would have to trek days to get a decent rack.

But this, what was happening to him now, was unexpected. Hell, who would have ever anticipated . . . Why now? After all this time, why now?

A loud snap brought his head around.

"Can't be," he muttered, looking in the direction of the brook. "How would he know where I got out?"

Maybe the blood at the bottom of his feet left some sign where he had stepped out, but still, the water should have washed away enough of it, at least enough to make it very, very difficult. This was too much, too much. It was as if he had known exactly where Al would go, anticipated his every thought.

He could do that, Al thought sadly. He could.

He waited, squinted and saw a shadow moving through two tall hickory trees. He swallowed back his fear and stood up. Then he backed away from the tree he was at and turned to head across the clearing. If he made it, he could go through the little gully and head east toward the Glen Wild road. Once he broke out where there were traffic and people, he would be safe, he thought.

He walked fast, broke into a jog, and then started to trot again, when suddenly he heard his name.

"Al!"

He shouldn't have stopped. He should have kept running. Maybe . . . maybe he wasn't a good target. A man on the run is not an easy shot.

"Hey, Al," he heard.

It sounded almost friendly, like someone he knew would sound when he had spotted him and wanted to get his attention. It was all so confusing, yet it made him turn to look back, and he lost his balance. He fell, braking his fall with his right palm. Then he stood up, intending to continue, but the bullet came crashing through his chest, tearing into his heart.

The impact was like a small punch. It surprised him and for a moment, he tottered, confused, a stupid smile on his lips. Then he looked down, saw the blood streaming and raised his eyes toward the gray sky.

"Oh, Mother, no," he said as his legs gave out and he fell forward like a man about to vomit up breakfast. He was on all fours a good few seconds before he turned and fell over on his back.

He died with his eyes open, watching the swoop of a chicken hawk making its way toward Myer Bienstock's coops just on the other side of the ridge, where there were safety and longer life if he had made it.

But he didn't.

And so . . . it had started.

ONE

Willie Brand heard the phone ringing in his sleep. He actually dreamed about picking up the receiver and beginning a conversation. It was the same conversation he had dreamed himself having so many times in his life. The state bureau of criminal investigation was calling. They had changed their minds. They needed him; they actually needed and wanted him. He wasn't going to be stuck in this one-horse town after all. He fantasized running over to tell the old man. He expected as always to find him there still in his prison correction officer's uniform, but just as always, when he got there, the rocking chair on the front porch was rocking, but there was no one in it.

It was too late . . . too late to make him proud. Why was it always so important to do that anyway? Was it because the old man never expected he would amount to anything? When did he first decide that? When does a father look at a son and feel a deep sense of disappointment? Hadn't he built himself up, become athletic, and determined at an early age he would go into law enforcement? Other boys his age weren't thinking past the upcoming weekend or what new toy they would get. Why wasn't his attitude something in which his father could take pride?

He remembered the first time he wore his cub scouts uniform. How proud he felt strutting about the house in the blue and gold. He had already won a medal for his mastery of tying knots and making a fire on a camping outing. His comfort and expertise in the forest brought him compliment after compliment from his den mother. When he brought all that home, his father glanced at it with vague interest, barely uttering a grunt of pride. Why did he always see a stranger in his father's eyes, like something detestable that had been left on the doorstep?

He opened his own eyes because the phone was still ringing and keeping them closed didn't stop it. The numbers on the pad glowed back through the darkness at him, resembling a small creature with green neon orbs. It went in and out of focus, something that was happening to him more and more these days, making it harder to conclude about the reality of what he saw, what he heard. Was he awake? Or was the glowing phone in his dream, too?

His mother had heard the phone ringing one tragic afternoon. He could envision it all: the way she looked up from what she was reading, her hesitation, and then her slow, but resolved walk to the table in the hallway where the phone rested, in this case like a sleeping black snake. His mother was truly amazing. Sometimes, the phone would ring and she would say, 'There's trouble,' and sure enough there was. How could she do that? A ring was a ring to him.

Maybe it was that ability that finally drove her into the deep depression, a dark hole of sadness from which could not emerge, a hole which finally determined she had to be institutionalized. Was he responsible for that, too? Too bad he never had a brother or a sister. An only child has to bear the burden of his parents' troubles and their guilt as well as his own. It was too heavy a load. The shadows in the corners of his mind were growing like a cancer.

His phone continued to ring and the cold numbness that had seeped in under his face retreated. The phone became clear in his vision. Like it or not, this wasn't a dream. This was the crusty world of reality in which he resided.

He thrust out his arm and seized the receiver violently, slicing the next ring just as it had begun. Most of the local people, the old-timers, had never gotten used to the idea of calling the police station, especially this early in the morning. They either knew his number or found it out and called him directly. It didn't matter how early it was or how late it was. He knew people believed they could call him any time they wanted. He theorized that just because he wasn't married, they thought they could abuse him continually. How many times had he been jerked out of a well sought after sleep because someone had a dog barking too closely to his home or someone saw a strange automobile cruising his street? People were becoming more and more paranoid, even in the small Catskill hamlets and villages, miles away from big city life with all its urban headaches.

But country people watched television too, and, to some extent, he had to admit, it was creeping in . . . the evil was oozing up and down the New York State Thruway. There were more burglaries, more stolen cars, more of everything despite the flat growth in the year-round population. For the last few years, he had been pleading with the village board to expand the police force, but those arrogant bastards had ridiculed his requests.

"To do what," they asked, "enforce parking meter violations during the summer months?"

"The sheriff or the state police handle the big stuff," they said.

To him it was like rubbing salt in a wound, the wound being how little they all really respected him. He was here only for the nickel-and-dime crimes and problems, a discount law enforcement officer with little more importance than a school janitor scraping used chewing gum out from under desks and chairs.

"Brand," he snapped into the mouthpiece. In Centerville, his name had become synonymous with police. Small town or no small town, he was at least proud of that.

"Willie, this is Flo Jones. I . . . I'm sorry to bother you."

Then why do it? He wanted to say, but he didn't. Instead, he sat up and flicked on the table lamp. The dusty orange-yellow shade dropped a small pool of sickly white light over his thick muscular thighs and hairy lower legs as he rose. He seemed to rise out of his body and float above himself for a moment and then settle back into it. These crazy sensations were growing more frequent and more intense.

Got to lay off the brandy, he thought, but he knew he wouldn't. It was what got him to sleep most nights these days. The habitual insomnia had grown more intense and when he did sleep, he was tormented by a myriad of horrible images, some from the past, some so unfamiliar, he conjectured they might be from the future.

"It's all right, Flo. This is why they pay me those terrific wages," he said dryly. "What's up? The Benson kid shooting out windows with his air rifle this late at night?" Willie had great memory for complaints. Flo Jones had made that one nearly a year ago.

"No, it's nothin' like that. It's . . . I think I better report my husband's missin'. I was sittin' up all night thinkin' about it. Actually, all of us is up now."

"Missin'? Who? Al?"

He flipped open the small pad he kept on the table next to the lamp and turned himself toward it. Then he wrote the time and after that he wrote: Flo Jones reported her husband missing. He would do things by the book. No one was ever going to accuse him of being shoddy when it came to his work. Any other local policeman would do nothing, figuring this would probably prove to be no more than a wife reporting a husband who was on some drunken bender.

"Yes. He . . . well, he went out late in the afternoon, day before yesterday and hasn't returned. Went by himself."

"Went out? Out where, Flo?" he asked. There was so long a pause before she replied that he actually thought the phone had gone dead.

"Flo? Where did he go?" He would make her say it.

"He . . . went deer huntin'."

"Day before yesterday? Gun or bow?" he asked quickly, already knowing the reason for her reluctant answer. Hunting deer with a bow and arrow was legal day before yesterday, but Al Jones wasn't one to use a bow and arrow. He knew him well. Al was nearly fifteen years older than Willie, but in a small town like this, fifteen years one way or another didn't stop you from knowing each other pretty well. Also, Al's father and Willie's had been good friends who had hunted together often. Memories of their smiling, younger faces haunted him. Why did his father always have a better time with his friends than he had with him? Sometimes, he wished that he was nothing more than his friend.

"Gun," she said softly.

"But that was . . . that was before the season opened," he moaned.

Indignation and pride rose to the surface of his confused pool of thoughts. Why did everyone take advantage of him, break and bend laws expecting him to look the other way all the time? What sort of a policeman did they expect him to be? Aboveboard only when it came to strangers, tourists, but bending for the locals? It made him feel more like a hypocrite than a cop, than someone trusted with a gun and a badge and the lives and welfare of the people he served.

He would make her feel bad.

"That's a serious violation of the hunting ordinances, Flo," he chastised.

"I know. I told him not to do it, but he carried on. Said the city slickers get up here and fill the woods, drivin' the deer to kingdom come. Said they made it more dangerous than anything, shootin' at whatever moves first, and then lookin' to see. Remember what happened to Tom Singleman last year?" She spoke quickly, trying to convince through the intensity of her words.

"I remember Al blowing off about this in Sam's Luncheonette, but I didn't think he was that serious."

He paused for a moment. It was as if he lost track of what he was saying. Similar memories of his father exploded like flashbulbs. The long diatribes against tourists, the complaints about the highway department, a shopping list of moans and groans that made him, a young boy, wonder whether they did live in the greatest country in the world after all. He was tempted to ask what the highway department was like in Egypt, but he had no more courage to be satirical than he did to be contradictory. His father still believed a young boy's place was off in the corner, all eyes and ears and no tongue. It was the way his father had been brought up, and maybe to treat Willie any differently was to deny that his own father had done it right.

"Willie?"

"Yeah, well," he said, looking at his pad again. "Are you sure he's missing? Did he go far out, camping maybe?"

"He didn't take anythin' to camp with, Willie. I waited, thinkin' he mighta stopped at someone's place—Ted McNeill maybe, but Ted ain't seen him. He woulda called me if he a done that anyhow. They boys wanna go off lookin' for him as soon as it's light, but I don't want them lost too."

"You keep the boys home. It's my job now, Flo. Any idea what area he staked out?"

"Usually goes over to Dairyland, cuttin' in behind the Lake House, ya know, but I ain't sure."

"I think I remember him talking about that area. Okay, I'll see about getting up a party to sift through the woods. If you hear anything from him, call the station. I'll be there by seven."

"Thank you. I'm sorta on pins and needles up here. Maybe he's gone and shot himself in the leg or . . ."

"Don't start figuring on the worst things, Flo. You'll only get yourself sick with worry. Give me a chance to organize a search party."

"Thank you. I'm sorry about . . . about his goin' out before the season and all," she said.

"Me too." He paused a moment anticipating more, but she didn't reply. "So long," he added, and waited until he heard the click. He shook his head and then called Bruce Sussman, the patrolman on duty. It took nearly six full rings before he lifted the receiver.

"What the hell you doing?" he demanded.

"I was in the bathroom, Chief."

Willie grunted. He knew that his patrolman had been sleeping in his chair, probably with his feet up on his desk. He related Flo Jones's phone call.

"He's out drunk or shacked up somewhere, ten to one."

"Yeah, we'll save your predictions for the lottery. You pick up Jerry and have him stay in the office," he said. "I'll go right over to the luncheonette to work up a search party."

"These guys ain't going to like losing hunting time to look for a damn poacher, Chief."

"Tell me about it, Sherlock Holmes."

Willie had little respect for either of his patrolmen, but with the kind of wages the village was paying, he was lucky to have any help at all, the way he saw it.

"Get the Kuhns. They both got their deer the first day as usual, Chief," Bruce said, a note of bitter envy in his voice.

"You just pick up Jerry and let me worry about who to get," Willie said, and hung up the receiver so sharply he imagined the echo punching Sussman's ear. Then he lay back in bed and groaned.

"Fucking deer season," he said as if he was rehearsing his lines for the public. "I wish it was different," he muttered. It was such a simple wish, but he said it again.

He said it as if there were someone in the bed with him, but there wasn't. There had never been.

And the way he felt, there never would be.